LOVE ON THE PITCH

NEIL PLAKCY

Dedication

This book is dedicated to the openly gay athletes who have inspired me with their courage: John Amaechi, Billy Bean, Mark Bingham, Brian Boitano, David Kopay, Greg Louganis, Robbie Rogers, and Michael Sam—as well as all those who use their athletic ability and prominence to make the world a better place for those who follow.

Acknowledgments

This book was originally published by Loose Id with the help of a great team, including my fabulous editor, Maryam Salim. I'm also lucky to have the support of many wonderful friends and critique partners. While researching this book I read a lot about the special pressures on LGBT athletes, and their stories were very moving. I am delighted to see so many athletes coming out and hope that their honesty will make things better for all those who follow them.

The first book I ever read about a gay athlete was Dave Kopay's autobiography, and it was a window to me into a more diverse world than I had seen represented so far. Gay men could be masculine and play football? What an eye-opener! I hope Warren feels the same way when he reads the book.

Thanks to Kelly Nichols for a great print cover.

PARTY TIME

"You don't understand." Warren Updegrove crossed his arms over his massive chest and leaned against the wall. "Writers, artists, musicians. They spend years perfecting what they do, being totally devoted to it. And they keep on going for the rest of their lives. But athletes are different."

"If I don't understand, then explain it," his friend Thom Lodge said.

The rhythm of Latin music pounded through the big apartment, and Warren had to raise his voice so Thom could hear. "There are over four hundred thousand NCAA athletes, and for almost all of them, when they walk away from college, they're done competing in the sport they've trained for all their lives. If I was a baseball player, I could maybe play in the minor leagues for a while. If I was a runner or in some other individual sport, I could keep going on my own for at least a few years, maybe try out for the Olympics or something."

"You played football for a year," Thom said. "In Jacksonville."

Warren shook his head. "I was on the roster for a year. I played maybe a total of an hour the whole season. And then I got dropped. No more football for me. And I didn't realize what a big hole that was going to leave in my life."

Thom was skinny but deceptively well-built, and his polo shirts and khakis were always loose. His perpetual smile accented his good looks. "You've got a job, right," Thom said. "That personal training gig. You're still an athlete."

"It's not the same. I don't get the same rush, the same sense of being part of a team."

"Can't you find some pickup games or something?" Thom asked. "Don't you have friends in the same boat you are?"

"The guys I played with at FU have moved all over the place. And then there's the gay thing."

Warren looked around the crowded apartment. A mix of gay guys he'd known in college at FU, pretty Latinas, and strangers. They all seemed to fit in better at the party than he did.

"How does you being gay change anything?" Thom asked. "That college player came out, right? And he got picked up by an NFL team."

"And dropped almost immediately. Last I heard he was in Canada riding a bench for some third-rate team. I'll bet you they're already calling him faggot behind his back."

"Bitter, party of one," Thom said. "Seriously. So you can't play football anymore. Grow a pair of balls, pick yourself up, and find something else you love to do. People do it all the time."

Warren looked at Thom. "Fuck you. When I need some advice on being a real man, you're not the one I'm going to come to."

He turned and stalked across the room to the cooler full of beer. He fished around past the sissy microbrews until he found a real American beer, and grabbed it. He popped the top and drained half of it in a long gulp.

Fuck Thom anyway. Who did he think he was? They had met in college, when Thom was assigned as Warren's tutor. Right away Warren had pegged him as gay—skinny, geeky, a bright green stud in one ear. The stud was the shiniest thing about Thom; otherwise he was a mellow-looking guy with brown hair and brown eyes.

Warren had big-time internalized homophobia back then, a result of his Southern Baptist upbringing, and he had kept his own desires buried deep. Thom was openly gay, living in a gay fraternity on campus, and Warren had bitched at him and teased him for a while. Then finally one day Warren cracked open like an egg and jumped Thom's bones.

They had fooled around for the rest of senior year, but they both knew they were too different to make it as a couple. Warren was a jock to his core, while Thom was a nerd who hated sports. They had maintained a friendship after graduation, while Warren was in Jacksonville and then after he returned, and it was Thom who had convinced Warren to come to this party on South Beach, hosted by three of Thom's frat brothers.

Warren had known them all casually at FU, but he hadn't particularly liked them. Manny was Latin, Larry a geek, Gavin a stuck-up pretty boy. And they were all gay, gay, gay. Warren hated that kind of obvious display.

It was why he stayed away from South Beach. After he'd crashed and burned in Jacksonville, he'd returned to Miami, because it was a way better alternative than going home to his family in South Carolina. He'd gotten a job at a gym in Kendall, a suburb on the south side of the city, and tried to start a whole new life.

At which he appeared to be failing. He couldn't

even be polite to the guy who was almost his only friend. He looked around for Thom to apologize, but couldn't see him through the crush in the living room. He drained the rest of his beer and reached for another.

He knew he shouldn't be drinking so much. His boss at the gym had already pointed out, trying to be polite, that Warren's muscle was turning to fat, and he wasn't setting a good example for the clients. Fuck him too. The job sucked, and Warren would be glad to get rid of it.

He glared around the room. Fuck all this shit. He popped the top on a can and took a long swig. As he put the beer down, he saw a guy staring at him. Maybe thirty, tough-looking, with muscular arms and a dirty blond goatee. He wore a black ball cap imprinted with a white feather and the words *New Zealand All Blacks*. Warren met his gaze and narrowed his eyes, sending a "don't fuck with me" message.

The look had the opposite effect. The guy came up to him and said, "You ever think about being a loose head? You've got the build for it."

It was so not what Warren expected that he didn't know what to say.

"The loose head is the big tough guy who guards the hooker," the guy continued.

"I'm not a fucking pimp," Warren said.

"Not what I was saying. I'm talking about rugby, dude. You ever play?"

Warren shook his head. He'd known a couple of guys at FU who played, but it was one of those things you were either all in, or all out, and he'd had football.

"Here's my card," the guy said. "I'm trying to put together a team. If you're interested, give me a call." He smiled. "I'd like to see you on the pitch, dude."

Warren took the card and slid it into the pocket of his jeans, though he knew he wasn't going to call. He watched the guy walk away, noting that he had a great build, a V-shaped torso and narrow waist, with a shapely butt.

"He's cute," Thom said, appearing by Warren's side. "Who is he?"

"Just some guy," Warren said. "Listen, I'm sorry I bitched at you before. You're right. My life is a fucking mess, and it's all my fault." He drank another swig of beer. "I'm gonna hit the road."

"You okay to drive?"

Warren felt himself swaying on his feet. How many beers had he had, anyway? "Maybe I ought to sit down for a minute." He looked around, but there was no space on the sofa or any of the chairs. He slid to the floor. "This feels good," he said, and then he was out.

When he woke up, he was lying on his side on the floor, and daylight was streaming into the living room. The place smelled like beer, sweat, and cold, conditioned air. The debris of the party was all around him—beer bottles, plastic cups, paper plates. And guys. A half-dozen of them slept on the living room floor. Most of them were naked.

And fuck, so was he, and so was Thom, curled against him. Both of them what his mamaw called butt-nekkid, his dick half-hard and pressed against Thom's ass.

What the fuck had happened last night? The last thing he remembered was sitting down on the floor with a beer in his hand. Fully clothed.

Now, his throat was dry, he had a killer headache, and he had to take a wicked piss. As carefully as he could, he extricated himself from Thom and stood up. He looked around for his clothes, but he realized he needed the toilet, stat.

He stumbled down the hall to the bathroom, flipped up the lid on the toilet, and stood there pissing. It was all done up in marble and mirrors, like whoever lived there was too fancy to take a dump in a dump. He hated that kind of attitude, and it made him want to spread his piss all over the place.

But he wasn't drunk anymore, and he restrained the urge. As he finished, he got a look at himself in the huge mirror in front of him. Christ, his boss was right. He had put on weight. There was a layer of fat around his waist that hadn't been there when he was in Jacksonville. His arms felt saggy, and his pecs looked like they were becoming man-boobs.

Which reminded him that he'd been naked when he woke up. What the fuck had happened the night before? He checked his belly, his pubes, and his dick for cum stains. Nothing there. He turned on the faucet and drank heavily from his cupped hands, then stood up and wiped his mouth.

The door to the bathroom popped open, and he realized he hadn't locked it. But it was only Thom.

"Move over, big guy," Thom said, shouldering past him, his hand casually caressing Warren's ass. "Gotta drain the lizard."

Warren looked at him as Thom stood over the

bowl. Yup, he was still as slim and fit and sexy as the last time they'd had sex. Broad shoulders, concave belly, slim thighs. Christ, he made Warren feel like a fat pig.

Thom flushed and then looked at Warren. Thom was still sporting morning wood, and Warren felt himself hardening. Thom reached out and wrapped his hand around Warren's dick, and it felt so good his whole body tingled. "Good morning, big guy," Thom said.

"Morning," Warren mumbled.

"I was talking to your dick," Thom said. Then he knelt down to the tile floor and wrapped his lips around the head of Warren's dick.

"Oh, Jesus." Warren leaned back against the vanity.

"The name's Thom," his friend said, pulling off Warren's dick for a moment, though he still had his fist wrapped around the shaft. "Jesus is out in the living room. But he pronounces it Hay-Zeus."

That was Thom, Warren thought. Always a smart ass. And a world-class cocksucker too. Thom kept on fisting Warren's shaft and sucking the head, and Warren's headache disappeared. Thom was using his other hand to stroke Warren's balls, and every nerve in Warren's body was focused on the pleasure his buddy was generating.

The noises Warren made as he was about to come embarrassed him, but Thom loved them, and Warren let himself go, moaning and whimpering as his guts churned, and he couldn't hold back any longer. "I'm coming," he said in a strangled voice.

Thom kept on sucking him, and Warren shot

off down his throat. Then Thom stood up, with a shit-eating grin on his face. "I wanted to do that last night, but you passed out before I could make a move," he said.

"How did I get naked?" Warren asked.

Thom turned to the sink, washed his hands, and wiped his mouth.

"Thom," Warren said.

"A bunch of us were pretty drunk," Thom said. His face was reddening with embarrassment. "Somebody had this idea that we should see whose dick was biggest."

"Tell me you didn't take my clothes off while I was passed out." Warren grabbed Thom's upper arm.

"I knew you were the biggest," Thom said. "I just wanted to prove it." He tried to twist away from Warren's grip. "You're hurting me, Warren."

Warren let go. "Sorry. But that was not good."

"I know. I'm sorry." He toed the tile floor, and Warren knew there had to be something more.

"What?" Warren asked. "What else?"

"We kind of took some pictures," Thom said, looking down.

"Of me?" Warren was too angry to be embarrassed about the way his voice rose.

"Not just you. All of us."

"Who has those pictures?"

Thom shrugged. "We used a bunch of different phones. And I think one of the guys might have uploaded them."

"I thought you were my friend. Now I realize you're just as much an asshole as the rest of them."

Warren pushed his way past Thom and walked

out to the living room, not giving a shit that he was still naked. He found his clothes in a pile on the floor and started to pull them on.

Thom followed him. "Listen, big guy, I'm sorry."

"I have a name. Not big guy. Warren."

He didn't bother to button his shirt, just barreled his way past Thom, then stepped over sleeping bodies until he reached the door. He wanted to slam it behind him, but he remembered the anger management training he'd gotten in Jacksonville. Let it go. Dial back the rage, channel it into something productive.

He closed the door quietly behind him and walked to the elevator.

Warren stopped at a traffic light on Alton Road. The sun glared above, banking off the big glass store windows. Tourists in bathing suits were already on their way to the beach. The sidewalks were hot enough to fry an egg, as his mamaw used to say.

Why had he made such a big deal over the pictures with Thom? So somebody took a dick pic of him when he was passed out. If he'd been awake, and drunk, he might have jumped into the competition voluntarily.

There was something more to it, he knew. He was drinking too much, not exercising, not caring about his body or his life anymore.

He had anticipated getting released from the team in Jacksonville. He wasn't stupid, though studying didn't come easily to him. He could see the signs. He wasn't getting to play much, even in scrimmages. And no matter how hard he'd worked, he knew that he didn't have the natural talent that some of the other guys had.

Getting cut was still hard. To realize that the dream he'd had since he was a kid, of playing in the NFL, was over. Within a few weeks he understood that there was nothing else, no new dream to replace the old one. Thom was the one who had pushed him to get the job at the gym, he remembered.

He started out taking new clients at the gym in rotation with the other trainers, and he worked hard, analyzing their strengths and weaknesses, developing fitness plans with them. A lot of those first clients never came back, once they realized how hard it was going to be to get in shape. But Warren held on to a few of them, and they referred others, and he had a pretty good client roster for a while. But then he'd begun to lose interest, and the clients had sensed that, and started dropping off or switching to other trainers.

The week before his boss had called him in. *"I don't know what's wrong with you, Warren. You've got your head up your ass, and you're losing clients. That's not good for them, for you, or for our business. I'm taking you out of the new client rotation until you show me that you want to get back in the game."*

Warren had nodded dumbly and walked out. Without new client referrals, his income was going to be cut in half at least, and within a month or so he'd start having trouble paying his bills. He was sharing a house with another trainer and a guy who put up ceilings, and if he couldn't cover his share of the rent, he'd be out on the street.

Thom had convinced him this party would be

the remedy for his malaise, that he'd have a good time and get charged up again. Instead he'd gotten drunk and pissed off Thom.

By the time he reached his place, he wanted to crash. But he forced himself into workout clothes and drove to the FU campus. He did a couple of laps around the track, and then a couple of stadiums—running up and down the steps until sweat was pouring off him and his legs were wobbly.

He was slumped on a bench when a couple of guys from the football team came in. He watched them on the field, setting up a practice scrimmage, and he wanted to go down there and join them so badly it made his stomach hurt.

But he resisted. Those days were gone.

He had to find something else to do with his life. Should he go back to school, get a master's degree in something?

He shook his head. More school wasn't for him. And he knew he didn't want to be a coach. Somehow he didn't think it was right, a gay guy spending all his time around naked teenagers. Not that his interests ran that way, but all the negative stuff he'd heard when he was growing up had become ingrained in him.

But what else was there? He tried to think of someone he could call, a friend he could talk things through with. But his only real friend was Thom. And he sure as hell wasn't going there.

He went back to the house and threw his workout clothes into the dirty laundry basket, then took a shower. When he got out, he carried the basket to the laundry room and was relieved to find that nobody had bogarted the washer. He started loading his clothes in, and when he picked up the jeans he'd worn the night before something crinkled in the pocket.

He pulled out the business card the rugby dude had given him. His name was Victor Ragazzo and instead of a company name the card read *Property Inspections*. The address was on North Federal Highway in Fort Lauderdale. He stared at the card for a minute, remembering the guy's fit body, the way he'd carried himself like an athlete. Warren needed that in his life, an outlet for all the aggression and competitiveness inside him.

Rugby. Maybe.

He threw the rest of his laundry in the washer and went back to his bedroom, where he opened his laptop. He watched a couple of rugby videos, and he felt his adrenaline rise. What was that term the guy had used for the position Warren would play? Something about a hooker?

No, the position protected the hooker. He looked it up and found it was called the loose head, and then watched a couple of videos of guys pushing together, grabbing onto each other, and he had to admit it made his dick jump.

Hell, he needed the exercise and the motivation of being part of a team. He typed out a quick e-mail to the address on Victor Ragazzo's card. *Don't know much about rugby but I'm willing to learn,* he wrote. Then he hit Send.

The dude must have been checking his e-mail on his phone, because a message came back almost immediately. *Meet 4 dinner 2night & talk? Call me.*

Why not? He dialed the dude's number. "Hey, it's Warren. We met last night."

"Crazy party, huh?" Victor said. "I don't get down to South Beach much."

"Neither do I," Warren said. "It's not really my scene."

"I hear you. Lots of pretty boys who care more about what they're wearing than what goes on between their ears."

The "pretty boys" comment surprised Warren. He'd pegged the guy for a jock, not a brainiac. And his vibe had been all male. "I've got a job this afternoon in Wilton Manors," Victor continued. "But I should be done around six. Can you come up this way?"

"Sure. Tell me where and when."

"There's a sports bar on US 1 between Sunrise and Oakland Park. Left side of the street. Can't miss it. Six-thirty?"

Warren agreed and hung up. A sports bar? So the guy was a jock after all? He wished he could call Thom and talk it over with him. But no, that door was closed. At least for a while.

He put on the white jersey he'd worn in Jacksonville at home games, with his name in a half-circle on the back over his number. It was a little tight over his gut, a reminder he had a way to go before he was back in playing shape. A pair of jeans, running shoes with white socks. At the last minute he put on a silver and rope bracelet he'd bought soon after moving to Jacksonville because another player had one like it, and Warren thought it looked masculine.

He realized as he drove up the Turnpike to

Lauderdale that he was nervous. Fuck, it wasn't like this was a date or anything. He was just going to talk to another jock about playing sports, right?

He felt immediately at home when he walked in the door of the bar. The walls were hung with pennants from all the local teams, there were ball games and golf games playing on the big-screen TVs, and groups of guys clustered around pitchers of beer, cheering the teams and razzing each other.

He stood in the doorway for a minute, absorbing it all. Then he saw Victor waving at him from a table in the corner. He was dressed like he'd come from work, a collared shirt and khaki pants, and he had a big pilsner-style glass of beer in front of him.

Warren negotiated his way through the crowd. Victor stood up and offered Warren his hand to shake. "No trouble finding this place?" he asked.

"None at all." Warren liked his grip, strong and solid, not like the limp fish so many gay guys had. He slid into the booth, and Victor sat back down.

"I'm glad you could make it," Victor said. "I've been struggling to get a team going down here, and it's hard to find the right guys."

The server came over, a tall guy in a Heat jersey. They ordered a platter of nachos and a draft for Warren. After he left, Victor said, "I played rugby in college, and then for the Gryphons, a team in Philly. But after I moved down here, I couldn't find the kind of team I wanted to play for, so I decided to put one together myself."

Victor looked like a typical jock, from his Dolphins T-shirt to his ball cap, backwards now. Warren gave in to his indecision and said, "Can I ask you something?"

Victor picked up his beer mug. "Sure."

"Are you gay?"

Victor put the mug down. "Is that a problem?"

Warren shook his head. "No. But you should know that I am. And you might not want a gay guy on your team."

Victor laughed. "Warren. Did I neglect to tell you that I'm putting together a gay rugby team? If I did, I apologize."

"A whole team?"

The server delivered their nachos, and Victor scooped up a chip full of salsa. "There's a whole league, Warren. An international league. A couple of dozen teams in the US alone, with others in Europe, Australia, even South America."

Warren shook his head. "I had no idea."

"It's called the International Gay Rugby Team and Board, though we're very open to anybody who wants to play in a nondiscriminatory atmosphere. I have a half-dozen guys lined up already, a couple of them straight. We fool around on Saturdays at a field down the road from here. But I need a big guy like you to play loose head."

"I've never seen a game in person, but I watched a couple of videos this afternoon. I still don't understand what that means, loose head."

"Let me give you a quick primer on rugby," Victor said. "Maximum of fifteen players to a side. The field is called a pitch, and we play two forty-minute halves. The goal is to score points with either goals or tries."

"Tries?"

"A try is actually worth more points than kicking the ball over the crossbar and between the posts. The player has to be in the goal area either holding the ball and touching the ground, or on the ground over the ball."

He passed a couple of printed sheets of paper to Warren. "These are some of the basics. You can read about the game when you have some time." He leaned back against the wooden booth. "What do you do for a living?"

"Personal trainer at a gym in Kendall," Warren said. "But I don't think I'll be there much longer."

"Really?"

It was like something burst inside Warren, and he began to tell Victor everything he'd been feeling. "My undergrad degree is in recreation and sports management, because that was what a lot of the guys on the team chose. I didn't think my major mattered because I was determined to play in the NFL. And I did, for a year in Jacksonville."

"That's awesome," Victor said. "I recognized the jersey."

"Wasn't so awesome when I got cut," Warren said. "I looked around and realized that I didn't want to be a coach or work at a county park or anything like that. The only thing I really knew how to do was work out."

He picked up his beer. "I came back to Miami because I went to college here. A friend suggested I look into personal training, probably just to get me off his couch. But I suck at it. And now I don't know what else to do."

"I hear you," Victor said. "My degree is in

construction management. But I figured out real fast that twelve-hour days, outside in the Philly winters, wasn't for me. I floundered around for a while until I stumbled onto what I do now."

"What is that?"

"When people go to buy a house, they need an inspection before they close," he said. "Somebody experienced to come in and point out all the problems. I get to work my own hours, meet different people all the time, use what I learned in school and on the job. And it gives me the time and flexibility to organize rugby."

"That's awesome," Warren said. "I wish I could get into something like that."

"You've got to follow your passion, dude. Figure out what you really want from life and go for it."

That was the trouble, Warren thought, as he drove home later that night. He knew what he wanted—to play in the NFL. But that was done. What did he want now?

KEEP THE NOISE DOWN

Warren woke Monday morning with a new resolve. He was going to exercise every day, cut back on the beer, do his damn job. He went for a long run, then showered and went to the gym.

His first client was a thirty-something stay-at-home mom named Candy. About twenty pounds overweight, with flab under her arms. She didn't really want to get fit; she just needed to get out of the house now and then. She liked Warren because he didn't push her, and half the time they just shot the shit while standing around the equipment pretending he was explaining stuff to her.

That morning Candy wore a pink tank top, matching shorts, and pink sneakers with white pompoms on the backs. Even her fucking ponytail holder was pink. "You've been complaining about your upper arms," he said, as they walked into the machine room together. "Today we're going to start doing something about them."

He began leading her through a series of stretching exercises, then took her to the shoulder press machine, demonstrated how it worked, and positioned her properly. She did two reps then stopped. "This is hard," she said.

"It's supposed to be. That's why they call it a *work* out."

She complained, but she managed to finish ten reps. Then he walked her up to the oval track on the second floor of the building. They talked about her son's Pop Warner football league as they race-walked, and when they finished their second turn around the track he showed her an exercise she could teach to her son. "This way you can work out together. You'll be part of his training."

"Thanks, Warren," she said when they were finished. "This was a great session."

"All part of the service," he said.

He didn't have another client scheduled until two in the afternoon, so he pushed himself through a workout, showering and changing before his client came in. Ed was a guy in his sixties, recently retired, who was in poor overall health. His doctor had told him to get fit or die, and so far Ed was choosing the second option.

He didn't want to stretch. "Everything still hurts from the last time I was here," he said. He was a short guy, no more than five-six or so, bald head with one of those comb-overs. He wore a T-shirt from one of the cruise lines with a sappy slogan on it.

"Then that means you didn't stretch properly last time," Warren said. "Come on, give it a try." He lifted his arms above his head, and Ed followed.

"You must get a lot of girls with a body like that," Ed said.

He was about to spit out an anonymous comment like "as many as I want," but he decided that telling the truth was part of his new program. "Not interested in girls," he said. "Now stretch your right leg."

"You're gay?" Ed said, looking up at him.

"Right leg, Ed," Warren said.

When Ed complied, Warren answered. "Yup. Now your left leg."

"My son's gay," Ed said. This time he stretched

his leg without being forced. "Lives in Alabama, if you can believe that. He and his partner run a guest house."

They continued to talk about Ed's son as Warren walked him through his stretching, and then they went twice around the track without Ed complaining at all. He was packing up his gear when his boss walked into the employee locker room. "You were on fire today, Warren. Keep up the good work, and I'll put you back in the new client rotation."

He felt so good when he left that he slipped one of his motivational CDs into the car player for the ride home. This one was an audiobook by the Dalai Lama about happiness. He got so into listening that he missed his exit on the highway and found himself approaching the FU campus, as if he still had a homing instinct for the place.

He looked at the dashboard clock. Thom usually finished his tutoring gig in the math lab at FU by four o'clock. Warren knew he needed to apologize, so he turned in at the curving drive that led to the frat house zone.

An anonymous gay benefactor had donated the cash to build the Lambda Lambda Lambda house, and the university had provided the land, at one end of Frat Row. Warren pulled up on the street in front of the modern three-story building with the three triangles above the front door.

Two years before, he would never have considered walking past the house, no less going inside. He had been so far in the closet back then, as Thom said, he could almost see Narnia. Meeting Thom had been the impetus for Warren to start taking those few tentative steps out.

He owed Thom a lot, and he couldn't trash their friendship over a single drunken indiscretion. He got out of his car and walked up to the house's front door. The house manager, Fitz, was in the living room at his laptop. He was a laid-back dude with a surfer vibe, always wearing tank tops and tight shorts.

"Hey, Warren. What's up?"

"Yo, Fitz," Warren said. "Thom here?"

"In his room. We've got some new rush candidates coming over soon, so try to keep the headboard-banging to a minimum, all right?"

"No worries," Warren said. Funny, even a year before he'd have been as embarrassed as hell by Fitz's comment, and the idea that others in the frat knew what he and Thom were getting up to. Now it slid off his back like axle grease off a duck's ass.

He climbed the stairs to Thom's third floor room and knocked on the door. "In," Thom called.

"Hey," Warren said, staying in the doorway. "I came to apologize."

"Come on in. I'm the one who should apologize. I violated your privacy and that was uncool."

"Yeah, but I overreacted. What's a dick pic between friends, right?" He looked at Thom's laptop. "Are the pictures still online somewhere?"

Thom looked embarrassed. "Yeah. I meant to ask Larry to take them down, but I forgot."

"You know where they are?" Warren walked over to Thom's side and pulled up a chair. "Let's see how we all stack up."

"Larry put them up on his Instagram page," he said. "But at least he put a password on the files." He typed, and a gallery of dick pics popped up. Each one was captioned with just a first name. Each one was hard, posed with a ruler beside it.

"Jesus, you got a lot of guys to pose," Warren said, looking at the screen. "Or were they all drunk like me?"

"We were all kind of drunk. But you were the only one who'd passed out."

"Look at that," Warren said. "Nelson never got cut." He pointed to a photo of a stiff purple-black dick. In the first picture the foreskin was up, in the second it was pulled back.

"You're the biggest," Thom said, pointing. "Not the longest—that's Larry."

"No wonder he was willing to put all these pictures up." Warren leaned toward the screen. "There's you. Is that a little drop of precum at the end of your dick?"

Thom shifted in his seat. "Yeah. I, um, I took mine after yours."

Warren looked at him. "Was I hard already? Or did you enhance things?"

"Christ, Warren," Thom said. "You're not making this very easy for me."

"Who knows," Warren said, leaning over to kiss Thom's throat. "Maybe I want to make it hard for you. If I do, will you hold it against me?"

Thom groaned. "Warren, you know what that does to me."

"Yeah. And I do it deliberately." He nibbled on Thom's earlobe. "We're good together, Thom-Boy.

Right? We have awesome sex."

"Because we're friends, Warren. Friends with benefits."

Warren stood up and dropped his sweat pants. His dick swelled against the pouch of his jockstrap. "Here's a benefit for you, buddy."

Thom peeled off his T-shirt, and Warren noticed that Thom had been working out. "Your abs are looking good," he said.

"But you don't want to fuck my abs," Thom said. "Lube and condoms in the drawer by the bed." He turned his back to Warren, undid his shorts, and pulled them and his boxers down.

Warren grabbed the lube and a condom and turned back to Thom, who was leaning against the desk. "I promised Fitz we wouldn't make too much noise," Warren said, as he lowered himself to the carpet and leaned forward. He pulled apart Thom's cheeks and stuck his tongue in between them.

He had never thought he'd like licking ass as much as he did. He'd never even thought of doing it until the first time he'd fucked Thom, when Thom had warned him that Warren had to get him good and lubed up before trying to stick his dick in.

He'd seen a few porno movies, and without even thinking about it, he'd leaned down and started licking around Thom's hole. It totally turned him on, and Thom liked it too. It had become a regular part of their sex routine, back when they were both still college seniors, before Warren went off to Jacksonville.

The blowjob in the bathroom at the party had been the first time they'd had sex since graduation, and Warren realized he'd missed this. He'd had sex with other guys, but Thom? He liked Thom. They were friends. That was really all a relationship was, right? They got along; they had great sex. Who needed anything else?

Thom's ass, like much of his body, was covered with a layer of fine brown hair, and Warren loved to run his hands over the ass cheeks as he played with the hole. He took his time licking and tongue-fucking Thom's ass, until the muscles were loose and Thom was begging to get Warren's dick up there. Warren stood up and grabbed Thom's hips, feeling the smooth skin over the bone, and then gently poked his dickhead toward Thom's hole.

"Oh yeah, big guy," Thom said. "Fill me up. Make me your bitch."

Thom was a graduate student in math, and with his muscles covered by a shapeless polo shirt, with his glasses on, you'd take him for a typical nerd. But he had a dirty mouth, and Warren loved hearing him talk during sex.

"Yeah, bitch," Warren said back to him. "Gonna fuck this sweet ass of yours. Stretch you out so that no other guy will ever satisfy you."

"Oh God, you're gonna split me in two," Thom moaned. "Your dick is so big. You sure you're not fisting me instead?"

"If I were fisting you, you'd know it," Warren growled.

They went back and forth as Warren eased his bulk into Thom, then began a slow, steady rhythm. Before Thom, he hadn't known what to do, how to suck a dick, fuck an ass. Thom had taught him so much. Thom writhed beneath him, moaning and talking dirty, and Warren increased the speed and the pressure.

"You're killing me, you big fucker," Thom said. "Oh God, are those your pubes scratching my ass? Are you that far inside me?"

"I'm so far in that if I wasn't wearing a rubber, you'd be spurting my cum out your mouth," Warren said. "I'm so far in that my dick knows what you ate for lunch."

Thom sputtered a laugh. "I'm so close, Warren. Jerk me."

Warren wrapped his hand around Thom's dick, which was hot and pulsed against his skin. He didn't need to lube his hand; Thom's precum was enough. He rubbed and pistoned until Thom spurted in his hand and then Warren let loose with a roar as the orgasm swelled up inside him.

"So much for keeping the noise down," Thom said, panting.

MY TEAM

Warren spooned with Thom in his narrow bed for a while. Thom's single room was on the top floor of the building and had a tall glass window that looked out on frat row. Thom had hung a couple of travel posters of places in Europe along one wall and along the other he'd built a makeshift bookcase of plastic milk cartons and wooden planks. The shelves were overflowing with paperback novels, textbooks, and hardcover art books.

Warren's stomach grumbled so loudly that Thom laughed. "Gonna bring the roof down with that noise," he said.

Warren laughed too. "My mamaw used to say that," he said. It was funny how with Thom he felt comfortable talking about his family and his background. He sat up and stretched. "Guess I ought to get something to eat. You want to come?"

Thom shook his head. "I'm TAing for a professor in calculus for science majors, and I've got exams to grade. I'll nuke something later."

Leaving Thom was always awkward—were they supposed to hug, or kiss? Fist-bump? The whole friends-with-benefits thing was confusing sometimes. By the time Warren was dressed, Thom was sitting at his desk with a pile of blue books in front of him. Warren settled for a gentle tap to Thom's shoulder. "Later, dude."

Thom looked up. "That was fun. Come by any time."

Warren laughed as he left. He stopped at a drive-through Pollo Tropical and ordered the whole chicken and the Caesar salad, and he'd devoured the accompanying rolls by the time he got home. He felt good, for the first time in a while.

The next day he got an e-mail from Victor Ragazzo, one that had been copied to a bunch of other guys. Victor was organizing a practice Saturday afternoon at the field off US 1 in Fort Lauderdale. Who was in?

Warren hesitated. Did he want to get into this rugby thing? He'd never even watched a whole game, just had this idea anyone who played the sport was crazy. Quickly his inbox began to fill with "reply to all" responses from guys who were going to be there. What the hell, he thought, and e-mailed that he'd be there too.

That night he watched more rugby videos on YouTube. The game seemed to be an organized free-for-all—guys were passing the ball to each other, running with it, tackling each other with glee. He looked up the terms Victor had mentioned and tried to make the connections to what was happening on the screen, but some of the guys were so hot that he had trouble concentrating.

His dick stirred in his workout shorts. His mouth was dry and his pulse was racing, and he realized he was horny. He popped his dick out and began stroking it as he watched the guys on the screen tumble around in a scrum. Jesus, how did anybody focus on playing when there were guys all over you, hands on your butt, crotch in your face?

He rubbed his thumb just beneath the head of his dick, and he felt it pulse. He tweaked one nipple with his other hand and then began fisting himself, faster until his hand was a blur, and then he shot a load over his belly. He slumped down in his chair. Maybe this gay rugby thing would be a big embarrassment—what if he shot a load in the middle of a scrum? What if their locker room shower after games turned into an orgy?

He shook his head. It was a fucking game, just like football. Sure, he'd gotten turned on by a teammate now and then, but never during play. He had to focus on what was going on around him. He was sure rugby would be the same.

At least he hoped it would.

The next day he kept his head down and his brain focused. He trained his clients, he worked out, he watched what he ate and drank. Late that afternoon, he got a text from Victor. *Client in Kendall til 6. U free after?*

Warren texted back that he was, and a few minutes before six, his phone rang. He'd already finished with his clients for the day, and he was doing some stretching to cool down. "You know a place we could do some practice?" Victor asked. "I could show you some of the rugby drills."

Warren was surprised at how pleased he was. "Sure. There's a park near my house that's almost always empty." He gave Victor directions and arranged to meet there in fifteen minutes.

He felt nervous as he drove there, as if he was going on a date. But that was dumb; Victor just wanted to help him get ready for the practice on Saturday afternoon. He got to the park first, and stood in the lot leaning against his car waiting for Victor. It was a big empty space, lined with a row of palms along one side, with picnic tables and benches at the back, beside a square concrete building with restrooms and showers.

He'd often seen people playing pickup ball games there and wanted to jump in, but he'd been too shy. He worried he'd be jumping into some office party or local league, and he'd be told he wasn't wanted.

Though it was early evening, the sun was still bright and the temperature was in the eighties, with nearly 100 percent humidity. He began to sweat just standing there, and he was embarrassed that he got a hard-on thinking of Victor.

He was glad when Victor arrived so he could focus on playing. Victor was wearing street clothes. "There a locker room here where I can change?" he asked. "Otherwise I can do it in the car. Done that enough."

The thought of Victor taking off his clothes made Warren's stiff dick twinge, and he shifted posture to hide it. "Sure. That building at the back."

"Cool." Victor tossed a ball to Warren and said, "I'll meet you out there."

The playing field was empty, and Warren walked out there, carrying the diamond-shaped white ball. It was shorter and fatter than a football, but it felt good in Warren's hands. He practiced some agility drills while he waited, and he was surprised when Victor appeared behind him. "Looking good," Victor said, and Warren wondered if Victor had been only watching him play, or looking at his body too.

"The first thing to remember is that if you have possession of the ball, you can run with it, you can kick it, or you can pass it. But you can't pass it forward."

"That doesn't make sense," Warren said. "Isn't the idea to move the ball forward?"

"Yeah. And that's why you can run forward with it, or kick it forward. But if you need to get rid of it, you have to throw laterally or behind you. Them's the rules."

Warren shrugged. There were football rules he didn't understand either, but he followed them. "Let's do some running and passing," Victor said.

They darted around the field together, carrying the ball, then kicking and throwing it back and forth. A light breeze picked up, wicking away their sweat. It was a hell of a lot of fun, and it reminded Warren of fooling around in high school with his buddies, before things got so complicated, when it was a kick to be out on the field with a ball and another guy.

"Let's try a couple of tackles," Victor said, after a half hour or so had passed. He wiped a hand over his brow. His dark hair was sticking to his head, and his face was flushed.

"I don't want to hurt you," Warren said. "I'm a lot bigger than you are."

"I'm sure you are," Victor said, with a wink. "But I'm not just going to sit around and wait for you to catch me."

He grabbed the ball and started to run. Warren took off after him as Victor darted around the field, pivoting and twisting. He was a fast fucker; Warren gave him that. And Warren was accustomed to being on the defensive line, where guys ran at you and you just knocked them over.

"Come on, you big fairy," Victor teased him, turning around and running backward. "Flap your fairy wings and tackle me."

Warren wasn't the kind of guy who'd gotten teased much in school. He was too big and too strong. But he had always been scared that other guys would figure out his desires and hate him for them.

Fortunately, he was a shower, not a grower. His dick was the same size soft or hard, so it hadn't given him away in the locker room. But that fairy comment really frosted him, and he took off with a vengeance.

He caught up to Victor and tackled him around the waist, then dragged him to the ground. Victor squirmed and wiggled, trying to escape, but Warren was too big and too strong. He found himself over Victor on the ground, holding his arms down to the grass. Victor laughed. "This isn't wrestling, Warren. You can let me up."

Warren was embarrassed by how much he had liked being on top of Victor, the way his body had reacted to all Victor's wriggling. "Let's do that again," Victor said, standing up. His T-shirt was drenched in sweat, and so were his bright red shorts, which clung to his body. Where they sagged a bit Warren spotted the white waistband of a jockstrap. "Only this time chase me like you mean it."

They did a couple more tackles until Victor was panting and out of breath. So was Warren, but he was trying not to show it. "I'm gonna hit the shower," Victor said. "Assuming the water works in there. You coming?"

Warren felt like he had to put his tongue back

in his mouth so he wouldn't look like he was panting after Victor. "Sure. I've got street clothes in the car."

Victor had left his in a bundle by the side of the field, so by the time Warren reached the locker room Victor was already naked and standing under a stream of water in the communal shower. Warren couldn't help taking a peek as he stripped.

Victor's body was all muscle, with tattoos curled around his upper arms and lower legs. He also had a long sentence tattooed above his belly button, but Warren wasn't close enough to read it.

He walked into the shower room naked and took a place across from Victor. He turned to the wall and adjusted the water, then turned to face Victor as the water cascaded around him. The air in the shower was hot and steamy, and Warren felt every nerve ending in his body tingling.

"Jesus, you're packing a weapon there," Victor said. "I don't know that I've ever seen a dick that big in person before."

Warren felt his face reddening. "It's not exactly a bonus sometimes. You know, it can be too big."

"A dick can never be too big or too hard."

Warren's was hard by then. And so was Victor's. It wasn't nearly as big as Warren's, but then few men's were. Victor rinsed his body, the clean water sluicing off and flowing down the tile floor to the drain. He turned the showerhead off. "You mind if I give it a shot?" he asked.

Warren felt his heart rate accelerate. "I don't mind at all." He turned behind him and shut off the water, then leaned back against the cold tile wall.

Victor palmed him first, weighing Warren's

dick. "Man," Victor said. "You make me hungry just looking at you." He looked up at Warren and smiled. "Hungry for dick, that is."

He got down on his knees on the wet tile floor and wrapped his lips around the head of Warren's dick. It was such a hot scene that Warren's pulse raced. He'd never gotten sucked in a locker room before; the couple of times when he'd hooked up with someone that way, they'd gone somewhere else. And despite what people saw in porn movies, a pro team's locker room was all about business, and he'd never considered having sex in one.

But this shower room scene, it was something else. Victor couldn't take all of Warren in his mouth, the way that Thom could, but he made up for it in other ways. He was a masterful cocksucker, bringing Warren to the brink of orgasm again and again, then pulling back, until Warren found himself pleading to come.

Suddenly Victor pulled his mouth off and stood up. He turned his back and pressed his ass against Warren's dick and rubbed for just a minute, and then Warren was coming all over Victor's ass crack.

"Oh, man," Warren said, when he could catch his breath.

Victor smiled a shit-eating grin. "I've been wanting to do that since I saw you at the party. But just so you know, I still want you to play for my team."

"I thought that's what I was doing," Warren said, and they both laughed.

RITE OF PASSAGE

Victor had another job to do that evening in Kendall, so he went back under the shower to rinse off, then dressed quickly. "See you Saturday," he said as he hurried out of the locker room while Warren was still dressing.

Warren was confused. Was Victor going to be another friend with benefits, like Thom? Was that all there really was to gay dating, just meeting up and having sex? Maybe that's why his family disapproved of gay people so much.

He knew there had to be something more. He often saw gay couples walking together on South Beach, and he knew guys who were in relationships. Fitz, the house manager at the Three Lambs, had been together with his boyfriend Chuck since they were freshmen, though theirs was an open relationship that was more like a free-for-all.

Was he supposed to call Victor, he wondered, as he drove home? Say thanks for the blowjob? Or just ignore that it had happened, show up for the rugby team practice? Did Victor blow everybody—was it some kind of rite of passage for the team?

He wanted to talk to Thom about it, but he was embarrassed. He and Thom had just had sex twice that week, and Warren was already getting blown by somebody he barely knew. That made him feel like a slut, which he didn't like.

So he didn't call Victor, and Victor didn't call him. He focused on his job, his diet, and his workouts, and by the time he showed up for the practice on Saturday afternoon, he was on his way to getting back in shape. He parked as directed behind a library branch at one side of the park, and walked out to the field, feeling self-conscious. Victor was all right, but what if the other guys were a bunch of bitchy queens or status-conscious pretty boys?

He almost walked right past a group of about a dozen regular-looking guys. Two of them were kicking a ball around, while the others were talking and laughing. Victor veered away when he spotted Warren.

"Hey, glad you could make it," Victor said. "Guys, this is Warren. Our new loose head."

"Look more like moose head." The thirty-something guy who spoke had an accent that reminded Warren of Boris and Natasha from the *Rocky and Bullwinkle* cartoons. "I'm Leo." He was showing off big guns with a T-shirt with the sleeves ripped off.

The other guys introduced themselves, and Victor organized them into two teams of six to practice. Nobody said anything about sex, about who was doing who or who had done who, and so Warren kept his mouth shut and looked for cues to Victor, who seemed to have forgotten all about their locker room interlude.

Warren was assigned to Leo's team. "You know what to do?" Leo asked.

"Protect Victor," Warren said. "Right? He's the hooker."

Leo nodded. "Anybody comes near whoever has the ball, you block him." He patted Warren on the stomach. "You're big guy. You will do fine."

From the inside, the game was fast-paced,

chaotic, and crazy. Warren tackled with glee, rolled on the ground like a little kid, even jumped up and down when his team scored. By the time night began to fall, he was a rugby convert.

Leo told him he and a couple of the other guys were heading to that sports bar for beer and chicken wings and invited Warren to join them. He breezed through a yellow light and arrived at the bar first. He stood outside waiting for the rest to arrive, worried for a moment that this was a prank played on the new guy.

But Leo rolled up a minute later, in a van emblazoned with the logo of an online site called GetBalled.com. At first Warren thought it was a sex site, but he realized from the illustrations that it sold sports equipment. Leo got out of the front and flexed his arms and legs. "Shit, I am old man," he groaned.

"Stretching is the key to staying flexible," Warren said.

"Yeah, I know. So, Victor say you played in NFL?"

Warren shrugged. "More like hugged a bench for a year. In Jacksonville."

"Hey, they are good team. You must have been excellent player to make it."

"It's over now," Warren said. "Gotta get my jollies from rugby from now on."

"Excellent!"

The rest of the guys arrived, and they staked out a big round table in the corner of the bar. Their server was a young guy named Nathan with geek glasses that kept sliding down his nose, and he was obviously their regular because they razzed him about coming to play with the team sometime. "Your boyfriend will appreciate your moves," Victor said.

"He already does," Nathan said.

"Nathan's an awesome athlete," Victor said. "You should see him do a jeté."

"A what?" Warren asked.

"Ballet," Nathan said. "I dance with a company in Fort Lauderdale. You should come see us sometime."

He took their orders and left. "I don't think of a ballet dancer as an athlete," Warren said, when he was gone.

"Are you kidding?" a guy named Pete said. He looked like the kind who went to the ballet. He was slender but wiry, and fast on his feet, and taught computer graphics at the community college. "You should see the way those guys work out. Make the rest of us look like pansies."

"Which we are," Victor said, and they all laughed.

Except Warren, who was never going to call himself a pansy, even if he sucked dick and played on a gay rugby team. He could only stretch so far.

They talked as they ate, about the game, their jobs, their families. Leo said something about his wife and Warren did a double take. Jesus, what kind of a woman would marry a gay guy? Unless he was talking about a guy he called his wife because he was the boss in bed? It was confusing, but Warren kept his mouth shut.

The guy beside Victor was Brendan, a tough-looking accountant with wiry forearms who looked like a real gym rat. He lived in Wilton Manors and had a mostly gay clientele, and he crowed about the extra work he was getting as long-time gay couples got married and had to change their tax status.

Warren was curious, but none of the guys seemed to be dating each other. Pete had a boyfriend. Jerry, who managed a coffee shop in Wilton Manors, seemed to date his baristas, sometimes more than one at the same time. Brendan was a horndog who had sex wherever he could.

Warren didn't think he'd ever be friends with these guys. Their lifestyles were so different from his. Even Brendan, who was a jock, geeked out about accounting.

The bar was loud and rowdy, groups cheering on teams on the big-screen TVs. The wings were crisp on the outside and juicy inside, and the beer kept flowing. When the bill came, Leo insisted on treating. "GetBalled is going through roof. We are so busy; I need to hire a guy."

"To do what?" Jerry the coffee-house manager asked. He was dead skinny and could slip through the narrowest gaps between offensive players. Warren thought he was kind of good-looking, with a two-day old beard and floppy dark hair.

"We need more products," Leo said. "Right now, we have football, baseball, basketball, soccer, rugby. All very excellent sports with many players. But I want expand to other sports. I must find guy to go to trade shows, read sports blogs, find all newest coolest products that jocks want."

"Gay jocks?" Warren asked.

"All jocks," Leo said. "We are like team here, don't discriminate. Gay, straight, bi, in closet, out of closet, whatever. As long as they like play sports."

"In case you haven't figured it out yet, Leo's our token straight guy," Pete said.

"What about Evan?" Jerry asked. "He's straight."

"Yeah, if you believe what he says," Pete said. "You wait. One day he's going to drop trou in the locker room and offer that dick of his up for sampling."

"Our official policy is that we're a nondiscriminatory sports team," Victor said to Warren. "We welcome anybody who wants to play rugby."

Warren was confused, but that was his new normal these days. He'd assumed that all the guys were gay, because of the way they talked. But Leo really did seem to have a wife, a female one. And there was at least one other straight guy on the team.

When they were all paid up, Warren lagged behind, waiting until it was just him and Victor. They walked out together into the humid night and Victor said, "Listen, about the other day."

Here it comes, Warren thought. It was a mistake, yadda yadda. He tried to shortcut the inevitable regrets by saying, "I appreciate the time you took to give me those pointers on the field. It really helped me out today."

"We call it the pitch," Victor said. "Not the field. But that's not what I meant."

Warren started to speak, but Victor held up his hand. "Let me say this, all right? I feel like a real dumbass because I'm worried that I moved too fast with you. You're the kind of guy who presses all my buttons, Warren, and I was thinking with my dick. But I like you, and I want to get to know you better. Please don't think I'm the kind of asshole who fucks around with every guy he meets."

"As long as you don't think the same thing about me," Warren said. The neon signs in the bar windows cast colorful glows on the parking lot. Behind him, Warren could hear guys cheering, and out on US 1 cars and trucks dashed past like their drivers were eager to get to wherever their weekend was starting.

"You're not dating anybody else, are you?" Warren asked.

Victor shook his head. "My last relationship went up in flames a couple of months ago. Guy who couldn't understand why I was always working out, playing rugby, running, whatever. But that's who I am."

"You're a jock," Warren said.

Victor nodded. "I swore then that I wasn't going to get involved with anybody who didn't share my passion. It's carried me this far, and I'm hoping it will carry me a long way ahead."

Warren looked across the highway to a row of big-box stores, their parking lots full, their windows glowing. "I don't know what my passion is. I thought it was football. But now that's over, and I don't know what else to do."

"I know just how you feel."

Victor was quiet for a moment, and Warren tried to relax, enjoy the buzz, being close to this interesting, sexy guy who was on his wavelength.

"You in a hurry to go somewhere?" Victor

asked. "Because there's something I want to show you."

Warren said that he had no plans, and Victor said, "Great. My apartment is just a couple of blocks from here. You want to follow me?"

"I do," Warren said. Wherever Victor was going, it was probably going to be better than the directionless wandering Warren had been doing.

PIN COLLECTION

Warren figured that what Victor had to show him would involve nakedness, and he was up for that. Literally. He'd been feeling a chubby off and on all evening, whenever one of the guys touched him or looked at him, and he was looking forward to getting off. And Victor was a cool guy to hang out with too.

He followed Victor's car into a neighborhood of low-rise apartment buildings. Palm trees clustered along the narrow street that led into Victor's complex, long rows of townhouses with parking spaces in front. People had customized the small squares in front of their houses with hibiscus and bougainvillea, orchids hanging from the branches of oak trees, cute little statues of cats and rainbow flags.

Victor pulled into a space, and Warren snagged a guest spot a few cars down. The night hummed with the sounds of insects and air conditioners, and street lamps that could have come from Victorian England cast tiny pools of light on the pavement.

"Nice place," Warren said, as he reached Victor.

"I like it," Victor said. "I grew up in New Hampshire, where it was cold and white all winter, and summer only blossomed for a couple of months. Never knew there was any place like this in the world." He waved his hand to encompass the palms and banana trees, and, Warren assumed, even the little gecko lizard slithering past into the underbrush.

"I didn't either," Warren said. "I just knew I wanted to get the hell out of South Carolina, and FU offered me a full ride."

"Yeah, I got a ski scholarship to UNH," Victor said. "I stayed on the team all four years, to keep my money, but my freshman year I found my real passion."

He opened the front door, and they walked into a small lobby with mailboxes along one wall. "Sex?" Warren asked.

Victor shook his head. "You'll see when we get inside."

They climbed to the second floor, and Victor opened the door to his apartment. "Welcome to the shrine," he said.

Warren had no idea what to expect, but he walked in. The first thing he saw was a poster-sized photo of a younger Victor, in a red long-sleeved shirt and black ski pants, with a bright blue helmet. He was sitting on a black sled in a tunnel of ice, with his feet stretched ahead of him.

Warren walked up closer to the picture, and that's when he saw a collection of lapel pins mounted on black velvet, under glass. At a quick glance, they looked like they were from the Winter Olympics. "You collect these?" he asked Victor.

"I did. In Vancouver. See, that one's from the opening ceremonies, and that one's from the closing. That square one with the snowflake was the official pin for the luge team. I got a whole bunch of them and then traded them for most of the rest of these."

"That's cool," Warren said. "I watch the Olympics on TV. It must have been so awesome to actually be there."

"I knew you'd understand," Victor said. "After it was over I was lost. I had no idea what else I wanted to do with my life. I spent years chasing that dream, and I had nothing to replace it with."

Warren looked at him curiously. "You spent years wanting to watch the Olympics in person?"

"Not watch, Warren. Compete." He pointed to another photo, this time of a guy lying flat on a sled. "That's me, only you can't really tell because of the helmet."

"Hold on. You competed in the Olympics?"

"In Vancouver in 2010. On the luge team."

Warren wasn't even sure what a luge was, though obviously it was some kind of sled. They didn't get enough snow in South Carolina for a lot of winter sports, and to be honest he mostly watched the skiing on TV, not the other offbeat sports. But he knew how hard you had to work to achieve anything in sports, and he was awed.

"I feel like I should do that thing, you know, where the guy bows down and says, 'I'm not worthy,'" he said. "I've never known an Olympic athlete before."

"And I've never known a guy who made it all the way to the NFL before," Victor said. "That's why I thought you might understand."

Warren nodded. "I'm starting to. How come you stopped?"

"You want a beer?" Victor asked. "This could take a while."

Warren agreed, and he continued to study the photos and the pins while Victor went into the kitchen. He had a box full of stuff of his own, things like field passes with his name, a photo of him at the NFL draft. But he hadn't wanted to face it so he'd pushed it to the back of his closet.

He started to laugh. "What's so funny?" Victor asked, as he returned with two bottles of beer.

"I was thinking about the stuff I have from my time in Jacksonville, and how it's stuck at the back of my closet." Warren took the bottle from Victor and clanked it against Victor's. "Something else to keep in the closet."

Victor laughed too. "Yeah, I was seriously in the closet when I was competing. Not that any of us had time for sex anyway. When I was in college, I'd go to class, work out, ski, and train on this natural luge course up in the mountains. That was it. In the summer, I'd stay up in New Hampshire and keep training, all day, every day."

"Football wasn't that intense," Warren said. "And I couldn't skate through my classes at FU. I had to study." He remembered Thom then, and how their friendship had begun with tutoring. But that's all it was, right? Just a friendship. Friends with benefits, Thom had said. Leaving the way clear for Warren to do whatever he wanted with Victor.

"But still. You get it, in a way that most guys, especially most gay guys, don't. That waiter at the bar, Nathan? He gets it. He's been studying ballet since he was eight years old, and he gave up everything else in order to get as good as he is."

Victor sprawled onto his dark blue futon. "Come on, take a load off. I want to tell you why I quit."

Warren sat down gingerly beside him. He was always afraid to sit too hard on other people's furniture for fear it might break under him. Victor leaned back beside him, touching his lower leg against Warren's. "For like a year or so before Vancouver, I started getting these killer sinus infections," Victor said.

He paused to drink. "I doped myself up with antihistamines and kept on working. Nothing was going to stand in my way. I'd knock it out, and then a month or two later it would come back. It started affecting my stamina and my ability to breathe."

"Wow," Warren said.

"But I pushed on. I just wanted to make the team, you know? I knew that we didn't stand a chance of medaling. But just to be able to compete at that level."

"I know what you mean."

"I made it through my heats, but I didn't make it to the semi-finals. It didn't kill me, though. I stuck around until the closing ceremonies, partying, trading pins, hanging out with other athletes. I even met a few who were gay."

He got a faraway look in his eyes, and Warren wondered if that meant that Victor had hooked up with someone there, maybe even fallen in love. "Had to change planes twice to get home, and by the time I got there I was sicker than I'd ever been. I went to the emergency room, and the doctor admitted me. I had this thing going on called biofilm."

"Sounds very high-tech," Warren said.

"It's very low-tech, actually. A group of bacteria get together in a moist environment and form, well, a film. Happens all over the place in nature. But in my case, it was happening in my sinuses. I'd taken so many antibiotics and antihistamines that whatever was up there had become resistant to treatment."

"Wow. How did you get over it?"

"I didn't, not really. I had an MRI, a cat scan, surgery to widen my nasal passages, anything the doctors could think of. I got it under control, but I still get bad infections at least once or twice a year."

"So that killed your chance to compete."

"Exactly. I didn't have the stamina anymore."

"But you can play rugby."

Victor nodded. "Rugby was my saving grace. I moved to Philly for the doctors there, and one of them played on a team. He introduced me to the sport, and I started to feel like I could be an athlete again. I could still train, and play, but at an amateur level. And if I get sick, I stay in bed and take care of myself until I'm better."

"When you saw me at the party, did you know who I was, that I'd made it to the NFL?" Warren asked.

Victor shook his head. "I just got a vibe from you. I knew we needed a big guy like you for the team, and I thought you looked like an athlete."

"I'm glad you came up to me," Warren said. "And not just because, you know. I need something in my life like you have. Maybe rugby will do it for me too."

Victor smiled. "I hope so."

Warren leaned forward and put his empty beer bottle down on the glass coffee table. "I'd be happy to have you in my life too. On whatever terms."

"Oh, Warren," Victor said, and he shook his head. Warren was worried that he'd said the wrong thing, that Victor believed their shower sex had been a mistake. "Don't settle for anything. Figure out what you want and go for it. Be the winner you are inside."

Warren couldn't help himself. He started to laugh.

Victor crossed his arms over his chest. "What?"

"I'm sorry," Warren said, struggling to control his giggles. "But you sound just like one of my motivational CDs." He paused to catch his breath. "I know what I want. You." Then he leaned over and kissed Victor on the lips, hard.

Victor struggled against him. "Whoa, Warren. You don't have to push that hard."

Warren looked down at his lap, embarrassed. "Sorry. I don't have much experience kissing."

"We'll have to remedy that, then," Victor said, and took his hand.

Warren lost track of time, but he figured they had to have spent at least a half hour kissing on the futon.

Victor stood up and reached for Warren's hand. "See, it's all about practice," he said, tugging Warren up from the futon. "You can't expect to be good at anything without practice."

"And I'll need a good coach." Warren stood and wrapped his arms around Victor. "I can see I'm going to need a lot of sessions with you."

"We can work that out," Victor said, and there was a devilish smile in his eyes.

ENJOY THE NOW

"I may be fast on the pitch, or on a luge run, but I like to take my time in bed," Victor said, as he led Warren into his bedroom. "I hope that's all right."

The room was dominated by a king-size sleigh bed made of dark wood, with a brown and white comforter in a geometric print. "Take things as slow as you like," Warren said. "As long as we get where we're going eventually."

"I like the way you think. Would you mind if I took your clothes off for you?"

"Mind? Hell no. Go for it."

Warren had worn a double-XL rugby shirt, in blue and black stripes, to the practice, and he had it tucked into his jeans, which were uncomfortably tight, a reminder that he still had some weight to lose. Victor tugged the tails of the shirt out, and then slipped his hands up underneath it.

"I know, I'm fat," Warren said. It wasn't like it had been in the shower at the park, where they were both naked. He felt uncomfortably on show, especially since Victor was so well-muscled.

"You are not," Victor said. "You're a big guy; that's all. And I like my men big, so you'll never hear me complain about size."

"But you're so fit," Warren said, as Victor ran his rough-skinned hands over Warren's smooth belly.

"Shut up, Warren." Victor tugged on Warren's chin, and Warren leaned down. Victor went up on his toes, since Warren was about three inches taller than he was, and pressed his lips to Warren's. The kiss was even more awesome with Victor's hands reaching up, up, to Warren's nipples and tweaking them.

Warren groaned with pleasure. Victor backed off from the kiss. "You're going to have to duck your head down for me to get this shirt off," he said.

Warren bent over, and Victor tugged the shirt off. When he stood back up, Victor said, "Oh, man, you are just fucking gorgeous."

Warren blushed. "Nobody's ever called me that before."

"You just didn't meet the right guys," Victor said. "Until now."

He unbuckled Warren's belt and opened his jeans, and Warren took a deep breath at the relaxation. Victor leaned forward and rested his head on Warren's chest, and Warren wrapped his beefy arms around Victor and held him close.

Victor began nibbling at Warren's left tit, which made him crazy. His dick was stiff and pressing against the protective cup of the jockstrap he'd worn for practice. Victor reached down to rub him. "Wow. You feel even bigger than before. Hold on down there. Don't you get ahead of me."

"I'll try," Warren said, his mouth dry. "But that's…that's not all me. It's a cup."

Victor laughed. "You get better and better, Warren. You are truly my wet dream come to life." He pushed Warren's jeans to the floor, and Warren kicked off his sneakers. He was left in white socks and his white jockstrap.

Victor dropped to his knees, still fully clothed, and pressed his face against Warren's jock. "Oh, yeah. Oh, Jesus, Warren. I'm about to come in my pants just thinking about you."

"Then you'd better get naked fast," Warren said. "I don't want to miss anything."

Victor laughed. He stood up and pulled his shirt off, then tossed it aside. He undid his jeans and shimmied out of them, dropping a pair of silk boxers with them.

Warren thought he knew what Victor would like. He grabbed Victor by the waist and pulled their bodies together, back to front, so that the cup was pressed against Victor's ass. Victor was breathing fast, and Warren rubbed against him. He reached around and grabbed Victor's dick, hot and wet and pulsing, and began to jerk him. His dick chafed against the hard plastic, but he didn't care; there was no way he was stopping now.

Victor yelped and squirted cum, and then he twisted around so that he was facing Warren. He stuck his hand inside the cup and began to jerk Warren, and then bit down hard on Warren's tit. Warren felt like he was losing consciousness, so overwhelming was his orgasm. He spurted into Victor's hand.

"Go for the gold," Victor said, looking up at Warren and smiling. "Always go for the gold."

Victor went into the bathroom and returned with a wet towel, and Warren dropped his skunky jock to the floor. As Victor approached, Warren got a good look at his body.

Warren had been forced to take anatomy and introduction to sports medicine as part of his degree, and he'd never been able to memorize all the muscle groups. But if he'd had Victor as a study partner, he thought, he probably would have done much better.

Victor was a walking model of muscular layout, and Warren hoped he was going to have a lot of time to study him.

Victor cleaned him up, and then yawned.

Warren took the hint. Guess he wasn't going to make it into that big, comfortable-looking bed—at least not that night. "I should get back home," he said. "I have a client at the gym early tomorrow morning."

"Just don't give any of them the kind of workout you give me." Victor leaned up and kissed Warren's cheek. "I'll talk to you this week, all right? I might have another client in Miami one day."

Warren didn't bother to put his jock back on when he dressed, liking the feeling of going commando. He left Victor's place suffused with the pleasant afterglow of great sex, and as he walked back to his car he passed a pair of guys holding hands. "Have a good night," Warren said to them, smiling.

"You too, sweetheart," one of them said, and instead of cringing as he normally would have, Warren just laughed.

He got back into his car, adjusted his junk in his rugby shorts, and threaded his way back through the narrow streets to I-95. It was a long drive back to Kendall along bright highways, but Warren hardly noticed the time passing, so caught up in happy endorphins.

He resolutely decided to ignore any possible complications in the future, just enjoy the now, as one of his CDs counseled. He wanted to share his happiness with someone, and the only one he could think of was Thom, but for some reason he didn't want to tell Thom about it.

Had he ever told Thom about sex with anyone else? Not that there had been a lot of guys besides Thom, but there had been a few, mostly in Jacksonville. It was funny that he could talk about anything with Thom except sex. He had no idea if Thom had sex with other guys, but if he did, it wasn't Warren's business, right? If Thom was his friend, he ought to want his friend to be happy.

By the time he made it back home, he was running on empty, ready to crash, but he spent an extra moment in the bathroom, staring at himself in the mirror. "This is what you look like happy, bud," he said to his reflection. "Remember this."

He went back to work on Sunday, picking up new clients from the rotation. But even though he was determined to do his best, his heart just wasn't in it. He was lonely, for one thing. He needed to be part of a team, and since the other trainers were also consultants who came and went, he hadn't connected with any of them, not even the one he shared the house with. His only friend in town was Thom, and Thom had his own life, his studies, his part-time job, his brothers at the frat.

His housemates were nice enough, but hadn't made any overtures to befriend him, and he was always uncomfortable about pushing himself on others. He wondered if the guys on the rugby team might become friends someday.

He remembered that Leo ran a website, and went online to check it out. Maybe that would give him something to talk about the next time the team met.

GetBalled.com had a good selection of

products, including some things Warren had never seen before. The website was slick and professional, with lots of pictures of athletes using the equipment, and sales copy that was so persuasive Warren found a bunch of things he wanted for himself.

But the site didn't seem finished, somehow. It was missing a lot of sports, the offbeat ones that only a few people practiced, but those few were fanatical in their devotion, always looking for the newest best gear. Leo ought to get onto that.

Maybe Warren could put some ideas together for Leo, a first step toward establishing a better friendship. He had a pretty good background in sports management, from his college courses, and he knew a little about almost every sport played. He had worked summers at sporting goods stores, first in South Carolina and then in Florida, and he knew that he could talk about gear and sell people on it.

He sat back against his chair, his brain whirring. He searched online for the most popular amateur sports. No surprise, soccer was number one. GetBalled.com already had that covered. Number three on the list was tennis, and Warren was surprised that Leo wasn't already competing there. Tennis used balls, right? And golf. There had to be a lot of competition in that space, but maybe there was room for Leo to get his foot in the door.

Boxing, swimming and diving, and cycling were also very popular, and though none of them used balls, it sounded like Leo was ready to expand beyond his initial concept. Probably too much of a stretch to throw in skiing or ice hockey—this was Florida, after all, and who knew anything about winter sports here? Then again, Victor had been on the ski team in college and competed in the luge. And Warren had seen notices for ski clubs that went on vacation together.

He started making notes. He wasn't sure what he'd do with the information, maybe just casually drop some ideas the next time he was hanging out around Leo. He found an academic study on the sports industry, and though a lot of the business jargon was beyond him, it was interesting to see the ideas it brought up—the difference, for example, between sports, recreational activities, and games of skill like chess or poker. Running was a sport, jogging a hobby, for example.

That distinction didn't matter when it came to selling products, though. Runners and joggers both needed quality footwear, and there were so many new gadgets for tracking performance.

It wasn't until he'd been working for over an hour that Warren realized that this was the first time since college he'd been engaged by anything other than studying football plays. He worked until it was time for bed, and by the time he shut down his laptop he'd covered a couple of pages of a legal pad with scribbled notes, statistics, and questions.

Maybe there was an opportunity for him somewhere—if not with Leo's company, then another one in the sports industry. He looked at the clock, wanting to call Thom and share this new insight, but it was already late. Better to save it for the next time they met, when they could celebrate Warren's new direction.

LIFE DECISIONS

Monday morning, Warren was on duty starting at eleven, and he had a couple of clients during the day. Mid-afternoon, as he was finishing a training session, Thom showed up at the gym. Warren waved at him through the big glass windows and saw Thom settle down in the lobby with a book. When the client's session was over, Warren took a quick shower and dressed. "What brings you out here? Going to join?"

Thom closed his book and stood up. "I wanted to talk to you. You free now?"

"Sure. You want to go to the juice bar next door?"

Thom agreed, and they walked out into the humid Miami afternoon. Dark gray storm clouds massed over the Everglades, and the air was heavy with automobile exhaust. A bright green gecko skittered past as Thom opened the door of the juice bar, a narrow space painted sunshine yellow.

They ordered power smoothies and settled down at a wrought-iron table with a rickety leg. "What's up?" Warren asked.

"I'm trying to figure out how to say this," Thom said. "But you know how when you make one of those big life decisions it's really hard?"

"I usually sit back and let the decisions get made for me," Warren said. "You know I got recruited to FU. Then I went into the NFL draft, and Jacksonville picked me up. Then dropped me. So I'm not the best guy to ask for that kind of advice."

"But you and I, we, you know, we've been

friends for a while."

Warren was confused. Was this about their friendship? Their occasional sex? Did Thom want to stop? Or did he want to be Warren's boyfriend?

His brain was scrambling through all those ideas. What would that be like, to be Thom's boyfriend? Would they go to the movies together, hold hands and shit?

Thom took a deep breath. "Here's the thing. I hate teaching."

Warren was surprised. So this wasn't about the two of them dating? He kicked himself. *No, you big dumbass. It's not all about you.*

"But you're getting your master's degree," Warren said. "I thought that was because you wanted to be a math professor."

Thom shook his head. "I like math. I like the way that numbers always do what they're supposed to do. I like studying math. I just don't like teaching it."

"Why not? I remember when you tutored me. You were really good."

Thom smiled. "I was good at helping you because I had ulterior motives. And it was a challenge, figuring out how to get you interested enough in math to pass the course." He sat back. "But being a TA for a class of a hundred kids? It's boring the shit out of me. I teach a couple of recitations, and most of the kids are there just because it's a core requirement. They don't care about the math."

"Won't it get better after you graduate? When you're the one in charge?"

Thom shook his head. "I've seen some

professors who love to teach, and it shows. But there are others… I think they went into math because they didn't want to have human contact with anyone. I'm afraid I'd turn out like that."

"What else can you do?" Warren asked.

"That's where I'm getting hung up," Thom said. "I've been so focused on getting ready for this semester, the classes I'm taking and the ones I'm teaching, that I haven't been thinking about the future. It's like I finally woke up." He looked at Warren. "And when I needed somebody to talk to, you're the first guy I thought of."

"I appreciate that," Warren said. "And I want to help you; I really do. But jeez, you know how I am with math."

He remembered the job that Leo's website had. Though he'd been thinking of it for himself, maybe it was what Thom needed. "I met this guy through the rugby club," he said.

"The rugby club? You mean at FU?"

"I didn't tell you? I will. But first let me tell you about this job." He explained what GetBalled.com did, what kind of person they were looking for. "You could do it," Warren said. "You're smart; you can do research. Leo's a good guy. You'd like him."

"It sounds great," Thom said, and Warren's heart sank a little, though he really did want his friend to be happy. "For you."

"For me?"

"Of course, Warren. It sounds like a great gig for you. You should totally call the guy. You could get out of the gym you hate."

"But what about you?"

"I don't know what I'm going to do. But I'm glad I could talk to you. Just saying it out loud helps." He drained the last of his smoothie. "I need to get back to campus. I have a lot of prep work to do for tomorrow."

Thom left, and Warren sat back in the juice bar. Customers he recognized from the gym stopped in before or after workouts. They all seemed to have a purpose, places to go, things to do. Why didn't he? Could working for Leo be the direction he needed? But he wasn't a salesman, and he had no head for business or numbers, the way Thom did. He was a guy who used his body, not his brain.

The storm clouds had moved closer, and it had begun to pour. Warren dumped his cup in the recycle bin and headed out in the rain.

When he got home that night, Warren called Victor. "I was thinking about talking to Leo about that job he has. What do you think?"

"You'd be terrific at it," he said. "I should have thought of that myself."

"I'm worried I'm not smart enough," Warren said. "I don't have much of a head for business."

As soon as he said it, though, he remembered all the research he'd done the night before, all that business stuff he'd read. Sure, he hadn't understood it all, but he could learn. He'd made it through college, right?

"You understand the jock mentality," Victor said. "That's the biggest part. And I'm sure Leo has an accountant or a bookkeeper to handle the numbers."

After he hung up with Victor, Warren went back to the research he'd done. For one of his sports management classes, he and a couple of classmates had to come up with a business plan, and he dug through a box of his old papers to find it.

It was pretty lame, he realized. They'd written about buying an old RV, refitting the inside as a personal gym, and driving around to clients' homes. It was short on actual numbers, but they had put a lot of work into specifying particular pieces of equipment that they could carry around with them easily, like kettlebells, medicine balls, and dumbbell sets.

He couldn't present something like that to Leo. Hell, how did he know that what he'd come up with was any good?

He called Thom. "Hey, you got a couple of minutes?" he asked.

"For you? Sure. What's up?"

Warren told him about the research he'd done on sports equipment. "But what if it's just dumb stuff that anybody could figure out? I don't want to embarrass myself."

"Tell me what you found," Thom said.

Warren went through it all, stopping now and then as Thom asked questions. When he was done, Thom said, "You need to believe in yourself more, Warren. What you've put together is really awesome."

"You think so?"

"I do. This guy Leo would be lucky to have you on his team."

After he hung up with Thom, Warren thought about what his friend had said, calling Leo's company a team. From all his years playing football, as well as other sports, he knew that a solid team was composed of players with different skills. Some of his teammates could run fast, while others had golden hands that latched onto any ball in the vicinity. Big guys like Warren who could block for the quarterback and place kickers who could put a ball right in the center of the uprights.

Maybe there would be a place on Leo's team for him.

BROMANCE

The next morning, Warren had no clients scheduled, and he called the number on Leo's business card around ten. "Hey, Leo, it's Warren. From rugby. I was wondering if I could talk to you more about that job your company has. If it's still available, that is."

"Yes. I have no time for hunting for right guy. But maybe we can talk at lunch?"

"I have nothing scheduled until late this afternoon," Warren said. "I could come up and meet you whenever."

They arranged for noon at a Mexican place near Leo's office on University Drive, off I-595. "You can bring resume, please," Leo said.

Warren agreed and hung up, smiling and pumped. Cool. This was a lot easier than hunting for a personal training job. He'd had to scour the online ads, visit corporate websites, and fill out complicated applications, then wait around hoping someone would call.

He popped open his laptop and looked at the resume Thom had helped him prepare when he returned to Miami. Compared to others he'd seen, his was pretty skimpy—just the couple of part-time jobs in high school and college, and a big section on playing football at FU, and then in Jacksonville. Thom had helped him focus on the teamwork, communications, and leadership skills he had gained on the field.

For Leo, though, the jobs Warren had held in sporting goods stores would be important, and he looked those over with an eye to improving them. He went to a couple of resume sites to see what they suggested. He changed "sold sporting goods to customers" to "helped customers analyze their needs and suggested appropriate equipment, then provided instructions and training tips."

It was more than he'd actually done—most of the time he'd stood at the register and rung up sales. But he could have analyzed and suggested, if he'd been given the chance.

Thom had also impressed on him the importance of the job objective statement at the top of the resume, and so Warren hit the Delete key and removed what was there. He opened a web browser and went to GetBalled.com to see what he could learn about the company.

Thom had told him to look for key words in job ads and then use those in his objective. But how could he do that when there was no ad to respond to? He looked at the "about us" page for clues. GetBalled was a site for jocks, by jocks, he read. *We only want the best equipment for our own workouts and games, and that's what we provide for you. We listen to the ideas our customers provide, and bring new products to market based on their ideas, suggestions, and even their complaints.*

Warren nodded and then started to type. *A position with a dynamic sports-oriented company, where I can search out the best products in exercise and leisure sports to help clients make the most of their fitness experience, using my background in college and professional sports with an emphasis on teamwork.*

He sat back. Looking good. Thom would be proud of him. He'd have to show it to Thom the next time they got together.

He printed up a clean copy and put it into a bright blue folder with the Jaguars' snarling cat on it. He looked in his closet and dug out a polo shirt with the same logo, combed his hair and put on his best smile. If that wasn't enough for Leo, then all he'd have wasted was time and gasoline.

Even though Warren was early, Leo was already at the restaurant, standing in the shade of the awning and talking on his cell phone. He ended the call when Warren approached. "Hey, thank you for coming up to meet me," Leo said.

Warren was glad to see that Leo was wearing a polo shirt with his company logo, rather than a suit. He didn't think he'd want any job where he had to wear a jacket and tie to work every day, even if it meant all he could do was pick up trash in a public park somewhere.

They went inside, and the hostess greeted them in Spanish. Leo responded in the same language, and Warren was impressed. "How many languages do you speak?" he asked, as they slid into a booth.

"Russian, Ukrainian, Yiddish, Hebrew, English, Spanish," Leo said, counting them on his fingers. "Is six. I am trying Mandarin Chinese, but is very difficult."

"Wow," Warren said. "I took a couple of semesters of Spanish in high school but usually the best I can manage is *una cerveza, por favor*."

"In my business, language we speak is sports," Leo said. "And I know you can talk that." After they ordered, Leo repeated what he'd said earlier about the job. "You know about products?" he asked. "What sports? How many you play?"

"You mean beyond football? When I was a kid I swam and dived, played in Little League, some basketball, a little soccer. I've tried my hand at racquetball, skiing, and tennis. And last summer I spent some time as a grinder on a big yacht. You know, one of those guys who works the winches that raise and trim the sails, move the boom."

"Yes, is pretty big-ticket sport. Too rich for us."

"I don't think so," Warren said. "I read that there are something like seventy-five million recreational sailors in the United States. And if they sail, they probably swim and dive too. So you've got all kinds of water sports gear you could be selling them."

Leo cocked his head. "You think about this stuff?"

"Only since I met you," he said. As they ate, he talked about the research he had done. "How come you haven't gotten into tennis or golf? Both of those are huge sports with balls."

"Lots of competition in that space," Leo said. "And they are individual sports, not team."

"All the more reason why you should sell to them," Warren said. "When you're on a team, you often buy the shit your teammates do, right? You see somebody has some cool shoes, or sunglasses, and you buy them. But if you play on your own, or just against a friend or two, you don't have that resource."

"Interesting." Leo pushed his empty plate toward the edge of the table. "You have resume?"

Warren handed over the folder and Leo scanned the page. Then he looked up. "One thing worries me. You have not much real work experience. Just sporting goods store?"

By then, Warren had decided that he really wanted to work for Leo, and he was going to pull out all the stops to get it. "If by work experience you mean showing up for a job, doing your hundred-ten-percent best, then you've got to consider my time with the Jaguars," he said. "You have to be incredibly determined and focused to get a spot in the NFL. Sure, other players had more natural talent than I did, and I only stayed on the roster for one season. But I can bring that determination to work for you, and I promise you won't be sorry."

Leo picked up his iced tea and took a long sip, and Warren felt like he was holding his breath. "All right, I give you chance," Leo said, when he put his glass down. "My only problem, I need you yesterday. How soon you can start?"

"I'm not on staff at the gym," Warren said. "I'm just a freelancer. If you give me a day to rearrange the couple of clients I want to hold onto, I could start on Thursday."

Leo was pleased about that. "Job is small salary plus generous commission. My secretary get all paperwork ready and e-mail you. Then if you have questions, we talk again."

Warren felt like his heart was wriggling around in his chest like a worm on a hook. "That's awesome." He couldn't wait to get out of the restaurant and call Thom.

Leo paid the bill, and they walked out together. "Call me after you see papers." Leo reached out to shake Warren's hand. "Thursday you meet rest of team and get started."

Warren's head was buzzing as he drove back home. That research he'd done had really paid off. He was so thrilled, and as soon as he got off the turnpike he called Thom to crow. "I got the job. I start Thursday."

"Congratulations, dude," Thom said. "That was awful quick, though. Isn't there something a little suspicious about that?"

"Suspicious? What do you mean?"

"Well, usually companies want to interview a bunch of people, check their references, all that stuff. Remember when the gym brought you on? Even just as a part-timer they had all those hoops you had to jump through."

"That's because the gym is a big corporation," Warren said. "This is Leo's company. If he sees somebody he wants to hire, he does. And he told me he needs me, like, yesterday. So business must be good."

"Just be careful, big guy," Thom said. "Have you looked at any of this company's financials? Are they really doing the business he says they are?"

"I thought you'd be happy for me, dude," Warren said. "Instead, you've got all this negative energy. Just because your life is crashing and burning doesn't mean mine has to."

"Hey, I'm happy for you," Thom said. "But you always say you don't have much of a head for business. I just want you to be careful."

"Everybody treats me like some big, dumb hunk of meat," Warren said. "I have a brain, you know. I have a college degree."

"I know, Warren. Remember, I tutored you in math. I've seen what you can do when you set your mind to it."

"Well, watch me now," Warren said. "I'm setting my mind to this. Listen, I gotta go. I'm at the gym." He hung up, even though he was still miles away. He didn't need Thom's negativity bringing him down from his high.

But what if Thom was right, he thought, as he stopped at a traffic light on Kendall Drive. What if Leo's business wasn't as good as he bragged? Suppose the company tanked?

Well, then he wouldn't be any worse off than he was, he thought. As long as he could keep his hand in at the gym for a while, he'd still have it as a fallback.

IN HIS CORNER

Warren worked with Candy again that afternoon. She was wearing baby blue that day, from her top to her pompoms. "I did what you suggested," she said. "On Saturday I went out to the backyard with my son, and we practiced those things together, the squats and the sprints and all."

"How'd that work out?"

"He killed me," she said, laughing. "But afterward he said it was the most fun he'd ever had. We're going to keep doing it a couple of times a week. But here's the thing, Warren. I can't manage that and training with you too. So I'm going to stop for a while."

"No worries," Warren said. "Actually, I got a new job, and I start Thursday, so I have to work things out with my clients."

"You did! That's great! What gym?"

"Not a gym. Come on, let's walk around the track, and I'll tell you about it."

"You're going to make me work, even after what I told you?" she protested, but Warren could tell she was kidding.

They climbed the stairs to the second floor and began the circuit. The big room reverberated with the sound of machines squeaking, people talking and laughing. Warren described GetBalled, and the job he was taking. "I'm kind of nervous about it. I've never worked in a real office. Just, you know, in stores and gyms."

"Make sure you get a good night's sleep tonight," she said. "And leave early for work, so you don't get nervous if you run into traffic. Get yourself a little pocket notebook, and take notes—who you meet, what their names and jobs are. Otherwise it can all be pretty overwhelming."

"That's great, Candy. I'll do that."

"Don't be afraid to ask questions. You're the new guy; they'll expect that. And make sure you really listen to the answers."

Warren nodded. "Before I let you go, I'm going to write all this stuff down. How'd you learn all this?"

"I used to be in human resources, before I got knocked up." Warren was startled, and she said, "Don't worry, it was all planned. My husband and I both agreed that the most important job I could have while the kids were little was being there to raise them. I'll be in your shoes in another year or two, looking for a job, starting over."

How many times did you have to start over in one life, Warren wondered, after Candy had gone home. When you're a kid, you think every new school year is a whole new start—new teachers, new classes. Then you get to college and you think you can settle down for four years.

But every year he had to fight for his place on the team, and then came the NFL draft, and walking into the locker room in Jacksonville on his first day. Sure, he'd known he wasn't going to last, but it had still been hard to come back to Miami and start over.

"Come on in, Warren," his boss said. "I'm glad to see you're back to your old self."

"Not quite," Warren said. "Listen, the thing is, I got offered this job." He explained about it. "But I'm not sure it's going to last, so I was hoping I could still keep some clients here, nights and weekends."

"If the clients are willing to work with your schedule," his boss said. "And you can't do this forever. I need trainers who are committed. Say three months?"

Warren nodded. That would give him until January. If things hadn't taken off with Leo's company by then, he'd come back to work full-time.

When he got home, he called Victor, but got his voice mail and had to leave a message. He was as nervous as a cat at the dog pound, as his mamaw used to say. He kept pacing around the house, trying to remember all the things Candy had told him. He found a little note pad he could carry in his pocket, and he went to the GetBalled website to write down the names of people he might meet and get more familiar with their products.

It was hard to concentrate because his stomach was churning, and his head started to hurt. Finally he broke down and called Thom. "Can you look at this website with me?" he asked, hating the whiny tone in his voice. "I start tomorrow, and it's all starting to swim around in my head."

"Sure. You want to come over here?"

"I feel kind of sick. You think you could come here?"

"My gas tank is low, and I have to wait until I get paid on Friday to fill it up," Thom said. "Can we do this over the phone?"

Warren agreed, and on his end Thom brought up the GetBalled website and started to look through it. "I'm impressed," Thom said, after a couple of minutes. "They've got some sophisticated software behind all this."

"How do you know?"

"I took a couple of programming classes at FU," Thom said. "I can do some basic coding myself, and I can recognize when somebody knows their shit. Whoever put this site together does."

They looked through some screens, practiced placing orders and after an hour Warren realized he wasn't feeling so sick anymore. "I really appreciate this, dude," he said to Thom after they finished reading all the FAQs together. "I feel a lot better about tomorrow."

"Cool beans," Thom said. "We should get together this weekend and celebrate. Saturday night?"

"Playing rugby Saturday," Warren said. "Not sure what time we'll finish." And he wanted to keep his schedule open in case Victor invited him back to his place again. "How about Sunday?"

They made plans to meet, and then Warren hung up. It was so good to have Thom in his corner, he thought. Sure, they had their little arguments and disagreements, but in the end he knew Thom was always there for him, and he was there for Thom. That must be what having a boyfriend felt like, that sense of the two of you against the world. Somebody there to hold your hand when you were having a bad day, to kiss away all the hurt.

Kissing reminded him of Victor Ragazzo. Warren looked at the clock and realized he needed to get to sleep. But Victor hadn't returned his call. What was up with that?

In the morning, though, there was an e-mail. *Sorry, had to work really late,* Victor wrote. *Big house out in Plantation, and the owners could only let me in after dinner. But I should be free tonight. Call me in the afternoon.*

Warren only had one client that morning, and the rest of the day free. He spent it going around to every sporting goods store he could find, walking up and down the aisles, looking at the equipment. Most of it was very generic stuff, workout clothes, baseball bats, tennis rackets, and so on. Only a few specialized stores had gear for elite athletes, and he couldn't find many of the products he'd seen on the GetBalled site at any store.

By the end of the day he was back in Broward County, near where Victor lived. He called, and Victor answered.

"I got the job," Warren said. "With Leo's company. I start tomorrow."

"Wow. You're a fast mover, Mr. Updegrove. But then, I saw that on the pitch."

"The thing is, I'm scared shitless I won't know what to do." Warren explained about all his research. "But I still need to process everything."

"A cool down talk," Victor said. "Yeah, I can help you with that." They arranged to meet at the sports bar.

Warren was so eager that he couldn't just go inside and wait for Victor; he had to pace around out front until Victor pulled up. "You look just like a puppy," Victor said. "So happy."

"I'm excited," Warren said. "I mean, the new job, and playing rugby, and meeting you. My life has taken a complete 180 from like two weeks ago."

"Let's hope you don't get too disoriented from

the spin," Victor said. They went inside and sat at a booth, and Warren was disappointed that Victor hadn't tried to kiss or at least hug him. It was a sports bar, so a little bromance wouldn't have been out of place. But Victor was all business.

"So, tell me what you've been doing," Victor said.

Warren explained about looking over the site with Thom, then going around to stores, in between ordering drinks and nachos.

"All this is fine," Victor said, when Warren was finished. "But it's just a bunch of data. You need a way to put it all together."

Victor thought for a minute. "What are the top five most popular sports in America?"

Warren shrugged. "Football, baseball, basketball. Soccer? Hockey?"

"Let's see what the Internet says." Victor pulled out his cell phone and typed. "Good for you, Warren. You got the top five. But remember, a lot of those sports are popular more for watching than for playing. How many adults with disposable income do you know who actually play football?"

Victor held up his hand. "Outside of NFL players, that is."

"Not many, I guess," Warren said. "Maybe pickup games at parks?"

"Yeah. Same for baseball, I think, though I know there are a lot of companies that have softball leagues. Basketball, I think a lot of guys still try and shoot hoops. But mostly I think adults are playing golf and tennis. And running."

"And cycling," Warren said, remembering the

research he'd done.

They brainstormed for a while, coming up with ideas Warren could take to the office for sports and products that GetBalled could get into, and Warren felt almost as excited as he had at the thought of playing in the NFL. Was it just the new job? Or spending this time with Victor? He didn't know.

After they'd finished two beers each, and big platter of nachos, Victor said, "Well, it's been great seeing you, Warren. But I've got an early job tomorrow so I need my beauty sleep." He stood up. "I'll get this. You can treat the next time, once you have a paycheck."

Warren was confused. So he wasn't going home with Victor? Yet there was going to be a "next time."

"Maybe we can get together this weekend," Victor said. "After practice on Saturday. We'll see how things go."

"Sure, that would be great," Warren said. It wasn't exactly a date, but at least it was something. Victor slapped some bills on the table, waved to the ballet-dancing waiter, and walked out.

Warren sat there for a while, zoning out to the background noise of laughter and TV sports. Why was this whole business so complicated—finding a job, finding a guy? Would it ever get any easier?

He felt his stomach begin to churn again, and stumbled to the men's room, where he leaned over the toilet and threw up the beer and nachos. He held onto the partition for a minute afterward, steadying himself. He took a couple of deep breaths.

He was tough, he thought to himself. He'd

never been afraid on the field—not of tackling, of getting knocked down, of screwing up. He just had to channel that into the rest of his life. Mamaw used to point out the rooster in her yard, the way he strutted around. *"He act that way 'cause he got balls,"* she'd say. *"You got 'em too, Warren. You just got to remember that."*

GET BALLED

Warren took Candy's advice and left earlier than he thought he needed to get to Leo's office for his first day, which was a good thing, because he had a hard time finding the place. He got off I-95 at Sheridan Street and drove through a maze of narrow streets that dead-ended, making U-turn after U-turn. Then he remembered he had a map program on his phone. He pulled into the parking lot of a furniture company and plugged the address in.

He saw where he was, and where the office was, and began driving slowly in the right direction, watching as the moving dot that represented his car got closer. Finally he pulled up in front of a large warehouse building with about a dozen bays. A couple of the signs were in Spanish, one in what looked like Portuguese. A Canadian flag flew outside the office of a French-language newspaper.

He parked in front of the bay with the GETBALLED sign, walked up to the door, and turned the knob. It was locked, and he looked around for an intercom or some way to communicate with the inside. Nothing.

He knocked. No answer. He looked around; the parking lot was shared by all the companies in the warehouse, so he couldn't tell if any of the cars belonged to GetBalled workers. He didn't see Leo's distinctive van either.

What the fuck? Had he gotten something wrong? Maybe this was the warehouse, not the office. But it was the only address on Leo's card. He pulled out his cell phone and dialed the company number. A young woman's voice answered with a message: the office was closed, but he was welcome to leave a message and someone would get back to him.

What was he going to say? I'm here for a job, and where the fuck is everybody else? He ended that call, and then dialed Leo's cell.

It sounded like Warren had woken him up. "Um, Leo? It's Warren."

"Hey, Warren. I am looking forward to your first day at work."

"Yeah, that's the thing. I'm maybe lost. I'm at this warehouse address on your card, and nobody's here."

"Shit, I guess I don't tell you," Leo said. "Much work we do is with West Coast and with China, so we don't open until ten. Michelle will open door few minutes before then. Starbucks up on Sheridan, go chill."

"Sure, no problem," Warren said. "I'll see you at ten."

He hung up. What a way to start his first day. He drove up to the Starbucks, bought an overpriced cup of coffee, and hung out in the air-conditioned space until it was ten. This time, when he tried the door to GetBalled, it was unlocked, and he walked into a small reception area of two metal chairs and a sliding window into an office.

The girl behind the window was petite and blonde. "You must be Warren." She stuck her hand through the window. "I'm Michelle."

He shook her hand and said, "Hi."

"Come on through; I'll show you around," she said. "These guys are a bunch of night owls, so it's just you and me right now."

The door opened into a cavernous space lined with metal shelves. Half were empty, the other half filled with a kaleidoscope of colored boxes in all sizes and shapes. At the far end of the room, he saw rolling doors. "This is the warehouse," Michelle said. She was older than he'd originally thought, mid-forties, and she wore a multi-colored tie-dyed T-shirt over jeans and Birkenstocks.

She pointed toward the rolling doors. "Merchandise comes in by the truckload. Jackie and Cesar are our pickers and packers; they'll be here later. They unload the cartons and stock the shelves."

They walked as she talked. "This terminal here is where they pick up the orders," she said. "They pull the order sheet and pack the box, then print out a label and seal the package up. UPS comes every day at five to pick up, but half the time one of us is running out to the office at the airport with late deliveries."

She opened a side door and led him into a cube farm. "This is where the coders work," she said. "Buzz and Pritap. They keep the website running. That's Leo's desk in the corner, and the one next to him belongs to Moises. He's one who does all the contracts."

Each of the cubicles was elaborately decorated with sports posters and memorabilia, from All-Star game jerseys to Dolphins giveaways. "That empty desk over there is yours," Michelle said. "Have a seat, and I'll bring your gear over."

Warren nodded and walked across the industrial gray carpet to his cubicle, with walls on two sides. He was across from Leo, with the programmers diagonally across from him. It was weird standing there, like he was in some science fiction movie where the earth had been decimated of people, while leaving all their crap untouched.

Not that different from an empty locker room. A locker room never really came alive until there were guys in it, changing, comparing game notes, talking smack about each other.

He pulled out the pad Candy had recommended he bring, and he wrote down the names Michelle had mentioned, along with their jobs. Then he checked out their cubicles for which sports and which teams were their favorites, and wrote that information down too.

Michelle returned as he was finishing, carrying a couple of boxes. "This is your laptop," she said. "If you need help getting it set up, one of the programmers can give you a hand. And here's your company cell phone, and a bunch of blank business cards you can write your name on until I get some ordered for you. Leo didn't exactly give me a lot of notice you were coming."

"Me neither," Warren said.

"We can use you," Michelle said. "This place gets crazy sometimes." Then the phone rang, and she left him in the empty room with his boxes. Warren unboxed the laptop and the phone and got them charging. Leo came in with another guy of about his age. Warren couldn't tell if the guy was black or just had a really deep tan.

"This is Moises," Leo said. "Moises, Warren. Moises is one who keeps place running."

"Pleased to me you," Moises said, with a hint of a Latin accent. "Moises Caminero. Attorney, accountant, fill-in picker and packer."

"Hell, we all fill in when we got to," Leo said. "I check my e-mail then we talk."

The two programmers came in a few minutes later, and after introductions they sat down at their computers with headphones on and went to work. Warren felt lost, sitting there watching software load on the laptop and bars grow on the cell phone. This was just what he'd feared—he had no idea what he was supposed to do, and it scared him.

He heard a loud grinding noise he assumed was the back doors opening. In the background he heard people talking, the sound of a forklift moving around. Everybody around him had something to do except him.

Finally Leo waved him over. "So, what we going to do with you, Mr. Warren?"

"I did some research," Warren said. "Ice hockey is the only one of the top five sports in the United States where you don't have any product coverage. Why not?"

"Good question," Leo said. "We start business here in Florida, where there almost no hockey. But now hockey my number two priority for new products."

"What's number one?"

Leo leaned back in his chair. "You tell me."

Warren thought for a minute. Had to be either tennis or golf, because the other popular sports he could think of, auto racing and wrestling, weren't so much for participants as spectators. Or maybe swimming? If Leo did a lot of business in Florida, then any one of three could be possible.

Leo was watching him. "Swimming and diving," Warren said finally.

"Interesting. Why no golf, no tennis?"

"You told me the other day that there's a lot of competition in that space. And I read an article yesterday that said golf equipment sales are way down," Warren said. "Golfers are playing less and are more reluctant to replace their clubs with new equipment. And there's so much product out there that the price competition is stiff."

"Smart. And tennis?"

"Just a gut feeling. I know people like to watch pro tennis, but how much equipment do you really need to play? A racket and a can of balls, right? And unless you're one of those assholes who smash rackets all the time, how often do you need to buy one?"

"So. Swimming."

"I watched the last Summer Olympics," Warren said. "And I saw all those new swimsuits for competitive racers. I think maybe that's filtering down to ordinary people. Swimming is good aerobic exercise, and you need at least a couple of suits if you're swimming frequently. Not to mention goggles and ear plugs and then all the recreational stuff, like boogie boards and swim fins."

"I like way you think," Leo said. "Is just way I think too. So we jump into pool, see what kind splash we make."

"Even though there aren't any balls involved?" Warren asked. "I mean, isn't that your name?"

"Do Amazon sell rain forests? Zappos sell magic wands? Name is just name, way to get foothold in business." Leo leaned forward. "But is something I need first, before that. You have been on our site?"

"Sure," Warren said. "First place I looked."

"Which area our weakest?"

Warren frowned. He hated having to criticize his boss on his first day. But he had noticed that they weren't as deep in the soccer category as in the others. "Soccer?"

"Exactly. Whole World Cup thing really threw us, even though Moises come from Mexico and supposed to be expert."

Moises looked up from his work. "Fuck you all the way back to Ukraine," he said, then went back to reading.

Leo laughed. "But we don't want just throw in bunch of crap. What are best products in each category? You work that first, and when you finish, then dive into swimming." He poked Warren in the arm. "I make joke! Dive into swimming!"

Then his cell phone rang, and Warren was on his own again. Pritap, a skinny Indian guy with tattoos up his arms, helped him get his computer connected to the network and the Internet, and Warren got to work researching soccer. Of course, since the rest of the world called the sport football, there was a lot of confusion.

When he'd gone to sporting goods stores, all he'd found was a basic selection of balls, jerseys, and socks. One store had the equipment necessary to set up a goal, and another had one box of something called a soccer trainer, basically a ball on a rope that you kicked for practice.

There had to be more out there, he thought. He went online and started searching. There was a lot of variety in shoes and in jerseys, from plain cotton to fancy fibers to wick away moisture. Most of the shirts had the logo of one team or other—Emirates was the biggest one, apparently.

As he dug deeper, he found pop-up goals, scrimmage vests, and equipment for training like sticks and ladders. Nobody did as good a job with soccer as GetBalled did with other sports, in his opinion, so there was definitely room to improve. He started making lists of items that GetBalled didn't carry, then researching the best in each category.

He had to put the work aside late in the afternoon, when things got very busy in the office. A website glitch had Buzz and Pritap cursing, and then a flood of orders required the rest of them to pitch in with fulfillment. Leo and Moises helped with the picking, and Jackie, a tall Jamaican woman with cornrows in her hair, showed Warren how to use the machine that shot out strings of air bags, and how to use the tape machine to seal the boxes up. Then he plastered on the labels and handed them off to Michelle, who entered them in the UPS system for pickup.

He loved the feeling of teamwork—it was the first time he'd felt comfortable that day. Everybody joked with each other. Skinny Pritap pretend-staggered under the weight of big boxes. Jackie spoke in a rapid Jamaican patois, criticizing every uneven run of tape, every misplaced label, but always with a big smile.

Warren was the biggest guy, so they had him stack all the large boxes on the forklift. Nerdy Buzz showed him how to drive it up to the back door where the delivery truck waited, and then they alternated passing boxes over to the driver who scanned each one. It was like a smoothly operating machine.

Maybe there would be a place there for him after all, Warren thought.

RULE BOOK

Warren didn't leave the office until nearly seven o'clock. It was still light out, though a couple of street lamps had come on, and the air buzzed with the hum of insects and the noise of tiny lizards skittering through the brush. It reminded him of evenings walking back to his dorm from football practice, the feeling of having accomplished something that day.

He thought about calling Victor to tell him about his first day. But Victor had been kind of cool the night before, making it sound like he wasn't interested in hearing from Warren until Saturday.

Instead he called Thom.

"Hey, big guy, how was your first day at work?"

That was Thom, Warren thought. He knew what a big deal this job was to Warren and was right there, ready to hear about it. He was about to say that it had gone well, but he could be honest with Thom. "Up and down," he said. "For a while I was confused about what I was supposed to do, but then things started to click."

"That's the way it is anywhere," Thom said. "You don't just walk into a new team and know everything."

"That's so right," Warren said. He talked about all the packing they had to do at the end of the day, how it felt like a team to him.

"This is going to be the best thing for you," Thom said when he finished. "I'm so stoked that you've got this job."

Warren hung up and wondered why he

couldn't feel so easy with Victor. He really had no clue how to do this dating thing. It wasn't like there was a manual you could get, an official set of rules like the ones published by the NFL. You could go to their website, and download the rule book, a summary of signals and penalties, and a casebook with each rule and its categories and subcategories. There was room for interpretation, but at least you had a place to start. Why didn't somebody do something like that for gay dating? Player conduct, out-of-bounds rules, goals and fumbles and when the clock stopped on a play.

When he got home he sat up in bed with his laptop to look online for a rule book for gays. Some of the rules he found were funny, like the one that said dating guys was like shopping for a sofa at IKEA. You might think he looks good in the store, but do you really want him in your living room? And if you were looking for a prince, go for a William, not a Charles—one who wouldn't cheat on you with some horse-faced slut.

Some of them were more serious, though. Like the "don't have sex on your first date" rule. He'd broken that for sure, if you considered that practice session with Victor, and their shower sex afterward, as a first date. "Save some of the magic for the future," Warren read.

Well, fuck. And he'd thought things were going so well with Victor once Victor had shown him the Olympic memorabilia and confessed his own failed dreams, and how he had come back from them. But was he doing that because he saw Warren as a loser who needed to be rescued?

Another one of the rules had to do with letting go of the past, with stuff like getting bullied as a kid, or the trauma of coming out, because that held you back from being able to form real relationships. But how could he get rid of that, when he hadn't experienced it?

Warren had always been big enough and tough enough as a kid that no one had dreamed of bullying him. He had never told his family, or even most of his friends, that he was gay, so he didn't know for sure how they'd react, but he suspected it wouldn't be pretty.

He wanted to talk about it with Thom, but he wasn't ready to confess what he'd done with Victor yet. And Thom had his own problems, with figuring out what he wanted do if he didn't want to be a math teacher. Warren had enough on his plate without getting into that.

But when he saw Thom on Sunday, he'd have to say that things were heating up with Victor; he wasn't going to be some sleazeball and have sex with two different guys at the same time.

He could feel himself getting angry, and he gave up and slotted one of his relaxation CDs into the player. If he had fucked up with Victor, then he had to use it as a learning experience and move on.

He was surprised late that night when Victor called. "I'm on my way home from a job. How was your first day at Leo's?"

"It was good," he said. He felt like he'd talked through everything important with Thom. "Leo's a good guy. I think I can learn a lot working there."

They talked for another few minutes, and then

Victor said, "I'm pulling up at my friend's house. I'll catch you on the flip side."

He hung up before Warren had a chance to ask who the friend was. Someone from the rugby team? A friend with benefits? Why had he said he was on his way home when he wasn't?

Warren went back to work the next day, researched products and suppliers, and helped out where he was needed. He kept his head down and his dick in his pants. He'd never had an office job before, and he had worried that he'd get bored and fidgety after a few hours, but there was no time for boredom at GetBalled.

That afternoon Leo called a time out and gathered the guys in the warehouse for a quick game of touch football, him, Warren and the male packer, Cesar, against Moises and the two programmers. Jackie and Michelle stayed on the sidelines making sure nobody crashed into products.

With Warren blocking for him, Leo completed pass after pass to Cesar, a skinny Nicaraguan who had played soccer back home. They only stopped because Moises took a tumble into a tower of UPS boxes, and Michelle yelled at them.

Warren left that day feeling happy. He'd worked out some aggression playing with the guys, and it was looking like this job could be a keeper. Now all he had to do was figure out what was going on with Victor.

That night he got a group text from Victor reminding them all of the practice Saturday afternoon. Warren wasn't sure what to expect from Victor. Would he be distant? Friendly? Romantic?

* * * *

Saturday morning Warren got to the gym well in advance of his first client so he could warm up. The quick game the day before had been his only exercise for a couple of days, and he was feeling stiff. He had three clients scheduled, an hour apart, and none of them showed up. At least Ed, the old guy, called to cancel.

Warren realized that he didn't care. He had enough money put aside to carry him until he got a paycheck from GetBalled, and he knew in his gut that he wouldn't be able to balance both gigs. So he pushed himself through a punishing workout, then went back home and napped until it was time to leave for rugby practice.

Though he knew he'd just get sweaty again, he showered before he left the house. He shaved again, sprayed on cologne, put some gel in his hair. When he got to the soccer field, there were a couple of cars in the parking lot but no one on the pitch. He heard raucous laughter coming from the locker room, so he walked over there, carrying his workout gear.

Victor, Brendan, and Pete were inside. Victor was still in street clothes, while Pete, the guy who looked like he watched ballet, was in his shorts and rugby shirt, putting on his shoes. Brendan, the wiry, fast-talking accountant, was buck naked, in the middle of a story. Warren nodded to them all and walked over to a locker.

"So I think the guy's just being friendly," Brendan said. As Warren kicked off his shoes he took a quick glance at Brendan's body. The guy had blond stubble and tatted arms, zero percent body fat and six-pack abs. His ass was high and tight, with a thin line of dark blond hair. He sure didn't look like an accountant.

Warren went back to changing as Brendan continued the story. "I say hello to him and keep on walking into the ocean. The water's warm, and I'm getting a boner from being naked out there."

"You get a boner from anything," Victor said. "Trust me, I know."

The guys laughed, and Warren took another glance. Victor had pulled off his shirt, and Pete had his shoes on, but Brendan was still naked. He'd half-turned toward Warren, to include him in the story, and Warren noted with satisfaction that Brendan's dick was on the small side. Yeah, he thought, you build up all those muscles, but you can't do anything about the one that counts.

"The guy comes back up to me, and he grabs my dick," Brendan said.

"Right there in front of everybody on the beach?" Pete asked.

"We were in the water up to our waist, and we were facing away from the shore," Brendan said. "I was surprised, and I tried to back away, but he had a grip on me. He didn't even look me in the eyes, just kept looking out to sea and jerking me. Didn't take long before I spurted."

Jerry, the coffee shop manager, walked in then. "Not another story of Brendan's awesome sexual conquests," he said.

"Sounds more like Brendan was the conquest," Pete said. "And some random chubby guy at the gay nude beach at Haulover was the taker."

"Hey, he didn't take anything I wasn't willing to give." Brendan reached for a jockstrap. "I was just surprised."

The rest of the guys filtered in, and when they were all changed they walked out to the pitch as a big group. "Good news, guys," Victor said. "I have a game set up for us next Saturday afternoon."

"All right!" Jerry high-fived Victor. "Who are we playing? High school girls, I hope. Somebody we can crush."

"Sorry, Jerry. Our first opponents are all male. The club at FU in Miami."

Brendan turned to Warren. "Didn't you go to school there? You ever play with those guys?"

How did Brendan know where Warren had gone to school? Warren was pretty sure he hadn't mentioned anything about college. "Nope. I was focused on football. And the rugby dudes seemed really crazy."

"All rugby dudes crazy," Leo said.

"Yeah, but these dudes know the rules," Victor said. "So I want you all to take a look at the rule book sometime this week so we don't do anything stupid on the pitch."

They ran through a bunch of drills and then split up into teams to play. Victor and Brendan were the hookers for their squads, which put Brendan in Warren's sights. There was something about the dude that just didn't sit right with him, though he didn't know what it was.

When Brendan had the ball, Warren had the chance to tackle him, and he did, putting all his power into it. In the resulting scrum, he found himself on top of Brendan, and he was embarrassed to realize that he had a hard-on.

Brendan knew it. "Jesus, Warren, you packing a baseball bat in your pants?" he said, when Warren rolled off him.

"Warren's a big guy." Victor reached down to give Brendan a hand up. "And you know that's what I like."

"He must be as big as that black dildo you have," Brendan said.

"Excuse me?" Warren said. "I'm right here." He felt his face reddening as his anger built. He was fucking sick and tired of gay men teasing him about his dick size, especially after that dick pic episode at the party.

"Come on, Warren, you gotta have a sense of humor," Victor said. "Everybody on this team envies you."

"Not everybody," Leo said. "If I have dick like Warren's, I split my wife open."

"Front or back?" Jerry asked.

"All right, enough!" Victor said. "Let's get back to play."

Warren was still in a lousy mood by the time the practice ended. He was the first one back in the locker room, and he was already changed by the time the rest of the guys arrived.

"You in a hurry?" Victor asked him.

"I've got stuff to do," Warren said. "I'll catch you later." Then he strode out of the locker room without looking back.

EXTRA LARGE

Warren was pissed. He was angry at Brendan and Victor for teasing him, and he was angry at himself for reacting so badly. And for walking out on a chance to spend the evening with Victor.

But he knew himself. When he got a head of steam up, he had to have his space and calm down, at his own pace. If he'd stuck around, he might have exploded, and that was not a good thing.

Back in high school, he'd had much less control of his emotions. His mamaw had said he was like a teakettle always on boil. The only places he had been able to stay calm were at home and in church. Warren was the middle child of three, sandwiched between Wanda, two years older, and Winona, two years younger. Wanda was the smart one. She wore nerdy eyeglasses, got straight As, and had gotten her teaching degree at the University of South Carolina. She was engaged to a guy who worked for his father's car dealership.

Winona was the pretty one—nearly six feet tall with a heart-shaped face, big breasts, and a tiny waist. She began competing in beauty pageants when she was six, and the year before she'd been the reigning Miss South Carolina. Their mother had been a pretty woman once, Warren could tell from old pictures, though the stress of working full-time and raising a family had taken its toll on her.

Warren's father was six-three and all muscle. He worked at the local steel mill and crewed for a shrimp boat in season. Warren had been dragged along a few times as a kid, but as he got older, summer and fall meant football practice, and football was the only thing more important to their father than church.

Winston Updegrove was a petty tyrant, exploding over the smallest infractions—a dish left in the sink, failure to straighten the hall rug. Simple shit. *"None of you all is ever gonna be too old or too big to feel the wrath of my belt,"* he often said. Warren could only imagine how he'd cope with a gay son.

Fear of his father had kept Warren in line at home, and fear of God had done the same thing in church. He came from a long line of Southern Baptists, and his father bragged that deep in their past the Updegroves had been Pentecostals—snake handlers, up in rural Kentucky.

Warren and his sisters had gone to Sunday school as kids, and their parents made them go to church every Sunday as long as they lived at home. From the time he reached puberty, Warren had known that he was a sinner. All men were, of course, because they were conceived in sin and would die in sin. But Warren knew he was worse than the rest of the men because of his sinful desires.

He had begun playing Pop Warner football when he was five years old, in the Tiny-Mite division, and he had spent his youth on playing fields, basketball courts, and in locker rooms. He was always surrounded by other guys, and half the time they were in various stages of undress. He was fourteen before he realized that other guys didn't seem to react the same way he did.

He remembered it clearly. He was in the locker room in junior high after gym class, and a bunch of the guys had clustered around a skinny, effeminate boy named Luther. *"Luther's got a boner,"* they'd teased him. *"Luther's a fag. Only fags get boners around boys."*

He didn't join in the teasing, but after that he was careful whenever he was in the shower to keep his dick soft, thinking about math problems and female teachers whenever he wasn't distracted by conversations or thoughts about games.

As he got older, the guys he played with were always talking about girls, about getting to first or second base, about which girl had the biggest tits. He remembered a joke he'd heard that he hadn't understood for a long time. *"How do you make a hormone?"* one of the guys had asked him.

Warren shook his hand. Science was a mystery to him.

"Do it with a baseball bat!" the other guy had crowed, and everyone had laughed. It wasn't until a year later that he got the joke.

After spending so much time in all-male environments, he was awkward around girls and never knew what to say. He went on group dates with guys from the football or baseball teams, and occasionally a girl would ask him to the movies or a school dance. Sometimes the guys would tease him about being shy, and he accepted it because he didn't want them to figure out the real reason why he wasn't interested.

He had fumbled with girls from time to time, though he got no pleasure from kissing them or feeling up their breasts. The one time he'd tried to have sex with a girl, toward the end of his senior year in high school, he had been so awkward trying to get the condom on that he was ready to flee in terror.

Sarah Jane had a reputation as being easy, and she was certainly more experienced than Warren. "My, you are a big boy," she said to him, in her southern drawl. "Here, let me help you."

He had a couple of condoms he had picked up at a high school health fair, but none of them were big enough. "Let me see what I have," Sarah Jane said. They were in her frilly pink bedroom, her parents away for the weekend. She opened her bureau drawer and found one. "Here we go. Extra large!"

She held it up, and Warren felt mortified. "Don't you worry, sweetie," she said. "Some girls like a really big man."

She had taken over then, opening the condom and rolling it down over his dick. She couldn't tell that he wasn't hard, because of his size. She had kissed him for a while and then opened her legs and tried to guide him in, but he wasn't interested, and she wasn't big enough. In the end, she had wrapped her hand around his dick to get him ready for a blowjob, but he'd ejaculated before she could even wrap her lips around him.

He had been mortified for days that word of his inability had spread around school, but it seemed all Sarah Jane had said to her girlfriends was that Warren was the biggest boy she'd ever had. In college, he talked a good game in the locker room about a girl back home he was sweet on, and that relieved some of the pressure.

In the fall of his freshman year, he and a bunch of his teammates were rushed by one of the fraternities on campus. One Saturday night, the guys gathered at the frat for a movie night. Warren was so naive he was expecting some action picture, but when the lights went down and a naked girl and a donkey appeared on screen, he realized how dumb he had been.

The frat brothers had filled squeeze bottles with mayonnaise and at one point in the movie, when two guys were boning the same girl, they squeezed them off and everybody made a big joke. Warren had been enthralled by that scene, even though the two guys never even touched each other. Just the idea of being naked with another guy gave him such a boner he was afraid he'd come in his pants.

The brothers had passed around a bunch of dirty magazines, and one of them had mentioned that he had bought them at an X-rated bookstore on Bird Road, not far from the campus. *"You would not believe how kinky this place is,"* the guy had said. *"They have everything there. Guys with chicks, chicks with dicks, guys with guys."*

A couple of weeks later a friend with a car had asked Warren to drive him to the airport, with the offer that Warren could keep the car for the weekend if he'd pick the guy up on Sunday. Warren agreed, and on the way home from the airport he found himself on Bird Road.

* * * *

He was ambling along, looking at the scenery, when he spotted the X-rated bookstore. He couldn't help himself, he turned in and parked. His pulse was racing and his dick was stiff, but he sat in the car for a while, not sure of what to do.

He knew what Pastor Tice would have said. There was a devil inside Warren, and Warren had to fight against his baser impulses. But Pastor Tice had been married three times and had four kids, so he must have given in to sex now and then. Warren walked into the store, his hands shaking, not knowing what would be behind that black-painted glass door.

It was so ordinary that he was confused—just fluorescent lights and wire racks, like a K-Mart of porn. Some instinct drew him right past the straight porn at the front to the gay racks at the back, where magazines, books, and movies were displayed face out. Naked guys alone or having sex with other guys. Dildos and cock rings and other stuff whose purpose he had no idea.

The store was empty except for a bored clerk at the register. Warren browsed through the magazines, finally starting to see his desires. He skipped over the black guys, the she-males, the carpenters, and plumbers. What really made his dick jump were the locker room fantasies.

"This isn't a reading room," the guy at the register called to him. "Buy something or move on."

Warren grabbed a couple of the magazines and walked up to the register. "Sorry," he mumbled.

"You wouldn't believe the shit that guys get up to in here," the clerk said, as he rang up Warren's purchases. "I gotta keep an eye out."

Warren handed over the cash, grabbed his bag, and walked out. His whole body shivered like a plucked guitar string. It took him a couple of minutes to calm down enough to be able to drive.

* * * *

He was angry back then too. Angry that he had these desires, angry that people disapproved of them. Angry that he had no idea what his future was going to be like.

And now here he was, angry again, driving home alone after walking out on Victor and the rugby team, without even a porn magazine for company. Oh, well. At least there was the Internet now. When he got back to the house, he went to his room and shut the door. He stripped naked and lay back on his bed, with his laptop in front of him.

He had a favorite site with a mix of amateur videos and clips from movies you could download for a price. The amateur ones were his favorites, particularly the ones with sports themes. The commercial pictures weren't believable enough for him. He'd seen too many where guys had blacking under their eyes and wore football pads, jock straps, and nothing else. But they didn't have the right physique to be athletes. They were too skinny, not muscular enough. The guys who pretended to be coaches weren't old enough or tough enough.

He skimmed through the recent uploads, hoping for a jerk-off session with a guy in a jock strap, or two hunky-looking guys out in the woods somewhere. He ended up watching a pair of big, hairy bears in a bedroom with a shaky hand-held cam.

He could tell they were amateurs. They were too awkward, not buff enough. But they were definitely into each other. He could see that from the way they looked at each other, the way they kissed, the ease they had with each other's bodies.

He wanted that, he thought, as he rubbed the head of his dick with his free hand. He wanted a guy who looked that way at him. Could he have that with Victor? They'd certainly had fun the couple of times they'd been together. And he felt a more than casual kinship with Victor, based on their shared background.

Both of them had dedicated themselves to achieving an athletic goal. Warren in the NFL, Victor at the Olympics. Had Victor had sex with any of the other Olympic athletes? He closed his eyes and pictured Victor on his back on the luge, only this time he was naked and hard, his hand on his dick. He was smiling up at Warren, encouraging him.

Warren jerked his hand faster and faster until he erupted in a stream of cum across his belly, pushing the laptop out of the way at the last minute.

He lay there, luxuriating in the post-ejaculation feeling. After a while his stomach started to grumble, and he got up, cleaned himself, and stuck one of the extra-large TV dinners from the freezer in the microwave. While it cooked he sent Victor a text, apologizing for walking out.

Though he kept his eye on the phone for the rest of the evening, there was no answering text from Victor. Had Warren screwed things up so quickly?

ALL IN

Warren was up early Sunday morning and ran a loop around his neighborhood. Then he went to the gym and worked out before his first client showed up. He went through the motions with him, and the two after him, and then slipped out to return home.

Still no response to his text to Victor, so he called. Got voice mail and tried to leave an upbeat message.

He spent the rest of the day online, researching sports equipment, until he met Thom for dinner at a restaurant near the FU campus. "How's it going?" Thom asked.

Warren shrugged. "I'm still having some anger management problems. I got pissed off after practice yesterday and stormed out. I'm afraid I might have screwed the pooch this time."

"In what way?" Thom asked. "You think they won't let you keep playing?"

"Not that. It's just, I started, you know, seeing this guy."

Thom raised his eyebrows. "A guy connected with this rugby club?"

Warren nodded. "He's really cool. He was in the Olympics. A luger."

"A loser?"

"No, dufous, the luge. You know, that sled thing? Don't you watch the Olympics?"

"Only the summer ones, where the guys don't wear so many clothes, like swimming and diving. I do watch the figure skating sometimes, though."

"You are so gay," Warren said.

"And you're not?"

"Not in the same way. I don't like ballet and opera and shit."

"Neither do I. Come on, Warren, you have enough experience to know there's all kinds of gay guys."

"Yeah, I keep learning that. Did I tell you it's a gay rugby team? Well, almost gay. There's one straight guy."

"Really? Do you guys get it on in the locker room after practice?" He nudged Warren with his knee, and Warren felt his face reddening. "Warren!" Thom leaned forward. "Really?"

"I don't want to talk about it."

"Come on. You can't tease me like that and then not spill the details. What was it, some group orgy like in porn movies?"

"It wasn't like that at all. It was just once, in the shower."

"Let me guess. One of the other guys spotted your sausage and gobbled it up."

"I am not my penis!" Warren realized that he had spoken too loudly. "Christ, everybody makes such a huge deal. Warren has a big dick. So fucking what?"

"Calm down, big guy," Thom said. "You know I think more of you than that."

"But you can't let it go," Warren said. "It's the first thing you think of when you think of me."

"What do you think of when you think of me?" Thom asked.

Warren looked down at the table. "You're smart," he mumbled.

"That's it? You're more interested in my brains than my body." He huffed, and Warren had the sense that Thom was pretending to be annoyed.

"You have a good body," Warren said, looking up. "And you can suck dick like a vacuum cleaner. I'm just more enlightened than you are."

Thom guffawed. "Yeah, right."

"So anyway, our rugby club is playing the FU team on Saturday. You think you could come and watch?"

"Can I get in on some of the locker room action too?"

Warren glared at him.

"Okay, not funny," Thom said, holding up his hand. "You're all serious athletes. Sure, I'm happy to come watch. You want me to wear a cheerleader outfit?"

Warren thought that might be sexy, but he didn't say anything. Then his phone buzzed with an incoming text. *Missed u last nite,* Victor wrote. *C U this wk?*

"Excuse me," Warren said to Thom. "I have to answer this." Warren's thumbs were too big for texting, so he used his index finger to type out a quick message back to Victor and hit Send.

"So are you getting serious with this guy?" Thom asked when Warren was finished.

Warren shrugged. "I don't know. Maybe?"

"Have you ever had, like, a boyfriend?" Thom asked. "An actual relationship with another guy?"

"You mean besides you? Because we do have an actual relationship, don't we?" Warren sure hoped the answer to that question was yes, because he felt closer to Thom than to anyone else in the world.

"Of course we do. But you know that's not what I mean."

"No, Thom. I have never had what you would consider a boyfriend before." Warren crossed his arms over his chest.

"Well, I think it's great that you're opening yourself up to that," Thom said. "Are you two going to be monogamous?"

"We've had like two dates," Warren exploded. "We haven't talked about that kind of stuff yet."

"But you're being careful," Thom said.

"Yes, Mom. Can we change the subject now? Have you thought about different careers besides just being a math teacher?"

Thom shrugged. "I've been reading up on stuff. But there are no jobs out there."

"Come on; that can't be true. A smart guy like you, with your talent with numbers? Are you really looking?"

It was funny to be the one giving Thom advice, Warren thought, as they talked through some of Thom's options.

"I just don't see myself a business guy," Thom said. "Wearing a suit to work every day? Sitting in a cubicle crunching numbers?"

"You'd look good in a suit." Warren felt his dick rise. Nope, not gonna go there. He was not having sex with two different guys at the same time.

Unfortunately that made him think about having sex with Victor and Thom together and that was even worse. He struggled to get his focus back. "It doesn't have to be like that," Warren said.

"GetBalled is a company, but it's not stiff and formal."

"They need anybody to crunch numbers for them?" Thom asked.

Warren shook his head. "They already have a guy for that. But there have to be other places out there you could work. Have you been to the placement office at FU?"

"Yeah. If I had a degree in engineering or hotel management, they could help me. But there are like ten people in my program at once, and almost all of them are going on for PhDs or planning to become teachers."

"I had this meeting with a counselor, part of my severance package with Jacksonville," Warren said. "He gave me this handout—a list of all the skills you develop as a professional athlete, compared to a list of things that employers are looking for. It was really interesting to see how much crossover there was."

"Earth to Warren," Thom said. "I'm not a professional athlete."

"That's not what I'm saying." Warren stopped to gather his thoughts. "See, this handout said that employers look for is the ability to learn new systems, because nobody ever comes out of college trained for the exact job they get. This counselor said that having to learn complex plays and then execute them showed I could do the same thing at a company."

He picked up a nacho. "You have a master's degree, so you've shown that you can learn new material and apply it, right?"

Thom nodded.

"And you had to be determined in order to

finish that degree. Employers like follow-through, people who can start a task and finish it."

"When did you get so smart?" Thom asked, with a smile.

"I was never that dumb," Warren said. "People have this stereotype that big guys who play sports have nothing upstairs."

Thom started to protest, but Warren stopped him. "Not you. You know me better than anybody. But football is a complex game, if you play at the highest levels. You have to be able to remember and execute plays, understand anatomy, nutrition, and muscle development. If you're too dumb, you never make it out of high school ball."

"You're absolutely right, Warren. And I'm sorry that I implied you weren't smart."

"Oh, I'm not a book-smart guy like you. But I know a few things."

"I can testify to that," Thom said, and the smile on his face sent those signals back to Warren's groin.

Warren figured it was time to say what had been on his mind. "You know I like having sex with you, Thom. But I kind of want to stick with Victor for a while. Just to see how things go. I know I would be pissed if we were starting to get serious, and I found out he was having sex with someone else at the same time."

"I understand completely," Thom said. "Here I am, unemployed, uncertain of my future, and you're taking away the only pleasure I have in life."

Warren's heart sank. "Oh, Christ, Thom. I'm sorry."

Thom laughed. "I'm just joking with you, big

guy. I could meet Mr. Right tomorrow and be the one saying the same thing to you."

"I'm not sure he's Mr. Right," Warren said. "But I won't know unless I give it a try, right? Gotta go all in for the win."

HOT AND BOTHERED

Victor called late that night, as Warren was getting ready for bed. He usually slept naked, because even the loosest of pajama bottoms or boxer shorts were too constraining for him. There was something very sexy about talking to Victor while he was naked, and his dick began to stiffen.

"Listen, I'm sorry I got pissed and walked out yesterday." He explained about the dick pic that Thom had taken at the party, how he was tired of having people focus on something that was such a small part of who he was.

"I hear you," Victor said. "Brendan was out of line, and I told him so. You're going to keep playing with us, aren't you?"

"Of course. I'm looking forward to the game this weekend."

"Maybe we can get together sometime before then?" Victor asked.

This time Warren was pleased when his dick reacted. He reached down and rubbed his thumb over the head. "Absolutely. You just tell me where and when."

"My calendar's all messed up this week. Jobs in Miami, jobs in Lauderdale. I'll text you when I know I can get away."

They talked for a couple of minutes and then Victor had to go. After he hung up, Warren sat back on his bed, his legs outstretched. His dick stuck up at an angle, and he wrapped his fist around it and began jerking himself. He closed his eyes and imagined that it was Victor's hand on him, Victor's teeth on his nipples, Victor's strong, smooth body pressed against his.

* * * *

It was like those first jerk-off sessions after he had discovered porn magazines at the X-rated bookstore on Bird Road. He was sharing a dorm room with another guy on the team, and he kept the magazines in a box in his closet, with textbooks and notebooks piled on top, and only pulled them out when he knew his roommate was going to be busy. Within a couple of weeks, the magazines were well-thumbed, some of the pages stiff where he'd accidentally come on them.

One afternoon he borrowed a Vespa from a teammate. He felt like a circus clown riding on a tiny bicycle. But it moved, and it got him where he needed to go. It was early evening when he pulled up in the bookstore's parking lot and locked the bike up.

His nerves were frayed from dealing with Miami traffic, and the excitement of going back to the store, and he hesitated outside for a moment to center himself. A skinny black dude, maybe forty, came out of the door carrying a paper bag and held the door open for Warren, so he had to go in.

The place was busier than it had been when he was there before. Was there a porn rush hour, he wondered? A couple of white guys in their twenties ribbed each other near the big-busted girl porn, an older guy in a suit hovered in the tranny corner, and a muscle-bound bald dude stood in one of the gay aisles.

Warren's heart was pounding as if he'd just

played all four quarters of a game. He pretended to browse in the interracial section, hoping that the bald dude would finish what he was doing and leave the area free. But he just kept pulling magazines off the shelf and looking through them.

A different clerk was behind the desk, and he didn't seem to care about moving the customers out. He was playing a hand-held video game and the *boops* and *beeps* started to get on Warren's nerves. Finally he moved over to the aisle across from the muscular bald guy. He wanted to grab a couple of magazines and get out of there.

He was flipping through a locker room magazine when the guy appeared beside him. "That'll make your dick jump," he said in a low voice.

Warren looked up, his body jittering.

"They got some great movies like that in the back," the guy said. "You want to take a look? My treat." He held up a couple of quarters.

Warren was confused. Did the guy want to give him the money? For what? To pay for a movie? Why?

Then the dude said, "We gotta keep it quiet, though. The clerk don't care as long as he don't see us go into the booth together."

Warren's mouth was dry, and he licked his lips. That must have been the wrong signal, because the dude said, "Third booth. I'll be right behind you." He handed a couple of the quarters to Warren, who took them because he didn't know what else to do.

"Go on," the dude said, nudging Warren's thigh with his hip.

In a sex-fueled haze, Warren walked to the

third booth and pulled back the curtain. It was a small space, with a wooden bench and a TV screen set into the wall. He stepped inside and tried to catch his breath.

A moment later the bald guy was inside with him, the two of them crammed together in the tight space. "New at this, huh?" the dude said. "I'm Joe."

"Wa—Walter," Warren said.

Joe slipped a couple of quarters into a slot, and a movie started playing on the TV screen. Two young guys in jockstraps were kissing in a locker room.

Joe put his hand on Warren's groin and rubbed. "I like a big guy," he said. Before Warren knew what was happening, Joe had opened Warren's zipper and grabbed his dick.

This was the first time another guy had touched his dick. Warren nearly came right then. Joe's hand was warm and rough, and he ran it up and down Warren's shaft, then pulled the dick out through his pants.

He looked at Warren and smiled in the light of the TV screen, then got down on his knees and licked Warren's dick. Then Joe swallowed all of Warren's dick, sticking his nose into Warren's crotch.

Warren struggled to control himself, but he couldn't. Within seconds he felt his orgasm rising, and he tried to back away, but Joe wouldn't let him. He shot off down Joe's throat.

Joe coughed a couple of times, and some of Warren's cum spilled out onto his chin, but he wiped it off and smiled. Warren quickly fumbled his pants closed and walked out, still holding Joe's quarters. He grabbed a shrink-wrapped package of magazines from a rack, not even caring what they were, and hurried up to the desk, where the clerk was still playing his game.

Warren laid the package on the counter and handed the clerk a twenty-dollar bill. He looked around once, hoping that Joe was still in the viewing booth. He didn't see him. He took his change from the clerk, and the magazines in a brown paper bag. It wasn't until he got out to the scooter that he realized he was still carrying the quarters Joe had given him.

Did that make him a whore, he wondered, as he took off toward the campus. Because someone had given him money for sex? Duh. It didn't work that way. As far as he knew the guy getting blown was the one who had to pay. But it was still a creepy thought.

* * * *

Sitting in bed, he realized that he hadn't thought of that moment for a long time. He had never seen Joe again, though he'd gone back to the store every couple of months for a fresh supply of porn.

The next morning he went to work at GetBalled. Over the weekend Leo had reviewed what Warren had found and already placed orders for some new merchandise for the soccer section. The next couple of days went by very quickly—a run in the morning, then work, then a stop at the gym for a circuit on the machines.

He talked to Thom every evening, trading stories of GetBalled with Thom's ideas about job hunting. When Warren was stressed, Thom grounded him, and when Thom was depressed Warren cheered him on.

It was Wednesday before Warren's schedule meshed with Victor's. Victor finished a job near the GetBalled office, and they met for dinner at a seafood restaurant in Hollywood. Victor looked trim in his tight-fitting polo shirt and khaki slacks, and Warren's dick pronged at the thought of the body underneath.

"Hey, Warren," Victor said, giving him a fist bump. "How's the job going?"

"Good. I'm learning a lot." The hostess led them past an empty lobster tank to a booth beneath a big red fishing net studded with glass globes and fake seashells. Stupid, he thought, to use fake shells when you could just walk out to the beach and pick up real ones.

"Do you know Moises?" Warren asked. "Leo's partner? He has me preparing the contracts for new products. It's just filling in the blanks, but I've been reading all the clauses and trying to understand them."

"I never went over to Leo's office myself," Victor said. "I'm more of a free range guy. That's why I like what I do. I don't get tied down to anything."

Warren considered that while they looked at the menu. Was Victor saying that he didn't want to get tied down to a boyfriend? Or was Warren just reading too much into everything?

Victor ordered the salmon, and Warren asked for a burger. "Really, Warren?" Victor asked. "A hamburger at a seafood restaurant?"

"I'm hungry," Warren said. And what the fuck was Victor's problem with a burger? That it wasn't healthy? Hell, what about all that beer and those chicken wings?

"I'm just saying, they have great fish here," Victor said, as the waitress stood there.

Warren handed her the menu. "Medium well on the burger, please," he said, and smiled at her.

Victor handed his menu over to the waitress, and she left. "Leo's a great boss," Warren continued. "He's really patient when I have to ask him questions."

"You still working at the gym?"

Warren shook his head. "I figured out fast that I can't manage two jobs and my own training. I've been running every morning, and most days I try to stop by the gym for a workout if it's not too late."

"You're looking good," Victor said. "Just don't lose too much bulk. I need that protection on the pitch."

Victor's phone beeped and he said, "I have to check this." While he did, Warren wondered what kind of a date this was. It was a hike to either of their places, so they probably weren't going to have sex afterward.

He guessed this was what straight people did when they dated. Maybe gay guys, too, for all he knew. Meet up for a meal and conversation, flirtation, maybe a little make-out session in the parking lot.

It was like the pregame practices to Warren. He wanted to get to the game. See Victor all the time, have sex, hang out, play rugby. This foreplay shit made him frustrated. He listened to Victor drone on about a mini-mansion he'd inspected.

"These people bought an old house on a small lot in the Lakes neighborhood in Hollywood," he said. "Most of them from the twenties and thirties, good, solid houses that just need some updating. But this woman wanted a new house, so they tore down the old one and built this monstrosity that crowds out the neighbors." He shook his head. "I hate it when that happens."

Warren didn't have an opinion about what rich people did with their money, so he said nothing.

"But they did it on the cheap," Victor continued. "Chinese drywall, low-end fixtures, and after a couple of years everything started to fall apart. The new buyers would have gotten saddled with a shitload of repairs if I hadn't found everything I did."

"Good for you." Warren was itchy to get on to something more personal. Like who was that friend Victor was visiting late on Sunday night? One of the players on the team? Or someone else?"

"So, you see any of the other guys on the team like this?" he asked. "Hang out and stuff? Go over their place at night?"

Victor cocked his head. "No, Warren, I don't see any of the other guys like this," he said, putting emphasis on the last two words. He stuck his leg out under the table until it made contact with Warren's. "I'm not saying I haven't fooled around with anybody, but I don't have anything going on now with anybody else. Just you."

Warren smiled and felt his dick swell. "That's good, Victor."

The waitress brought their food, and they dug in. "That burger does look good," Victor said. He had a reddish filet on his plate, probably just a couple of ounces, with some limp broccoli and a couple of roasted red potatoes. Warren knew he shouldn't, but he enjoyed his burger and fries even more seeing Victor pick at his over-done fish.

When they finished, eating, Warren reached for the bill. "This is my treat. I get my first paycheck from GetBalled this week."

"I'll pick up the next one then," Victor said. "I hate it when guys squabble over a bill, worrying about who had the extra cheese and who had two sodas. It's such a pain. Either you split things fifty-fifty, or you alternate paying."

At least there was going to be a next one, Warren thought. "Maybe Saturday, after the game? I live pretty close to the FU campus. You could stop by, I could show you the place."

"Sounds like a plan, man," Victor said.

Warren got his change, and they walked out to the parking lot. This was the part that always got him confused. Sure, they weren't going to fuck, but could they at least make out? Or was Victor going to shake his hand like some business associate?

Victor answered that question. "You want to come sit in my SUV for a couple of minutes?"

Warren felt like a big, eager puppy dog. "Sure."

"The back's kind of crapped up, but the front is clear," Victor said as he beeped open the car. "And at least there's no gear shift between the seats to get in the way."

Warren hopped into the passenger seat with such enthusiasm that the car bounced. "Hey there, boyfriend, don't break my car," Victor said, laughing. "I've got a lot of miles to put on this baby before I trade her in."

All Warren heard, though, was the word boyfriend. Did Victor consider the two of them as boyfriends? Or was it in the same way that some girls said girlfriend, with that sassy accent on the last syllable? It didn't matter because Victor was leaning toward him, and once their lips connected, Warren stopped thinking.

It was awkward in the front seat there, but they made it work. They kissed, and Victor's tongue probed Warren's mouth. Victor stroked Warren's thigh, and Warren wrapped an arm around Victor's back.

Warren was getting really hot and bothered when Victor finally pulled back from the lip-lock and Warren's grip. "Whew. Is it getting steamy in here or is it just that you are one smoking-hot dude?"

Warren blushed.

"I should get on the road," Victor said. "Got an early job tomorrow. And I don't want to get cum stains on my upholstery." He pushed gently on Warren's shoulder. "See you Saturday, Warren."

Warren couldn't resist. He leaned over for one last kiss, then backed away. "I'll be looking forward to it."

FRIENDS

When Warren got back to his car, his dick was pressing hard against his pants, his balls squeezed between his thighs. He unbuckled his belt and unzipped his pants, spreading them open. His dick pushed against the fabric of his boxers, and he pulled it out through the opening.

He didn't like the feeling of the air conditioning against his slick dick, so he rolled down the windows as he got onto the highway. There was something weirdly erotic about driving that way, his dick sticking up like a flagpole as he zoomed along. He wondered if anybody could see into his car—maybe a truck driver passing, happening to look down and get a good look at what everybody seemed to think was Warren's best asset.

What the fuck, he thought. Take a good look. He'd heard some of Thom's friends talk about a truck stop out at the edge of the Everglades, guys cruising out there to blow or get blown. He imagined walking around with his pants open and his dick out, like an advertisement or something. Get a piece of this big sausage.

His balls were clenched tight and starting to hurt. He thought about pulling off to the side of the highway. Put his blinkers on and rub one out. Maybe some hot cop would come up to his window to make sure everything was all right. See Warren's dick and want a piece of it.

He shook his head. Probably some clueless driver would rear-end him, and Warren's dick would get mauled by the airbag. He just had to suck it up and keep driving. When he got home he could take care of himself.

Or he could go over to Three Lambs and get a helping hand from Thom. Would that make him a cheater? It wasn't like he and Victor had pledged monogamy to each other. And wasn't that just some heterosexual thing anyway, that said one man and one woman should stay together for the sake of raising children?

He was so horny, and though he wasn't the most experienced guy, he was smart enough to know that thinking with the little head, not the big one, was a bad idea. So he drove home. By the time he pulled up in front of the house, his dick had gone down, and he was able to stuff it into his pants again, zip up, and walk inside without embarrassment.

As soon as he got into his bedroom, though, he pulled off his clothes and grabbed a bottle of lube and a book of erotic stories he'd bought years before. He had never been much of a reader, and he'd only gotten the book, with the cover ripped off, because it was sandwiched between a couple of magazines.

The paperback was called *Bathroom BJs,* and it was a collection of tales of guys getting it on in men's rooms in all kinds of places. He was sure that he remembered one at a truck stop, and sure enough, there it was.

He squirted some lube in his hand and started stroking himself as he read about married truckers looking for a little love on the road, cocksuckers and glory holes. He had never seen a glory hole in his life and had no idea what he'd do if he ever did. The idea of sticking your dick through a hole to some anonymous mouth creeped him out. What if the hole had rough edges? Suppose it was too small to fit him?

He jacked himself up and down. He knew there were guys who got off on having sex in public places, and he'd heard rumors that there was a men's room at a run-down mall where guys could go to meet up. He'd never been there, though.

One of the truckers in the story had a big cock. He walked around through the parking lot with his pants open, just the way Warren had imagined himself doing, looking for somebody who was man enough to take him.

A wiry guy with tattoos walked up to the trucker. "I need some meat," he said. "Got out of the joint a week ago, and I ain't had any since then."

"Go for it, you skinny fucker," the trucker said. The ex-con got down on his knees in the gravel parking lot and wrapped his lips around the trucker's cock. As he started to suck, a crowd gathered, guys taking bets on whether the ex-con could swallow it all.

Warren closed his eyes and focused on his dick, rubbing it up and down with a frenzy. Thom sucked him like that, he thought. Thom could swallow Warren's big dick whole and make him feel so good. His body stiffened, and he shot off, in an arc that sprayed up to his belly. He slumped back against the pillows. That was the problem with porn stories; you never found out how the story ended because once you got off you lost interest.

For the rest of the week, Warren channeled all his energy into working out and into his job at GetBalled. By Saturday morning, he was excited about the game against the FU team. When he got down there, he found a couple of the guys already in the locker room.

"Victor told me I ought to apologize to you," Brendan said. He was naked again, and Warren thought that was probably a bad move for a guy with such a small dick. "I didn't realize you were such a big pussy that a little teasing would make you cry."

"Brendan!" Victor said. "You're an asshole; you know that?"

"No problem." Warren had dressed for the game before he left home, in a T-shirt, nylon shorts with an elastic waistband, and a jock with a cup. He reached inside and popped his dick out, and wagged it at Brendan.

"My dick has been this big since I hit puberty, you know. And I've been in enough locker rooms since then to know that guys whose dicks stopped growing when they started getting hair under their arms are gonna be jealous."

He put his dick in his shorts and clapped Brendan on the back. "It's okay, little dude. I'm sure your dick gets the job done. Hey, you ever try having somebody suck you and someone else at the same time? I bet a guy with a loose jaw could manage that."

Brendan's face turned bright red, and the other guys guffawed.

"He told you, bro," Pete said.

"Hello, everyone!" Warren turned to see Leo in the door of the locker room, with a pile of shirts in his arms. "GetBalled provides you team shirts!" He handed one to Pete, who held it up. In black, it had the words Let's Get Balled stacked in block white letters. Leo looked around. "Well, who wants shirt?"

The guys lined up to get theirs as Victor put his arm around Brendan's shoulders and steered him away, talking to him in a low voice. Brendan did have a cute ass, Warren thought, and he wondered what it would be like to plow that ass with his big dick, make the little mouthy shit cry in pain.

"You got Brendan riled up; he's gonna destroy the other team," Pete said. "Good job!"

He went out of the locker room with Leo and saw Thom standing on the sidelines. "Hey, I want you to meet a friend of mine," he said. He walked Leo over and introduced him to Thom.

"Thom's a math whiz," Warren said. "He's the only reason that I passed math in college."

"You know anything about encryption?" Leo asked him. "We need better algorithms for site, and my programmers don't do that."

"I took a course in it, as part of my master's," Thom said. "And I've done some programming."

"Excellent! We can talk? This week?"

"Sure."

"Warren, you will make happen, all right?" Leo said. "Now I go out to warm up."

"Did you put him up to that?" Thom asked, after Leo had jogged away.

Warren shook his head. "I don't even know what encryption is. Some math thing?"

"It's a field where you use mathematical models to keep information safe," Thom said. "Like creating really complicated passwords for data as it travels between two servers, to make sure that no one can intercept the transmission and steal the data."

"If you say so." Warren flexed his back muscles

and swiveled his hips. "I should warm up. I'll see you after the game."

"Go get 'em, big guy." Thom gave Warren a light punch on the arm.

"Hey, we're a gay team," Warren said. "You can plant one right here." He put his finger to his lips, then leaned down. Thom was a couple of inches shorter than he was.

"I like this," Thom said, and he kissed Warren. Then as Warren turned to go, he patted his butt.

Warren joined the rest of the guys warming up, and then the game began. Though he'd watched a couple of games on YouTube, this was the first time he'd played in one, and he got caught up in the action quickly.

As he watched Brendan play, Warren was glad that they weren't scrimmaging again, because Brendan was an animal—charging into the opposing team, protecting the ball, and stampeding over anyone in his way. By the half, their team was leading. They looked really professional too, in their black shirts.

During the second half, though, the referee had to eject Brendan, because he was acting crazy, and Warren worried that he had razzed the guy too much. Brendan spent the rest of the game pacing on the sidelines looking very pissed off.

Without Brendan, they were a man down, and they narrowly managed to hold onto their lead until the final whistle. Victor immediately walked off the field with Brendan, and they were both gone by the time the rest of the team returned to the locker room.

"I didn't realize Brendan was so sensitive

about, you know," Warren said to Pete as they were drying off.

"Having a small dick?" Pete asked. "We all noticed, but nobody called him on it."

"You know what they say," Jerry said, thrusting his hips in and out. "It ain't the meat; it's the motion."

"You notice, you only hear small guys say shit like that?" Pete asked Warren with a laugh. He clapped Warren on the back. "Seriously, though, Brendan's wound really tight. But Victor will calm him down. A nice orgasm makes the whole world seem better."

Warren looked up. "You think they're going to have sex? Victor and Brendan?"

"They used to have a thing," Jerry said. "Brendan even asked Victor to marry him. Victor said no; he wasn't in love with Brendan."

Warren's mouth was dry.

"Then Brendan got royally drunk and wrecked his car," Pete said. "Got a DUI and had his license suspended for a year. Fortunately he works out of his apartment, but Victor had to drive him where he needed to go."

"And they're still friends?" Warren asked. "After all that?"

"Friends with benefits," Jerry said. "The best kind, right?"

He heard his phone buzz and discovered a text from Victor, that he'd had to look after Brendan. That was all right. Thom was there, and they could hang out. Who needed fucking Victor anyway?

"Absolutely the best kind," Warren said.

MONOGAMY

Warren's head was spinning as he finished getting dressed. So Victor was screwing Brendan, at the same time as he and Victor were dating. And Victor had never said anything about Brendan, that they had a history.

It was fucked up, he thought. This whole dating business was. Those rules he'd found online? They were bullshit, unless everybody agreed to them. Well, then, Warren Updegrove felt free to ignore them the way Victor and Brendan did.

Brendan's problem took some of the shine off their win, and the rest of the guys dispersed without any mention of going out. That was fine with Warren; he had Thom there.

"Awesome game," Thom said, when Warren walked out of the locker room. "That one guy, the one they kicked out? He's an animal. What does he do in real life?"

"He's an accountant," Warren said.

Thom laughed. "Then I'd sure as hell want him on my side if I ever got audited by the IRS."

"He's an asshole." Warren took a deep breath. "And he's Victor's ex."

"Really? Like Victor as in the guy you've been dating?"

"Exactly. And the guys on the team say that the only way to calm Brendan down when he gets like this is to fuck him."

"So you and Victor, you're…open like that?" Thom asked.

"Like I told you, we've only had sex a couple

of times. It's not like we're engaged or anything." He grabbed Thom's arm. "Come on; let's get something to eat. I'm starved."

They drove to a burger joint near the campus, and Warren ordered what he got during football season, when he was bulking up—two triple bacon cheeseburgers, a bucket of cheese fries, and a giant lemonade. Fuck Victor and his judgmental attitude.

They filled their cups at the dispenser then snagged a table and waited for their food to come out. "Are you jealous?" Thom asked.

"Of what?"

"Of this relationship between Victor and his ex. And the possibility that they're doing the horizontal mambo right now."

Warren sat back as he felt his anger rise. Cool down, he thought. This is Thom. Can't blow up again on your best friend. He struggled for something he could say that wouldn't make either of them crazy.

"I took this sociology course sophomore year," he said, as they waited for their food. "All the guys on the team were taking it, because it was a gut, and the professor was this real jock-sniffer who gave extra credit to athletes."

"Don't you just love that term?" Thom asked. "Jock-sniffer? Technically it's not even a gay term. You can be a straight guy who just likes to hang around athletes."

"I'm trying to tell a story here," Warren said. The clerk called their number, and Thom got up to retrieve the tray of food. When he returned, they both began to eat, and Warren was through his first burger and half his fries quickly. He burped and sat back.

"So one part of this course was on human sexuality," he continued. "One of our discussion questions was about monogamy. Was it necessary, or even possible?"

"Well, biology says that men have an imperative to spread their seed to as many women as possible, to perpetuate their genes," Thom said. "And women want to find one man who will protect and provide for them and their kids."

"That's what the textbook said. But most animals aren't monogamous at all, and maybe it isn't natural for humans either."

Thom nodded as he munched his fries. "And for gay men, all those arguments go out the window. A gay man doesn't need a husband to give him children or provide for him. And it wasn't even legal for two men to marry until a couple of years ago."

"What do you think?" Warren asked. "Is monogamy possible?"

Thom shrugged. "My parents have been married for forty years, and I think they've been monogamous, but I'm certainly not going to ask them." He sat back in his chair. "Think about it. People used to get married at like fifteen. Even our parents' generation were married off by their twenties. That means that for the rest of your life, you can only have sex with one person. The same person."

"Which is probably one reason why so many marriages break up," Warren said. "Men are horndogs."

"And by men, you're thinking of this guy Victor," Thom said.

"I think it's stupid. We're brought up by this

straight society to believe in all this shit—man plus woman plus two-point-one kids equals white picket fence and eternal happiness. If it doesn't work for straight people, why expect it to work for guys like us?"

Warren kept eating, and before he knew it the tray in front of him was empty.

"Jesus, Warren, at least you didn't eat the napkins," Thom said.

"Yeah, well, I still have an appetite for something," Warren said. "Can we go back to your room?"

"You don't just want to have sex with me because you're pissed at Victor, do you?" Thom said. "Because that's fucked up."

Warren knew the answer to that question was yes, and that he truly was fucked up. But he also knew that giving the honest answer would not get him into Thom's bed. "I just look around me to see who my friends really are, and it's you," Warren said. "And yeah, I kind of feel like shit because I thought Victor and I were going to be boyfriends. As long as that's not going to happen, why shouldn't you and I keep on having fun?"

Thom stood up. "No reason that I can see."

They went back to the Three Lambs house. Most of the brothers Warren knew had graduated, and there were a bunch of strangers hanging around in the living room smoking dope and drinking beer, along with Fitz, the house manager, and his boyfriend Chuck.

"Yo, Thom," Fitz said, waving a hand lazily. "You want a hit of this?"

Thom looked at Warren, who said, "Why the fuck not?"

They sat cross-legged on the wooden floor, and Fitz passed the joint to them. Warren took a deep breath and held it in as he handed the joint to Thom. The smoke flooded into his brain and for the first time since seeing Brendan in the locker room before the game he started to relax.

Across from them, two of the guys started making out, and Warren got the urge to do the same thing with Thom. He put his arm around Thom's shoulder and pulled him close, and they locked lips. Thom stroked Warren's thigh, and Warren felt his dick stiffening.

"There's a party over here," Chuck said, laughing and pointing at them. "Go, Thom! Go Warren!"

Thom tried to pull away, but Warren wouldn't let him. He squirmed around until he was lying flat on the floor, and then pulled Thom on top of him. "Oh, yeah," he said, as Thom dry-humped him through their clothes.

"Is this a private party or can anybody join in?" Fitz asked. He leaned in and kissed Warren on the lips as Thom rode him.

Warren was horny and high by then, and he wrapped one beefy arm around Fitz and French-kissed him. Chuck came up behind Thom and reached around him, gripping his nipples, and from then on it was a free-for all.

Thom stripped naked, and opened Warren's pants so that his dick jumped out. Things got hazy then, but somehow Fitz and Chuck were both naked too, Fitz's blond pubic hair, Chuck's dark hair and almond eyes.

Everybody wanted a piece of Warren once his dick was exposed. One of the strangers put a condom on Warren's dick and positioned his ass over it, and then one after another they were riding him like a bucking bronco. Warren had never had sex with more than one guy at once, though he'd seen enough porn movies.

Thom finally pushed all the guys aside and reached down for Warren's hand. "Come on, Warren. I want you all to myself."

Warren thought about protesting. He was having fun there, poking ass after ass. But he remembered something his mamaw had said to his sisters, about always going home with the guy who brung you. He sat up and giggled. Then he got to his feet, and he and Thom raced up the stairs naked to Thom's room, the staircase thundering with their steps.

"You all warmed up for me?" Thom asked breathlessly, as he slammed the door of his room behind him.

"You bet," Warren said. "But you'd better get your ass over here because I'm not sure how long I can hold out."

The condom had fallen off somewhere on the stairs as Warren's dick softened, but Thom had a fresh one out of its package, and he skinned it down over Warren's dick. The touch was enough to get Warren hard again, and he grabbed Thom and pulled him close, rubbing his five o'clock shadow against Thom's cheek as he caught quick kisses from Thom's lips.

Their bodies rocked together until Warren couldn't hold back any more. He grabbed Thom by the shoulders and flipped him around so he was up against the bedroom door. Warren put his hands under the globes of Thom's ass and pushed them up. "Prepare to be fucked, bitch," he said.

"I can take whatever you can dish out," Thom said. "Fuck me, man. Fuck my ass with that big baseball bat dick of yours."

Warren lined himself up and plunged in, pushing past Thom's anal sphincter without a thought, totally focused on filling up his best friend's hole.

"Lordy!" Thom gasped.

But Warren was too far-gone to worry about hurting him. He slammed in as far as he could go, then began pistoning Thom's ass. "You're breaking me apart!"

"You'll never have a guy better than me," Warren said. "I love you so much, Thom. Nobody makes me feel the way you do."

"Back at you, big guy," Thom said, between pants and whimpers. "Oh God, you make me feel so good."

Warren reached around and grabbed Thom's dick with one hand, and jerked him at the same time as he fucked Thom's ass, clenching his glutes and slamming forward, then pulling back just enough to tease.

Warren came first; he'd had a lot of ass already that evening. But Thom wasn't far behind, and then the two of them collapsed on Thom's bed together.

Fuck you too, Victor Ragazzo, Warren thought.

He remembered what he'd said to Thom, in the heat of the moment. Where did that declaration of love come from? He and Thom were just friends with benefits, right? Could you love your friends? Well, duh. Of course you could. And with that idea ricocheting around his brain, he dropped off to sleep.

BUDDIES

"I have got to stop doing this shit," Warren groaned the next morning, as he tried to sit up. His head was hammering, and his throat was dry.

"Which shit?" Thom said lazily. "The dope smoking? Or the smoking-hot sex?"

Though he felt like crap, Warren couldn't resist reaching over to squeeze Thom's limp dick. "Which do you think?"

"I sure hope it's just the smoking and drinking," Thom said. "Last night was something else."

Warren struggled to remember it all. "Did we have an orgy?"

Thom laughed. "You could call it that. But don't worry; nobody took any dick pics of you. At least not that I know of."

Warren sat up. "Where are my clothes?"

"Must be downstairs," Thom said. "I'm gonna get something to drink. I'll bring your stuff up."

"You have any tomato juice in this house?"

"Think so."

"Bring up about a gallon of that, with cayenne pepper, sugar, and lime. That'll help replenish our electrolytes."

* * * *

It was late morning by the time Warren felt well enough to drive home. He didn't check his phone for messages until he'd gone in, taken a long hot shower, and then taken a nap. There were three missed calls from Victor, and a text asking Warren to call.

Warren was tempted to just blow him off, but he did like the guy, and he liked playing rugby. So he called.

"Sorry to bag out on you yesterday," Victor said. "But Brendan was in a bad way, and I had to calm him down."

"Yeah, I'm sorry I teased him," Warren said. "I had no idea he'd go off like that."

"It wasn't the teasing so much." Victor hesitated. "I had breakfast with him yesterday before the game, and I told him that you and I were going out. He got jealous."

"Because he's your ex, and you're still banging him," Warren said. "Yeah, I get it."

"I'm not still banging him," Victor said. "Yeah, he's my ex, but this is one of the reasons I broke up with him. He gets nuts sometimes."

"And the only way to calm him down is sex," Warren said.

"What is with you, Warren? I just told you, I'm not having sex with Brendan. At least, I haven't for a couple of months now. It wasn't healthy, the relationship we had. Neither of us were seeing anyone else, but we weren't going to be together, either. So I called it quits. But I don't think it sank in with him until yesterday."

"So when you left with him…"

"I took him to dinner. The Cheesecake Factory, if you want to check my receipt. He ate himself into a stupor and then I took him home. To his place. Where I left him."

Warren felt like shit. "Jeez, I'm sorry. The other guys started talking, you know, and I just assumed."

"That's why I've been calling you. Because I like you, Warren, and I want to keep on seeing you. I didn't want you to get the wrong idea."

Which I did, Warren thought.

Then he remembered what he had done after the match. But he couldn't tell Victor that, could he? *Gee, bro, I was pissed off that I thought you were having sex with your ex, so I fucked a whole fraternity.*

"So can I make it up to you?" Victor said. "Dinner tonight?"

"Honestly, I got drunk last night with some college friends," Warren said. "I'm feeling pretty ragged. Can I get a rain check for later in the week?"

"Sure. I'll call you when I know what my schedule is."

* * * *

It was hellishly hot and humid, too hot for a run, so Warren went to the gym, where he did a circuit of the weight machines and then ran several laps around the track on the second floor. By the time he got back home and downed a bucket of fried chicken and a half-gallon of water, he was feeling more like a human being.

But he was still freaked out about the night before. How he'd gone crazy thinking that Victor was cheating on him, and then this afternoon, how he had lied to Victor. Well, it wasn't a complete lie; he had certainly gotten drunk and had a hell of a hangover. So more like a sin of omission in not telling Victor the whole truth.

Truth was overrated, though, he thought. He was watching TV later that night when Thom called him. "How are you doing, big guy?" he asked.

"Getting better. How about you?"

"Still feel kind of raw. But I wanted to check in with you about what your boss said."

Warren searched his memory. His boss? Leo? "What?"

"About maybe having some work for me," Thom said. "And that you could hook me up with him sometime this week."

"Oh, yeah, right. I'll check with him first thing tomorrow and then call you."

"Thanks. And by the way, last night was pretty awesome."

"Yeah, it was," Warren said. At least what he could remember was. But somehow he knew that if anything bad had started to happen, Thom would have taken care of him.

He wrote himself a note to ask Leo about a job for Thom, not trusting his faulty memory, and the next day he broached the subject with Leo as they stood at the coffee machine at the back of the warehouse.

"Yes, yes," Leo said. "Have him come. Today? I want he should talk to Pritap and Buzz, maybe Moises too."

Warren grabbed his coffee and turned away, but Leo called him back. "Listen, Warren, this week is big sporting goods show in Atlanta. I want you go with me, look for new products."

"Sure, Leo. When do we leave?"

"Thursday night. Show starts Friday morning

first thing, goes through Saturday. We come back Sunday morning. Michelle will give you all details."

Well, that was pretty cool, Warren thought. His first business trip, if you didn't count flying to games with the Jaguars. He went back to his desk and called Thom and made the arrangements, and then pulled up the website for the sporting goods show.

There were vendors listed from sports he'd never even heard of, no less wanted to play. He could see he'd have a lot of research to do before he could walk in the place with Leo. Curling? Was boomerang tossing a sport? Did people still play croquet and badminton? There was even something called sporthocking, which involved doing acrobatic style tricks with a rounded stool instead of a skateboard.

He watched a couple of videos and finally had to admit that sporthocking looked kind of cool. He particularly liked the synchronized tricks—guys tossing their stools in the same pattern, ending up sitting on the stool.

GetBalled probably couldn't sell many stools, but it might be something that made the site stand out. He'd taken a marketing course as part of his sports management degree, and the professor had made it clear that building a buzz was important for any operation. He started imagining how the site would look with a sporthocking video right up front, and wondered how they could take that video and make it go viral. A couple of really buff guys, and some smoking babes? Maybe a bit of wardrobe malfunction?

He was still daydreaming about dicks falling out of shorts while the stools twirled in the air when

Michelle called to say that Thom was in the waiting room, and Warren walked out to get him. "Hey, bro, come on in. Welcome to GetBalled."

They walked past the warehouse on their way into the office. "Impressive stock," Thom said.

"And you wouldn't believe how fast it turns over," Warren said. "Pallets of equipment coming in every day and then going right back out to customers."

He stopped in front of the office door. "Listen, bro, one thing," he said. "You know Leo is on the rugby team, right?"

"Sure. That's how I met him, remember?"

"Yeah. But that means he's tight with Victor too."

"So ixnay on the ex-say," Thom said. Warren must have looked as confused as he felt, because Thom leaned in close and whispered, "So I won't tell him that you and I have sex now and then."

"Exactly. And especially not Saturday night." His mouth was dry again, and he licked his lips. "Turns out Victor wasn't fucking Brendan like I thought."

"That's a good thing, right?"

"Yeah. But he said the reason why Brendan was so crazy is because Victor told him about me, that we'd been dating, that Victor, you know, likes me."

"Oh, snap," Thom said. "So here's your boyfriend being all loyal and romantic about you, and you're off fucking anybody whose ass can take your dick."

Warren felt his temper rising, but he tamped it back. "Yeah, that's about it."

"No worries. I won't say a word."

"You can tell him we're friends," Warren said. "Just not the benefits part. Now come on in. I'll introduce you. Oh, yeah, he's straight, and so is everybody else."

"I can do straight," Thom said.

Warren introduced him to Pritap, who was wearing a T-shirt that read, *BINARY: It's as easy as 01, 10, 11.* Warren was sure there was a joke there that he didn't get, but Thom seemed to, and he and Pritap fell immediately into geek-speak.

Warren went back to his desk to start his research on those oddball sports, beginning with curling, which at first he thought had to be some kind of women's sport involving hair dressing.

Instead, it looked like a cross between shuffleboard, which he had played at beach vacations with his family, and hockey, but with stones instead of pucks. The stones came from either an island in Scotland or a quarry in Wales. Warren couldn't see that there would be much market selling forty-pound stones online, but you never knew. There were also special gloves, pants, and shoes. Because it was such a niche sport there weren't many places online selling the gear, so it would be pretty easy for GetBalled to jump in.

From there he went to croquet. He learned there were a couple of different variations, from the kind you played in your backyard to an international level of competition. He shook his head at that. Imagine saying you were a world champion at croquet, how goofy that must sound.

Then he thought of Victor, whose Olympic

sport had been the luge, which had to be almost as obscure as croquet, and not even something you could play on your lawn. By the time he looked up, Thom was shaking hands with Leo.

"Thank you very much," Thom said. "I really appreciate the opportunity."

"Hey, if Pritap thinks you know your shit, I believe," Leo said.

Thom walked over to Warren's desk. "Did you know that there's an international croquet association in West Palm Beach?" Warren asked him.

"That's a pretty random observation," Thom said. "Don't you want to hear about my interview?"

"Sure." Warren pushed his chair back. "Come on; I'll walk you out."

They stepped into the warehouse, where Jackie was signing a touchpad for the UPS driver, and Cesar was already slitting open the shipping cartons with a wicked-looking box cutter.

"What did he say?" Warren asked.

"He doesn't have enough work to bring me on full-time, but I can work as a consultant," Thom said, smiling broadly. "Pritap's going to give me assignments, and I can work here sometimes, or at home if I want."

"That's awesome, bro," Warren said. "Congratulations." He wrapped an arm around Thom's back and hugged him, and almost immediately felt his dick prong. What was it about Thom that always got him going?

How would he manage having Thom in the same office with him and Leo? What if Thom accidentally said something that got back to Victor?

Crap. He remembered a line from a musical that Thom liked, something about no good deed going unpunished. Got that right.

But he was happy for Thom too. This could be the gig that launched him into a new career, something he'd like more than teaching. If he had to take the occasional kick in the balls so Thom could succeed, then so be it.

"It's awesome that they're willing to take me on with no real experience, and train me," Thom said. "I mean, hell, I'd work for free to get that kind of exposure."

"When do you start?"

Thom looked at his watch. "As soon as I get home. Pritap's going to e-mail me some stuff, including links to some basic encryption tutorials. I'm coming in tomorrow to get familiar with the operation." He elbowed Warren. "We'll be buddies."

Warren's mouth was dry again, but he managed to say, "Yeah. That'll be great."

CHINESE FOOD

That night when Victor called, Warren told him about going to Atlanta. "So neither of us are going to make practice on Saturday," Warren said.

"I think we could all use a week off anyway," Victor said. "But that's a bummer, that you won't be around over the weekend. How about if we have dinner tomorrow night? I have a job in West Palm, but I'll be back at my place by six. We could order in."

"Sounds like a plan, man." Warren leaned back against his pillows. "How was your day?"

"Same old, same old. Every house is different, you know, different age, structure, fixtures. But in the end they're all the same. Some have bad wiring, some have termite damage, some have cracks from the foundation settling."

"You must know a lot," Warren said.

"I know my share," Victor said. "Listen, I'm pulling up at Pollo Tropical. See you tomorrow night at my place?"

"Six o'clock," Warren said. "See ya."

Almost as soon as he hung up, his phone rang again, this time a call from Thom. "Can we drive up to GetBalled together tomorrow?" Thom asked.

"No can do, bro," Warren said. "I'm going to have dinner with Victor after work."

"Oh, well, bad for me, good for you. I'll see you there, then."

After he hung up Warren wondered what Thom meant by that remark. Good for Warren, sure, to have dinner, and probably sex, with Victor. But what was bad for Thom? Not being able to get a ride?

Or Warren continuing to see Victor?

He'd never really considered the whole friends with benefits thing from Thom's point of view. Warren had been so confused for so long about his sexuality that he couldn't look farther ahead than the next guy or the next date. But Thom had been cool about being gay for ages.

He hadn't mentioned dating anybody for ages. He'd been seeing someone during that year Warren was in Jacksonville, but it had only lasted a couple of months, and Thom didn't like to talk about what had gone wrong.

Maybe once Warren was on firmer footing with Victor, he'd see if Victor had any friends to fix Thom up with. They could go out on double dates and shit. But then he started imagining himself together with Thom and Victor, in some hot three-way. It was weird, though, that in his fantasy it was mostly him and Thom, with Victor just there.

He popped his dick out of his shorts and started stroking it, hearing Thom's dirty talk in his head, remembering the feel of Thom's mouth on his dick, of filling up Thom's ass and fucking him, fucking him…

Warren's dick erupted with a geyser of cum that splashed up onto his shorts and his T-shirt. Oh well, he thought. He had to do laundry soon anyway.

* * * *

The next morning he got to work at a few minutes after ten, and Thom was already there, huddled with Pritap at his cubicle. The three geeks went out to lunch together, and Warren felt curiously jealous. Thom was his friend, and he was getting coopted by the programmers.

That was dumb, though. It was just a work thing. When Warren left at five-thirty, Thom was hard at work at a laptop, his headphones on and his fingers flying across the keyboard. Warren tapped him on the shoulder and gave him a two-fingered salute, and Thom pulled the headphones off. "Have a good time tonight," he said.

It began to thunder as Warren left the warehouse, and he had to fight downpours and traffic all the way to Victor's apartment. He was a couple of blocks away when Victor called him. "I'm stuck behind an accident on I-95. Running about a half hour late."

"It's okay," Warren said. "Drive carefully. The roads are miserable."

"Tell me about it. Say, why don't you go over to that coffee shop where Jerry works and wait for me there? There's a good Chinese place next door. We can eat there."

Warren agreed and hung up. Was this just a ploy of Victor's to keep Warren from his apartment? Did that mean that Victor didn't want to have sex with him that night?

Christ, he was acting like a teenaged girl. If they had dinner, they had dinner. If they had sex, they had sex. He couldn't let himself get so caught up in his head that he forgot that he was playing a game.

Jerry was behind the register when Warren walked in, a ball cap turned backward on his head to show off the shop's logo. "Hey, dude, what brings you up this way?"

"Meeting Victor." He wasn't sure if Victor had told the rest of the guys that he and Warren were dating. "He's still giving me rugby pointers. And I'm going out of town for work this weekend so I won't be able to practice Saturday."

"Cool. Like your dedication. What can I get you?"

He ordered a big flavored iced tea and sat in a big armchair in the corner to wait for Victor. A couple of minutes later, Jerry joined him when someone relieved him at the register.

"So, weird shit last Saturday," he said. "Brendan is an animal, but I've never seen him so worked up that he got kicked out of a game. You must have pissed him off big time."

"Yeah, I'm sorry about that," Warren said. "Guys give me shit all the time about having a big dick, like it's the most important thing about me. I just figured I would give him some of the same shit back."

"You mean it's not the most important thing about you?" Jerry said in mock surprise.

"Ha, ha." Warren realized that from the way he was sitting, his pants were stretched tight against his thighs, and his dick was outlined. Though it wasn't hard, it was still visible.

He tried to shift his position, but all his shuffling did was draw Jerry's gaze down. Then Jerry leaned forward, close to Warren's ear. "I have a very flexible jaw," he said in a low, throaty voice. "You ever want to have a little fun; I'm your man."

Warren wanted to say, you mean you're a slut, but he resisted. That was his upbringing talking, and he had to learn to be more tolerant of others if he expected others to tolerate him. "Thanks for the offer. But right now I'm good."

The front door opened, and they both looked up to see Victor come in. Jerry backed away from Warren and stood up. "Keep me on speed dial," he said and he smiled a shit-eating grin.

Warren grabbed his iced tea and stood up, intercepting Victor as he was about to order. "Can we eat?" he asked. "I'm starved."

"Sure," Victor said, sliding his wallet back into his pocket. "The rain's let up. We can take our food to go."

Warren was happy to hear that. He followed Victor out the door and into the Chinese restaurant, where they placed their orders. "I was figuring we'd hang out in the coffee shop while we waited," Victor said. "But I guess Jerry freaked you out, huh?"

"He doesn't know that we're...you know?" Warren asked.

"I haven't made an announcement," Victor said. "But it's not a secret, either. Why? Did he ask to suck your dick?"

Warren nodded.

"Don't worry about that," Victor said. "Jerry asks almost every guy he meets."

Warren must have looked offended, because Victor quickly added, "I'm sure you would be a real trophy in his collection, though."

"He said he had a very flexible jaw," Warren said.

"And a throat like the Holland Tunnel." Victor held up his hand. "Before you ask, yeah, he's blown me a couple of times. Not when I was dating Brendan, though. I don't do that shit."

"Good to know," Warren said, having trouble swallowing. He forced himself to say that he didn't either, because he felt in his heart that it was a true statement, even if it didn't reflect his current situation.

Victor paid for their order, and as Warren followed him back to his place, he worried that Victor would find out about what he'd done Saturday night. How would he explain it without sounding like he was trying to blame Victor? It wasn't Victor's fault that Warren had gone crazy at the frat. Warren was an adult; he had to take responsibility for his own actions.

But that didn't mean he had to tell Victor about it. Just not do it again, right?

"You know what one of my favorite things is?" Victor asked, as they walked into his living room.

"What's that?"

"Eating Chinese food naked," he said, and he grinned at Warren.

"Never tried it, but I'm up for anything," Warren said.

"Let me show you." Victor laid the food out on a low table, and pulled two big floor pillows up, one on either side. Then he began to get undressed.

Warren followed his lead, moving slowly because he was watching Victor's body be revealed, from his tattooed abs to his muscular thighs, and everything in between.

When Victor was naked he walked into the kitchen, and Warren had a chance to admire him from behind. He had a light dusting of brown hair on his shoulders and buff upper arms. A thin line of similar hair flowed down the center of his back, where it almost connected to the hair rising from his ass crack.

His ass was a work of art, in Warren's opinion. High and tight, with a butt like two melon globes resting on his muscular calves. There was something hard and all-male about him. Thom, on the other hand, had a smooth back, almost like a woman's, and his butt was flatter, not so much of a curve down to his thighs.

Warren shook his head. He was here with Victor, not Thom. He had to stay focused.

Victor returned a moment later carrying a pitcher of cold water and a pair of glasses, his half-hard dick swinging against his hairy thigh. "Can I see your tattoos?" Warren asked.

"Sure." Victor turned sideways so Warren could read the words on his upper arm. "This one here is a tribute to Mark Bingham. You know who he was?"

Warren shook his head.

"Gay rugby player who was on Flight 93, one of the ones that was hijacked on 9/11. He said this, 'Let's roll,' right before he and some of the other passengers tackled the hijackers."

"Wow," Warren said.

Victor shifted to show his other arm. "*Deo Non Fortuna,*" Warren read.

"It means from God, not from luck," Victor said. "You know who else has this?"

Again, Warren didn't have an answer.

"Gareth Thomas. First professional rugby player to come out. His is much bigger, takes up his whole upper chest."

Victor pointed to the five Olympic rings inked on his right hip, just below the waist. "Got this done in Vancouver." He shifted again and pointed at an image of a rugby ball with flames coming out the back on his left hip. "This one's the newest. A present from Brendan to commemorate the first game we won."

"You guys have a history," Warren said. "I get that."

Victor sat across from Warren and used a remote to lower the light level to a dull glow. "That's true. But that's all it is. History."

He popped open the box of chicken, and the aroma of the sweet, tangy sauce made Warren's mouth water. The rice was fluffy, the egg rolls crunchy. They talked, a far-ranging conversation that covered bits and pieces of their growing up, past jobs, travel, and then dating.

"I'm guessing you've never had a serious boyfriend before," Victor said. "Unless Thom…"

Warren shook his head. "Like I said, we're just friends." He took a deep breath. "But you're right; I've never had a real boyfriend before. I mean, I've had sex, and I've gone on a couple of dates, but nothing ever worked out."

"Dating is a tough game," Victor said. "Straight couples, they can meet through family, friends, work colleagues. But we don't have those options, usually. We have to depend on the bars or the Internet."

"Or things like the rugby team," Warren said.

"Yeah, though I didn't set the team up in order to get laid," he said. "There aren't a lot of options for gay guys who like sports. There's bowling, and swimming, and then a bunch of stuff that comes and goes. For a while one of the bars had a country-western line dancing night, which was fun. And a guy tried to start a boxing club a couple of years ago, but it failed."

"Gay boxing?" Warren asked.

"You'd be surprised," Victor said. "You know who was one of the guys who boxed? Nathan, the waiter at the sports bar."

"The dancer?"

Victor nodded. "Boxing has a lot in common with dance. You have to center your body, then let your limbs follow, whether you're setting up a pirouette or a punch. You know what a plié is?"

"Just that it's some dance thing."

"It's where you bend at the knees," Victor said. "You must have seen that. Ballerinas with their hands up above their heads, their knees bent?"

"Yeah, I guess."

"Well, you do that in boxing too. Bend your knees. You need a good level of overall fitness for both."

"If you say so," Warren said.

Victor picked up a napkin and wiped his mouth. Both of them had cleared their plates by then. "You know what else you need a good overall level of fitness for?"

"Rugby?"

Victor laughed. "Well, I was thinking about sex, but rugby works too. Although if you were hoping we were going to play rugby after dinner, I hate to disappoint you."

"I'd say sex could be an appropriate

substitute." Warren uncrossed his legs and stretched them under the table toward Victor.

"I'm glad." Victor took Warren's right food in his hands and began massaging it.

Warren groaned with pleasure. "Fuck, we could just do a foot massage and call it quits. That feels so good."

"Nobody's calling it quits for a while," Victor said, grinning. Eventually Victor pushed the table out of the way and instructed Warren to lay on his stomach on the pillows. He sat on Warren, ass to ass, and began rubbing Warren's shoulders.

"Mmm," Warren said, mumbling into the pillow. "We didn't get massages like this in the NFL."

"Too bad," Victor said. "From what I've seen, some of the players could use them." He leaned forward and spoke into Warren's ear. "And some of them play like they need a good stiff dick up their ass."

Warren was hard against the pillow, lulled into a high-endorphin state by Victor's expert massage. "Maybe even some ex-players too," he said.

"I was hoping you'd say that," Victor said.

He stopped rubbing Warren's back and stood up. But he returned a moment later with a condom and a bottle of massage oil. "Let me get you good and relaxed first." Victor squeezed some massage oil in his hand and continued rubbing Warren's shoulders, then his lower back.

Warren was in ecstasy. He'd gotten rubdowns before, as part of regular workouts, but never like this. Victor's hands were strong and a bit rough, and he kneaded Warren's muscles with his knuckles, pressing his thumbs into the flesh. Then Victor pressed against the big globes of Warren's ass, and snaked a finger into his hole.

Warren was nearly asleep when he heard the rip of the condom packet. "You have massive thighs," Victor said as he tried to position his legs outside Warren's. He was panting. "This isn't going to work. Can you get up on your knees?"

"I can," Warren said. "But you know, I have a pretty big ass, and most guys can't make it in far enough to be worth the trouble."

"I'm not most guys," Victor said.

Warren lifted himself up, spreading his legs and opening his ass so that Victor could slip in. "Yeah, that's what I'm talking about," Victor said, as he eased his dick into Warren's ass. Victor grabbed his hips and balanced himself there, then began a slow in and out movement.

Warren had heard guys talk about getting fucked, about how a man's dick felt when it banged against your prostate. But he'd never experienced that. He'd only been fucked a couple of times, and in each case it hadn't been a big deal, more like feeling like he had to take a dump.

But there was something about the way Victor moved that began to float Warren's boat. Victor wasn't just banging in and out; he was moving around inside, rubbing his pubic hair against Warren's ass, massaging Warren's hips with his talented fingers.

Suddenly Victor grunted, and his dick fell out of Warren's ass. "Did you come?" Warren asked.

"Yeah," Victor said, panting.

Warren started to get up, but Victor said, "No. Stay right there."

He squirmed his way under Warren and took Warren's stiff dick in his mouth. He squeezed Warren's balls and tickled his perineum, and Warren felt like he was an airplane taking flight as his body swelled with pleasure. He moaned a couple of times, and then shot off in Victor's mouth.

Victor pulled out from under him, and turned on his side on one of the big pillows, a shit-eating grin on his face. Warren rolled down and turned to face him. "Gonna miss you this weekend," Victor said.

"Yeah," Warren said. "Me too."

LITTLE PIGLET

"I'm jealous of you," Thom said the next day at the GetBalled office. He was working at a cubicle right beside Warren's. "I've never traveled for work farther than the FU library."

He'd settled in a lot faster than Warren had, tacking a purple and gold FU banner up on the divider, with an FU bobblehead doll in a football jersey on top of it. Warren had brought in a couple of things from his playing days—a Jaguars all-access field pass, photos of him in his uniform, an autographed card from the Jaguars' quarterback wishing him luck.

"It's not all it's cracked up to be," Warren said. "Waiting around in airports, sleeping in a different hotel room every night."

"Come on; didn't you guys have your own plane?"

Warren shook his head. "The team chartered a plane, but we had to fit into those little seats. Only the most important players got to sit in first class. We had to pack and drag our own luggage, go through security, all that stuff. I had to share a room with another guy. We couldn't order room service or use the minibar, and we had a curfew."

"That's no fun," Thom said.

"Not supposed to be. Even though they call football a game, for us it was a job, and a hard and fucking serious one. And remember, there's over a hundred people who travel with an NFL team, so you're just one cog in a big wheel. And then you play, and if your team loses, everyone's in a shit mood, but you have to buck up and go right back to practice the next day."

It was weird having Thom there in the office. Though Thom was pretty much his closest friend, they'd never worked together or even spent a lot of time together, outside of fucking. Back when they were undergrads, Thom was busy with classes and his frat, and Warren was too freaked to be seen with a gay guy too often.

Since his return to Miami, they'd talked and e-mailed each other often, but Thom had been too busy with his coursework and his teaching to hang out too much. And Warren had been embarrassed about feeling needy and lonely and hadn't pushed him.

Now, it was cool to have him right there. Even though they were doing different things, he could turn to Thom for advice on something he was writing or a product he was considering. And Thom could ask him questions about the office, about why people bought sports equipment online.

Thursday, Thom worked from home, and Warren already missed him. He was glad to leave the office early so that he could drive home, pack, and meet Leo at the Miami airport. Leo hadn't been able to get them seats together, so Warren sat on his own, wedged between two strangers. Check this out, Thom, he thought. Glamorous travel.

It was late by the time he and Leo checked into their rooms, so they agreed to meet early in the morning for breakfast and strategizing. Warren realized that this was the first time he'd had a hotel room to himself, and he was tempted to raid the minibar just because he could. But he didn't want Leo to think he was taking advantage.

He sat on the bed, and called Victor, but the call went straight to voice mail. "Just wanted to say hi," Warren said. "I'm in Atlanta. Sounds like we'll be really busy at the show, but I'll try and call you tomorrow night."

He ended the call and stripped down, but he had trouble falling asleep. The trade show was a big deal, an opportunity to show Leo that he could manage this job. What if he couldn't? Suppose he screwed up, didn't get the information Leo needed?

He looked at the clock. Not too late to call Thom.

"Hey big guy, what's up?" Thom said. "You make it to Atlanta?"

Just the sound of his friend's voice was relaxing, and Warren leaned back against the pillows. "Yeah, squeezed into a seat like a sardine in a can," he said. "But now I'm here in my own room, and it's kind of, you know, lonely."

"Wish I could be there with you," Thom said. "We could have some fun. What kind of bed?"

"King-size," Warren said. He bounced up and down a bit. "Solid mattress. Big fluffy pillows."

"You already stripped down for bed?"

Warren felt his dick stir. Of course Thom knew that he slept in the nude. "Yup."

"If I was there, we could cuddle up together," Thom said. "You know how good it makes me feel to have your arms around me."

"I'm so screwed up. I really like Victor but, you know, you and I…"

"We have a history," Thom said, and Warren

remembered Victor using that same phrase to describe his relationship with Brendan. "You know, a little phone sex might relax you. And it wouldn't be cheating, right? Because it's not like you'd actually have your dick in my ass."

"Or in your mouth," Warren said. "I love the way you can…you know…take me all in."

"It's my pleasure," Thom said. "You've kind of spoiled me for other guys. Because you're so big, and so sweet, and so handsome."

"Aw, I'm not handsome," Warren said. He looked over at himself in the mirror beside the bed. He'd always thought his face was just too big to be good-looking. After all, you never saw fashion models over three hundred pounds.

"Beauty is in the eye of the beholder," Thom said. "And right now I'd like to behold your dick. You have an iPhone, right? Can we FaceTime?"

"I've never done that before."

"It's easy. I'll tell you exactly what to do." Thom led him through the app, and suddenly there was Thom, on his screen. He had his shirt off, but Warren couldn't see anything else.

"Hold your phone lower," Thom said. "I want to see that big dick of yours. And yeah, I know, you're more than your dick, yadda yadda."

"I'll yadda yadda you," Warren said, but he aimed his phone down.

"Oh, man, you're already hot," Thom said. "I can see the precum around your dickhead."

"Of course I'm already hot," Warren said. "I'm talking to you. But what about you, dude? Show me your dick."

The view on Warren's screen shifted down, and he saw Thom had his shorts open, his dick sticking up out of the waistband of his briefs. "Hey there, little guy," Warren said. "Wish I could be there to suck you in person."

"You and me both," Thom said. "Come one; let's jerk together."

On the screen he saw Thom's thumb begin to rub beneath the head of his dick. Warren grasped his dick in his fist and began rubbing himself, lubricated by the precum that kept flowing.

"Oh, yeah, rub that dick," Warren said. He leaned in close. "I never noticed how the head of your dick flares out like that."

"Yeah, because it's usually in your mouth," Thom said.

They kept rubbing and talking dirty to each other, and then Warren felt his orgasm rising. "Oh God. I'm coming just watching you jerk."

"Me too, big guy," Thom said, and then Warren spurted a stream of cum that ran down his hand and between his fingers. On screen he saw Thom shoot a load onto his belly.

Thom's face appeared on the screen. "Think you can get to sleep now?" he asked, smiling.

"Still wish you were here to cuddle with," Warren said. "But I'll manage."

He didn't even clean himself up, just ended the call and slid down against the pillows. When he woke up his hand and his belly were sticky with cum, and he stumbled into the shower to get cleaned up.

He got to the complimentary continental breakfast buffet in the hotel restaurant before Leo, and he loaded up his plate with croissants, Danish, and fruit, along with a big glass of orange juice.

The room was crowded, and he was lucky to snag a table by the window. Most of the people in the room looked like they were there for the trade show—a bunch of ex-jocks in polo shirts and khakis. One guy at the table across from him looked familiar. He kept staring at Warren, and Warren felt himself blushing.

Was this guy cruising him? Finally, the group at the guy's table stood up, and Warren hoped he'd leave without saying anything. But no such luck. He looked up to see the guy standing right beside him. "You're Warren Updegrove, aren't you?"

The guy was about his age, maybe a couple of years older. "That's me," Warren said.

"Rich Cantoro," the guy said, and held out his hand. Warren stood to shake it. "I was the backup kicker for Jacksonville three seasons ago. Never got to play much, and I only lasted one season, but I still watch the games and follow the players."

"I mostly rode the bench," Warren said.

"But you had great stats in college," Rich said. "They should have given you more of a chance."

Leo joined them then, and Warren introduced them. "Rich played for Jacksonville before I did."

"I'm a sales rep now for Little Piglet." Rich handed them both his cards. "Stop by our booth, and I'll show you our new product line."

When he was gone, Leo said, "Excellent! You are networking already. Good job, Warren."

Warren didn't tell him that he'd worried at first that Rich was cruising him. It was silly, of course. But had there been something to it? Was Rich gay too?

Warren knew that there had to be other gay players in the NFL, though he was sure they were all as closeted as he was. It was a statistical thing, as Thom had pointed out to him. If somewhere between five and ten percent of the population was gay, and gay men came in all shapes, sizes, and talents, then it made sense that there had to be a few ends who were tight in a different way, backs who liked to take it from behind.

Thom had even given him a book to read, an autobiography by Dave Kopay, the first pro football player to come out of the closet, though he'd done it years after his career had ended. He had also outed a couple of other players, dead of AIDS by then.

Cantoro said he'd been a kicker, which Warren had always thought was a pansy position. The kickers were on the "special" team, and all they needed to be able to do was kick a ball a long fucking way.

Leo was talking, and Warren realized he hadn't been listening, so he tuned back in. "What you say we start opposite ends of show and meet in middle?" Leo said. "Pick up lots of stuff on new products; then we go over together."

They walked to the convention center and got their credentials; then Warren was on his own. He dutifully began walking past booth after booth, but most of them were pushing the same old crap that GetBalled already sold. It was hard to find anything new or unique.

He was handed plastic tote bags, stress-relieving squeeze balls in various shapes and sizes, novelty pens and mouse pads and screen cleaners. By the time he reached the booth for Little Piglet, he was starting to worry that he'd never find anything worth showing Leo.

"Hey, Warren, thanks for stopping by," Rich Cantoro said, reaching out to shake Warren's hand again. He was a good-looking guy, Warren thought, with thick, wavy black hair and piercing green eyes. "So tell me, what are you up to these days?"

Warren explained about GetBalled.com. "You ever think about adding some of the less popular sports?" Rich asked, when he was finished.

"I've been looking into it," Warren said. "So far I haven't gotten a handle on it."

"Let me help you," Rich said. "You know anything about *boules*?"

Warren shook his head. "We think it's going to be the next hot craze," Rich said. "It's the generic name for a bunch of different games where you throw heavy balls toward a target. In France, the most popular version is called *petanque*, and seventeen million people play it. In Italy they call it *bocce*. Let me show you some of our products."

Warren listened as Rich described the differences. "There are two main versions of the game—one where the ball is tossed underhand, the other where it's rolled. The balls can either be hollow metal, wood or leather. We sell different kits for each variation."

Warren looked over the different kits, but the game wasn't ringing any bells with him. "You probably still work out, don't you, Warren?" Rich reached over and squeezed Warren's biceps.

"I do."

"You play golf?"

Warren shrugged. "A little bit. Not since I left Jacksonville, though."

"Exactly. And why did you play there? Because you were around a bunch of old guys, ex-jocks, right?"

Warren thought back to the couple of times he had played. Usually it had been as part of a foursome of older men, football supporters who liked having one of the guys from the team along. He nodded.

"See, that's the beauty of boules. You can play it at any age. Little kids, moms and dads, old guys too. It doesn't take much skill or flexibility, but it's good exercise. And all you need is a patch of lawn, a couple of balls and a *cochonnet*, the target. In French, cochonnet also means piglet—which is where our name comes from." He smiled. "You'll see; it's a great game. Low cost of entry, hours of fun."

He leaned in close to Warren. "And see, here's the thing. You're playing with balls."

Warren just looked at him. Was there some kind of innuendo there?

"And your site is called GetBalled, right?" Rich asked. "So you're a natural to carry our kits."

"Oh, yeah," Warren said.

"Listen, we're throwing a little party tomorrow night," Rich said. "To show off the product and give folks a chance to play." He reached over to the display table for a heavy white card. "Here's the invitation. Stop by, even if you only have a couple of minutes. You won't regret it."

Warren took the card and the product literature, and a small rubber ball with the word *petanque* and the company name on it.

After that, his day picked up, and by the time he met Leo he'd collected a half-dozen ideas for products. They had hot dogs and sodas from one of the food court booths, and then split up to cover the other half of that hall, because Leo thought two sets of eyes would help them not miss anything.

The show spanned two halls, and Leo wanted to cover hall one that day and hall two the next. By the time they got back to the hotel at the end of the day, Warren felt like he'd gone through a tough workout. His feet hurt, his calves ached, and his back was tense.

Leo, on the other hand, was still going. "We have dinner my favorite steak house," said. "Hard-working guys like us, we need protein."

"So, what you think of working world?" Leo asked after they ordered. "Very different from football?"

"Different in some ways, but similar in some," Warren said. "When I was a kid, I played for fun. In high school, I started to push myself because I wanted to get a college scholarship. That was a lot of pressure, but it was nothing compared to playing in college, once I figured out that I had a shot at the NFL, if I could reach my potential."

"But is good practice for real world," Leo said.

"It is. But I could manage all that pressure because I had a goal in mind. Once I made the roster in Jacksonville, though, it was different."

The server brought them wedges of iceberg lettuce drizzled with bacon bits and thousand island dressing, and Warren dug in. "On one hand, it was awesome, because I had dreamed of playing pro ball and there I was. But there were guys there who had so much more natural talent than I had. And they were willing to work just as hard as I was, or even harder. I was on this treadmill, struggling not to fall behind."

Leo didn't interrupt, and Warren kept talking.

"It was totally devastating when I realized I wasn't good enough to stay. I kept on working until the very last day, but I knew the end was coming, and it scared the shit out of me. I mean, I had spent my whole life wanting this, and now I had it, and it was going to be over, and I had no idea what I was going to do."

"I'm sure was tough," Leo said. "For me, I came to United States when I was eighteen. I was supposed to go to university in Moscow, but my family had chance to come here, and I was not to stay behind without them."

"Did you speak English already?"

Leo shrugged. "I study in school. And I can ask for hamburger, and where is bathroom. But not good enough to go to university, at least not right away. My parents are both engineers in Russia, but in US my father goes to work in factory, my mother cleaning houses. I was delivery boy for pizza company, taking English courses during the day. My younger brother and sister go to school, and I look over homework with them so I learn too."

"I can't imagine how hard that must have been," Warren said, as the server brought their entrees. The steaks were huge, accompanied by baked potatoes the size of small footballs.

"Makes me hungry," Leo said. "You, you must do same thing. Change direction, channel same determination into business."

"I promise you I'll do my best," Warren said.

He was too exhausted when he got back to his room to do anything more than strip down and fall into bed. Saturday was easier, because the hall wasn't as full and Warren felt that he could take his time.

He stopped at a booth for a publishing company that specialized in sports books. They weren't giving stuff away, but a book on math and sports caught his eye, and he thought it would be a fun gift to bring home for Thom. He was still tutoring at the math lab, and the book was full of stuff like "Can a jump shot be made with an initial angle of thirty degrees" and "What equations describe the mechanics of a golf swing?" Maybe he could get something from it to help one of the jocks he was tutoring.

He bought the book and dumped it into his bag. As he continued down the aisle, he remembered those tutoring sessions with Thom, the way Thom had managed to make the math more understandable. And then of course there was the way he'd felt sitting there next to Thom, knowing that his tutor was gay. The way he'd gotten so horny that he couldn't hold it in any more, and he'd mashed his lips against Thom's in the tiny library room.

He had to shift the bag over his crotch to avoid showing off his boner. He shook his head and got back in the game, looking over the products and trying to find the ones that would work for GetBalled.

That evening, he and Leo went to another hotel a few blocks away where Little Piglet had set up their bocce games.

"I am liking," Leo said, after he and Warren had bowled a game against Rich and his boss. There were about a dozen people there, most of them huddled around the bar. "I want set like this for my backyard."

"See," Rich said to Warren. "I knew once you guys tried it, you'd be hooked."

Warren wasn't hooked yet, but he was glad that Leo thought he'd found at least one good product. As they were getting ready to leave, Rich pulled Warren aside.

"We're about to pack this up," he said. "You want to grab some dinner? Talk about the old times we almost shared but didn't?"

Okay, Warren thought, there was something in Rich's eye that you'd have to be a total virgin to miss. And though he knew he ought to say no, he said yes.

KEEPING TRACK

Warren felt grungy after a day on his feet and then standing around on the bocce court in the last rays of the sun. He went back to his hotel, where he showered and changed, glad Thom had suggested he bring something extra to wear if he went out.

He wished that Thom was there to give him a read on Rich. It wasn't like he was going to sleep with the guy or anything, but it might be cool to talk to another NFL athlete about being gay. How could he broach the subject, though? Would Rich bring it up? Maybe he wasn't gay at all, just an ex-jock interested in rehashing his glory days?

Rich had suggested a barbecue joint a few blocks from the hotel, and Warren smelled the aroma as he approached, a shot back to his childhood at church picnics, drinking root beer and eating ribs and corn on the cob, chasing his sisters around the parking lot until they all collapsed in laughter.

The restaurant was in a rustic-looking wood building with sweet smoke pouring out of a chimney. Rich approached the place at the same time Warren did.

"Glad you could come out with me," Rich said. "We ex-jocks have to stick together, right?"

Would he be stuck with that for the rest of his life, Warren wondered, as they stood in line to order at a wooden counter plastered with license plates from around the country. An ex-jock. Somebody whose best days were behind him. Or was there something better on the horizon? Somehow, *business executive* didn't have the same ring as *NFL player*.

They ordered local micro-brewed beer and big platters of baby back ribs, hush puppies, and corn bread. "Man, this is just like home," Warren said, salivating.

"I grew up in upstate New York," Rich said. "For me this food is as foreign as French or Thai. I love to eat where the locals do when I travel."

As they drank and nibbled on sweet biscuits, they talked about the Jacksonville coaches, players they knew in common, the rigors of training, and road travel. "It's awesome being able to talk like this," Warren said, after they picked up their platters at the counter. "I never felt like I could talk to anybody that openly while I was still on the team, and then after I left I didn't have contact with anyone."

"I know what you mean. It's why I asked you to dinner. I don't get a chance to talk like this too often. " He paused. "And there was something else too."

Warren only had to look at him to know what that something else was. Without thinking, he said, "Yes, I am."

Rich looked stunned, then laughed. "That is so freaky. You knew what I was going to ask you."

"I got a vibe from you," Warren said.

"Gaydar?" Rich asked. "I come off that way?"

Warren shook his head. "It was just a feeling. I doubt that anybody who's straight would even notice it."

"Good. Because my boss is kind of a homophobe. I'm not comfortable talking to him, or anybody else at work, about my personal life."

"That sucks," Warren said. "Where's your

office?"

"Birmingham, Alabama," Rich said. "It's a nice town, but very conservative, lots of religious types."

"Tell me about it. I grew up Southern Baptist in South Carolina."

"How about you?" Rich asked. "You out at work?"

"I met Leo through this gay rugby team I joined, so he knew from the start."

"Your boss is gay too?"

Warren shook his head. "He's straight, but he likes to play rugby. He's a cool guy."

"You're very lucky. When people ask me what I did over the weekend, I have to say that I went out with a friend."

" A boyfriend?"

Rich nodded. "He works for his family business—paperboard distribution. So it's not like he can pick up, and we could move somewhere more tolerant." He shook his head. "I never expected to be able to be openly gay in the NFL, you know, before Michael Sam, but I thought it would be better in the workplace. Guess I was wrong."

They talked for a while longer about being gay in sports, and in sports business, and by the time dinner was over, Warren thought that he'd like to build a friendship with Rich. When they left the restaurant, they shook hands and promised to keep in touch. " And hey, maybe you'll order some little pigs," Rich said.

"From the way Leo liked it I'm sure we will."

He walked back to the hotel on his own, thinking about how lucky he was that he had stumbled into a job where he could be comfortable. He never wanted to be one of those flag-waving gays, to march in parades or slap rainbow flags on his bumper. But it was good to be able to be who he was, not have to hide.

When he got back to his room, he called Victor. "Listen, I'm kind of in the middle of something," Victor said. "When are you coming back?"

In the background, Warren could hear the sound of a TV going, a football game Victor must have taped for later viewing. "Tomorrow morning."

"Call me when you get in, and we'll see what we can work out. Catch you later."

He hung up before Warren could say good-bye himself. What was so urgent? If the game was taped, he could have just paused it. Was there someone with him? Brendan?

What if Victor had been lying to him, and he was still caught up with Brendan and his drama? He felt his blood pressure rising, and he caught himself. He and Victor were dating; that's all. If he was out of town, there was no reason why Victor couldn't spend time with his friends.

And if he was going to date Victor, he had to trust him, right? Victor said he wasn't having sex with Brendan anymore, so Warren had to accept that.

He sat back on the hotel bed. Maybe the problem was with the distance between them. He had already been thinking of moving to Broward to shorten his commute to GetBalled. Why not just do it?

The more he thought about it, the better the idea seemed. Victor's hours were so erratic that if they lived closer together, they'd be able to spend more time together on short notice. It could be Warren's place that Victor stopped by on his way home.

Or he could just jump-start things and move in with Victor, at least for a short time. See how the relationship worked out, then once they were comfortable with each other get a house together, maybe even a dog. He'd have to talk it over with Victor of course, but he went to sleep thinking about how cool it would be to be with Victor all the time.

Leo had plans to spend Sunday in Atlanta with cousins, so Warren took an early flight back to Miami on his own. He called Victor once he landed. "I was just going to go for a workout," Victor said. "You want to join me?"

"Sure." They both had memberships at the same gym chain, so Warren drove up to Broward to meet Victor at his branch. Victor was already lifting weights when Warren walked onto the gym floor, so he stepped over to spot him.

"How was your trip?" Victor asked, when he finished his set.

"Interesting. Learned a lot at the trade show, found some interesting products."

"Cool. Leo should be happy." They moved smoothly along the circuit, then went for a run upstairs, neither of them talking much. After they showered and changed, they went back to that sports bar on US 1 for dinner.

After Nathan had taken their order, then brought them their beers, Warren said, "So at the trade show, I met this guy."

Victor looked up. "What kind of guy?"

"He was a kicker for Jacksonville a couple of

years before I came on board. We knew a lot of the same people. And he's gay."

"Really? What's his name?"

"Rich Cantoro."

Victor shook his head. "Don't recognize the name, but I'm not a big football fan. Is he out?"

Warren shook his head and explained about the homophobic boss, the boyfriend stuck in a family business.

"That's a bummer," Victor said. "It's one of the reasons I like to work for myself. I can be myself without worrying about what a boss says."

"But you must have clients," Warren said. "Companies that hire you to do the inspections? Real estate agents who recommend you?"

"Of course. But a lot of them are gay too; so it's no big deal. And it's not like I show up to inspect somebody's house in a feather boa and a rhinestone jockstrap."

"You have those?" Warren asked.

Victor laughed. "Don't get your hopes up. Never done drag, never had an interest."

"I can't imagine doing drag," Warren said. "Even when I was a little kid I never wanted to try on my mother's clothes or anything. They probably don't even make women's clothes in my size."

"Oh, you'd be surprised," Victor said. "Is GetBalled the first place you've worked that you've been out?"

"I guess," Warren said. "I mean, I'm not really out at work. I don't talk about sex or who I'm dating, but Leo knows, of course, and I'm not sure who else."

"But still, doesn't it make you feel more

comfortable?"

Warren thought it was exactly the opposite, since Thom had come to work at GetBalled, but he wasn't going to say that to Victor, so instead he just said, "I guess. I mean, I like GetBalled, and I'm planning to stay there. So I was thinking I should just bite the bullet and move up to Broward."

"Great idea," Victor said. "There's a lot more gay life and culture up here, particularly around Wilton Manors, than you'll ever find in a suburb like Kendall. I can point you toward a couple of real estate agents if you want. You want to rent, or you thinking of buying?"

Warren took a deep breath. "I was thinking I might come stay with you for a while, see how things work out before I commit to a lease."

Victor looked stunned. "Warren, you can't just move in with somebody after two dates," he said.

"Five dates," Warren said. "This is our sixth."

"You're keeping track?"

"Of course, Victor. Aren't you? I want to be able to spend more time with you, and with your work schedule, it's hard to get together."

"Yeah, but Warren, that's not a reason to move in with somebody. Sure, move up to Broward, find someplace nearby, we'll hang out more. But I'm not ready to get married or anything."

"I didn't say we'd get married," Warren said angrily. "Just that I wanted to spend more time with you. If you don't want that…"

"Calm down, Warren. Of course I want to spend more time with you. I like you."

That was pretty tepid, Warren thought. But he

took a deep breath. "You're right. I like you too, Victor. I'm letting myself get carried away."

"Passion is great," Victor said. "Going for what you want is great too. But you didn't jump right to the NFL from high school football, did you? It takes time and work to get what you want."

"A relationship shouldn't be work." Warren crossed his arms over his chest.

"That's naive. Of course a relationship takes work. Even a good friendship. You have your ups and downs. You put up with the other person's crap; he puts up with yours. You work through your problems."

Victor leaned back in his chair. "Take your friend Thom. You must have had arguments with him, right?"

"I guess."

"Come on, Warren, work with me here."

There was that word again. Work. "Yes, Thom and I have argued. And we really don't have that much in common. But somehow we connected, and not just through sex. I feel like he's somebody who's got my back."

"Exactly. It's the same with me and Brendan. He may be a crazy bastard, but I know he'll always be there when I need him. And I'll do the same for him."

He motioned for Nathan to bring their check. "You seem pretty tense tonight," Victor said. "How about we go back to my place, and I give you another back rub?"

Warren felt like an eager puppy dog who had just been promised a treat. "Sure, great. Maybe you can show me what to do so I can do you too."

"I like the sound of that," Nathan said as he delivered the bill. "Who's doing who?"

"I'll send you a link to the YouTube video," Victor said, and handed over his credit card.

Nathan laughed and walked away.

"You aren't really videotaping us, are you?" Warren asked.

"Of course not. It's a joke. Jeez, Warren, lighten up."

Warren followed Victor back to his apartment. When he parked and got out of his car, he saw Victor still sitting in his SUV talking on his phone. Warren didn't want to stand by Victor's car as if he was spying on him, but he didn't know what else to do.

He decided to walk up to Victor's door and wait there, but as he passed Victor's car he couldn't help hearing Victor shouting, "I told you, B. Enough already."

He must have seen Warren passing, because he said, "I'll call you later." Then he was out of the car, slamming the door behind him.

"If this is a bad time," Warren began.

"There is nothing fucking wrong with the time." Victor opened the door of his apartment so heavily that it swung back against the wall with a thud. He stalked inside, and Warren hesitated on the doorstep. Something was very clearly wrong, but Victor didn't seem to want to admit to it.

"Well, come on in," Victor said. "You're letting out all the air conditioning."

Warren walked inside and closed the door carefully behind him. Victor came up to him then. "I'm sorry I yelled." He smiled at Warren. "If I told you I was a bad boy, would you punish me?"

"I'd do anything for you," Warren said.

FOOL MOON

Anything, in Warren's opinion, turned out to be some kinky shit, but he had to admit that it got his dick hard, and reminded him of some of those porn magazines he had gobbled up in the past.

"I want you to spank me," Victor said. "Would you do that for me?"

"Sure, Victor." Warren had never spanked anybody before aside from some fraternity rituals with wooden paddles, but he'd been spanked enough as a kid for misbehaving so he knew what was involved.

He sat down on Victor's couch. "Come here, Victor," he said, motioning with his finger. "Stand right here in front of me."

"You know you've been a bad boy," Warren said, when Victor was in place. "And you know what happens to bad boys, don't you?"

Victor looked down at the floor. "They get punished," he said in a small voice.

"That's right." Warren reached up and undid the drawstring of Victor's sweat pants, then tugged them down. Victor was wearing a pair of white jockey shorts so old the hem was frayed. Warren took hold of the waistband and ripped, and the noise was almost startling. Once torn, the jockeys fell to the floor, and Victor was left in his T-shirt and flip-flops.

Victor was hard, and Warren had to force himself to resist touching Victor's dick. "Lie down on my lap," Warren said.

Victor did, positioning himself so that his dick was against Warren's thigh, his ass centered in

Warren's lap. "Such a pretty ass," Warren said, stroking the buttocks gently with his hands. "Such a shame to make it red, but it has to be done."

He leaned back and slapped Victor's right cheek with his open hand. The smack was loud and satisfying, and Victor's body tensed, but he said nothing.

Warren smacked the other cheek, watching as his handprint appeared, then vanished. He ran his index finger down Victor's crack. He was already juicy back there. He began a pattern, spanking one cheek, then the other, talking dirty to Victor. Sometimes he flexed the muscles in his right thigh, making Victor's dick jump. He felt Victor's precum soaking into his pants.

"I think you're enjoying this too much," Warren said. His hands were starting to hurt, and Victor's cheeks were bright red, but Victor still had not complained, except for the occasional moan of either pleasure or pain, Warren couldn't tell which. "Stand up."

Victor stood, and Warren heaved himself up off the sofa. He wrapped his hands around Victor and pulled him close. He leaned over and spoke into Victor's ear. "You know I only do this because I care about you, don't you?"

"Yes," Victor mumbled into his chest. "Thank you, Warren."

He reached down and grabbed Victor's butt cheeks, squeezing them. Tears pooled at the edges of Victor's eyes. "You can say it, Victor," Warren said. "You can share your pain with me. I'm strong. I can take it."

"It hurts." Victor began to cry, his tears wetting Warren's shirt. "I'm such a fuck up. I can't do anything right."

Jesus, Warren thought. This was getting serious. "You're not a failure, Victor. Look at yourself the way I see you. You made it to the fucking Olympics, right?"

"But I didn't even make the qualifying rounds." Victor sniffled.

"Did you try as hard as you could?"

Victor didn't say anything, but his head moved up and down against Warren's chest.

"That's all that matters." Warren sat back down on the sofa and cupped Victor's dick in his hand. It was stiff and leaking precum. He pulled the dick toward him, and then took it in his mouth.

Victor's dick was hard as a rock and pulsing with heat. Warren stroked Victor's balls and sucked on his dick, and suddenly Victor was yelping and shooting his load down Warren's throat.

Warren pulled back and licked his lips, then looked up at Victor. "How'd I do?" he asked.

"You were awesome," Victor said. "I'm such a loser. How did I get lucky enough to find you?"

"Don't say that," Warren said. "You're not a loser at all. I'm the one who's lucky, to have found you."

Victor got down on his knees and opened Warren's pants. Warren leaned back to give him free access, and Victor tugged down Warren's boxers, freeing his dick. Victor began to suck him, and Warren spread his legs even farther, closed his eyes, and focused on the wet warmth surrounding him.

Victor sucked with a vengeance, as if he was desperate to swallow Warren's cum, and Warren couldn't hold out for long. His whole body tingled with tiny electric flashes, and his cum bubbled up in his guts and then spilled out.

Victor stayed on his knees, his head slumped down.

"You have some body lotion?" Warren asked him. "Your butt is going to sting."

"I want it to," Victor said. "Don't worry; I'll sleep on my stomach."

Victor looked so utterly exhausted that Warren stood up, closed his pants, then helped Victor to his feet. Warren put his arm around Victor's shoulders and steered him toward the bedroom. When they got to the door, Victor stopped and turned to face Warren. "You're such a sweet guy." He leaned up and kissed Warren gently on the lips. "I'm going to crash. I'll call you." Then he walked into his bedroom and flopped facedown on his bed.

Warren stood there for a moment, looking at Victor's red ass cheeks. There was something fucked up here, he thought. He just had no idea exactly what that was.

He drove back down to Miami under a full moon. He remembered a South American guy at FU, someone in one of his classes, who had a heavy accent, and had spoken about a "fool moon."

Yeah, that's what this was, Warren thought. Halfway home, his phone buzzed with a text, and he was sure it was from Victor. Instead of checking it, though, he left the phone on the seat beside him until he was parked in front of his house.

It wasn't from Victor, though, but from Thom, asking for a ride the next morning. Warren sent him a quick okay, then sat there in his car for a while, staring at that fool moon.

SUPERMAN

Monday morning Warren swung by the Three Lambs frat house to pick up Thom. "Thanks," Thom said. "My car's acting up, and I have an appointment to take it to the garage tomorrow. I didn't want to risk driving it all the way up to Broward and have it conk out on the highway."

"No problem," Warren said. "We could make this a regular thing, you know. For the days you're working up at the office. It would be nice to have some company on the drive."

"I can kick in for the gas," Thom said. "And it'll be fun to hang out together." He turned to face Warren. "I don't know if I've said it before, but I'm really glad you came back to Miami."

"Yeah, I'm glad too. But you watch. You're going to get some awesome job offer, and you'll be out of here like a light."

"Don't count on it. I mean, I'd love to get a great job. But for now I'm happy with what I have. So, how was your trip?"

They talked about what Warren had discovered in Atlanta, both about products and about Rich Cantoro, and they were so engaged in the conversation that Warren was surprised at how quickly the trip had passed.

When he took a break for lunch, Warren checked his personal e-mail, and there was a message from Victor there. *Sorry if I seemed like a head case last night,* he wrote. *There's stuff going on that's screwing me up. I appreciate having you there for me.*

That was sweet, Warren thought. *You can count*

on me, Warren responded. *I'm on your team.*

That sounded wrong. Sure, he was on Victor's rugby team. But wasn't he something more? He erased that last line and typed, *You're an awesome guy. Don't ever forget that.* Then he hit *xx* and *oo* with his index finger, and hit Send quickly.

He had never been one for adding hugs and kisses to his e-mails before. But maybe that was a sign of how much more open he was becoming. If he wanted Victor to be his boyfriend, he had to treat him that way, right?

Warren spent most of the day doing further research on products he'd seen at the trade show and writing up a report for Leo. He was so engrossed in his work that he hardly noticed the hours go by, until he looked up and the other guys were packing up to go home.

"You want to work out together on our way home?" Thom asked. "We could go by the FU gym. You've still got access there, right?"

"Yeah, but I can get you into my gym on a guest pass," Warren said. "Better equipment, and no skinny, pimply freshmen."

Thom winked at him. "Sometimes they can be fun."

Warren laughed. Thom needed workout clothes, so they swung past the frat house first. "You want to come in?" Thom asked. "I'll only be a minute."

"I'm good here," Warren said.

"What? You embarrassed you might see somebody you fucked the last time you were here?" Thom asked. Warren felt himself blushing, and Thom laughed. "Don't worry, big guy. You're already last week's news."

What did that mean, Warren wondered, as Thom ran up to the house's front door. Was there an orgy at the Three Lambs every weekend? Did Thom participate in them?

He had no right to be jealous. Thom wasn't his boyfriend, just his friend, and they'd suspended the whole friends with benefits thing, right? Thom came back a couple of minutes later in a loose T-shirt and tight workout shorts, and Warren had to force himself to think about something other than ripping those shorts down and blowing Thom right there in the car.

At the gym, he pushed himself hard, and Thom almost as much. "Come on, you can do another five reps," Warren said, spotting for him.

"No, I can't," Thom said, putting the weight bar back. "Not everybody is a Superman like you."

"I'm no Superman," Warren said.

"You're as close as I'll ever come to one." By then Thom's T-shirt was drenched with sweat and clung to him like a second skin. He really had a fine chest, Warren thought.

They showered at the gym, and Warren had to turn his back to Thom in the communal shower so that he wouldn't see him naked and get hard. Thom didn't seem to notice Warren's discomfort; he kept talking, forcing Warren to turn his head around to reply. He sped through his shower and grabbed his towel, going back to the lockers before Thom had finished washing his hair.

He didn't say anything more until they were back in the car. "Good luck with the garage tomorrow. Hope it's nothing major."

"Yeah. Me too." He turned to Warren. "You want to come up and hang out for a while?"

Warren shook his head. That would be a very bad idea—him, Thom, and a bed in the same room. "Nah, I'm wiped. I'm just gonna go home and crash."

"Well, thanks for the chauffeur service." Thom leaned over and kissed Warren on the cheek, then got out of the car.

Warren felt that kiss all the way home. By the time he got there, he was so horny he could hardly stand it. He hurried into his room and stripped down, but before he could get busy Victor called.

"You feeling better?" Warren reached down to scratch his balls. That felt good.

"Yeah," Victor said. "Sorry to dump all my shit on you like that."

"It's okay." Warren idly stroked the head of his dick with his index finger, but it appeared to have changed its mind, and it wasn't interested in getting hard.

"No, really, I appreciate it," Victor said. "How about it if I take you out for a nice dinner Saturday night, after practice?"

"I'm warning you, I've got an appetite," Warren said.

"Oh, baby, I know that," Victor said.

It was the first time Warren could remember Victor using an endearment, and his heart gave a couple of quick bounces, and his dick finally snapped to attention. They talked for a while longer, and by the time he hung up Warren had a serious case of blue balls. Between lusting after Thom at the gym, and then thinking of Victor, he was getting desperate for some relief.

He closed his eyes and brought up an image of Victor naked in front of him. He went down on his knees and took Victor's dick in his mouth. But when he looked up, it was Thom staring down at him, not Victor.

He snapped his eyes open. That wasn't cool. Victor had a killer body, he was a sweet guy, and he and Warren had so much in common. Thom needed to get the fuck out of his head.

He closed his eyes again, this time thinking of Victor's chest, the way he liked having his nipples sucked. Warren leaned in close, took one nipple in his mouth and began to lick and gnaw at it.

"Oh, man, big guy. You know what I like."

Crap. It was Thom's voice. There was something seriously screwed up.

Warren got up and dug through the bottom of his dresser for his porn. But he'd read everything a dozen times, and nothing got him going anymore. He picked up his laptop and went online, looking for anything to get his mind focused.

He skimmed through a bunch of pictures, but none of the guys floated his boat. They were too skinny, or too fat, too old or too young. The ones posed in locker rooms, in or out of jockstraps, looked like the kind of guys who'd had their mothers write notes to get them out of gym in high school.

He went to a movie site and scanned through the clips. The twinks didn't excite him, and neither did the bears or the out-of-shape amateurs. He was still hard, but no matter how he squeezed and rubbed his dick, he couldn't feel the rise of an orgasm coming.

What was wrong with him? He was horny as hell, but he couldn't get off. He logged into a gay chat room, but the guys there were either private messaging each other or just chatting, crap like what they'd had for dinner, the movies they'd seen.

He clicked a link at the bottom of the screen which led him to a repository of amateur porn stories. They were classified by type, and he scrolled through the list. The incest and urination stuff was too creepy, and he wasn't interested in first times or man-boy love. He clicked the link for "authoritarian," just to see what that was like.

The first story was called "Spank Me, Daddy," and he started to read it. It reminded him of his escapade with Victor, only kinkier. One dude had the other naked, in handcuffs, and was flailing away at him with some kind of rope. As the sub's balls got squeezed, and his tits pinched, Warren suddenly felt his orgasm rising, without even touching himself. He shot a load on his belly and then lay there, stunned.

Was this what turned him on? That was sick. He wanted a guy to love him and have fun with him, not somebody to torture and torment him. And he didn't think he wanted to be that Dom either, causing pain to someone. He shook his head. The thing with Victor had to be a one-off. He wasn't going to get into that anymore.

ROOMIES

The next day he drove to work alone because Thom was dealing with his car. It seemed like the trip took a lot longer than the day before, and the constant traffic irritated him. He blew his horn a lot, zoomed around slow drivers, and basically acted like a jerk. He knew he was doing it, but he couldn't help himself.

Soon after he got in, Moises called him over. "Leo gave me this list of products you and he talked about. I want to get in touch with the manufacturers and start the paperwork so we can add these to the site, but I need to go over some stuff with you."

Warren scooted his chair over to Moises's cubicle, and they looked over the list. "Talk to me about these soccer training mannequins. Why is this a consumer product? Seems like the market would be limited just to coaches and schools."

"See, that's what's cool about them," Warren said. "You can set them up in your backyard and practice just like you would with a coach. So many kids are getting into soccer these days, and this is something lightweight and easy to put up in your backyard, so your kid can practice kicking, dribbling, whatever, even without another player. We could market it as a way to give your kid a real advantage."

Moises nodded. "I like that. Can you write that up, so we can use it on the site?"

"I've never been real good at writing."

"Just write it the way you explained it to me. You can grab statistics and testimonials from the manufacturers' sites and product reviews. You're an athlete—you know what would make somebody want to click the Buy button."

"All right," Warren said.

They went through a couple more products. "What's this thing?" Moises asked. "Shuttle baseball?"

"Oh man, that's really cool," Warren said. "I remember when I was a kid playing softball and baseball, we had this gadget that would pitch balls at you so you could hit them. But it was a pain to go around and collect the balls afterward, because if you really wailed at it you could send the ball far away."

"And this?"

"It has this badminton shuttlecock thing going on," Warren said. "The plastic stuff around the ends of the ball catches the wind and slows the ball down. So you can really hit it, but you don't have to chase it to kingdom come."

"Where is that?" Moises asked. "Is that part of the ball field?"

Warren laughed. "No, it's just something my mamaw used to say. Someplace really far away. You could practice in your backyard, and not worry about breaking your neighbor's window."

Moises nodded. "I see."

"But there's more to this product. It's not as hard as a baseball, but firmer than a foam ball, so you can really knock at it. But if it hits somebody, it doesn't hurt them the way getting hit with a baseball would. So it's safer for kids to play with."

"You really know your sports," Moises said. "Leo did a good job finding you."

Warren was embarrassed by the praise. He had

never thought that his knowledge of so many sports would help him get a job, or succeed at work.

They spent another hour going through the products; then Warren went back to his desk and Moises started contacting the manufacturers.

Warren was so jazzed by his conversation with Moises that he went right to developing the copy for the products. That kept him busy until late afternoon, when Michelle buzzed to say that a package had arrived for him.

He went out front. It was from Rich Cantoro at Little Piglet, and inside was one of their top of the line bocce sets. "What's that?" Buzz asked when Warren brought the package back to the office.

Warren explained to him, Pritap, and Moises. "Sounds like fun," Moises said. "Let's give it a try. Why don't you set it up in the warehouse?"

Warren read the simple instructions and set up the cochonnet, the target, at one end of a cleared space between racks in the warehouse. It could be stuck directly into the ground, or sit in a little base. Then he borrowed a tape measure from Cesar and measured out the court, drawing the lines on the concrete floor with blue chalk. When it was finished, he called the guys, and they each took turns.

Leo went first, rolling his ball easily until it was close to the cochonnet. Then the other guys took their turns. Moises tried to knock Leo's ball away but missed by a few inches. Warren had done some bowling, so he knew the right stance and the right way to throw, and he aimed at Leo's ball.

With a thwack his ball hit Leo's and sent it caroming away. Warren's ball rolled right up to the cochonnet and rested beside it.

"You must have been practicing," Pritap said.

"He's fucking athlete," Leo said. "Is any sport you can't do, Warren?"

"I'm kind of a water buffalo on the tennis court," Warren said. "I've got a lot of power, but I can't dive for shots."

"Then we play tennis sometime, and I kill you," Leo said.

All in all, he thought on his way home, it had been a pretty good day at work. He was starting to feel more comfortable with his coworkers and with the job that they expected of him. After he got off the expressway, he called Thom. "You want a ride tomorrow?" he asked.

"Yeah, that would be great. My car has to stay in the shop for a couple of days, and it was too expensive to get a rental."

"How'd you get home, then?"

"I started talking to this guy in the waiting room," Thom said. "He's like forty, but he's in good shape, and we swapped stories about working out. When I found out I wasn't getting my car back, he offered me a ride home."

"That's nice," Warren said. "Say, you want to just crash at my place for a couple of days? That way you wouldn't be stranded."

"Thanks. But wouldn't your roommates care?"

"We each have our own bedrooms," Warren said. "I've got a king-size bed. You could just bunk with me."

Thom hesitated, and Warren waited to hear what he had to say. He was in bumper-to-bumper traffic on the expressway, stuck behind a lumbering SUV, so he wasn't going anywhere fast.

"He asked me out," Thom said.

"Who?"

"The guy who drove me home. Dusty."

"Dusty? What kind of a name is Dusty? Is he a cowboy?"

"His real name is Myron," Thom said. "But his last name is Rhoades."

Warren groaned. "Dusty Rhoades? Give me a break."

"Anyway, I kind of like him. And I need to focus on finding somebody, now that you have Victor."

"You can still share the bed with me," Warren said. "I promise, no funny business."

"If you're sure. You don't think Victor will care?"

"We've just had a couple of dates," Warren said, remembering his conversation with Victor. "It's not like we're married."

"Then that would be awesome," Thom said. "I was figuring I'd be stuck here at the frat for the rest of the week."

Warren swung by the Three Lambs house on his way home and picked up Thom, and then they went to Costco, where Thom could use the frat house membership, and stocked up on food for the rest of the week.

Back at Warren's, they binge-watched a comedy series on TV for a couple of hours, then Warren yawned. "Guess we should get some sleep," he said.

"Yeah, I'm beat," Thom said. Warren went into the bathroom first, and by the time Thom came out he was under the covers on one side of the bed, the other side turned down. Thom was wearing boxers, and he slid in beside Warren. "Thanks for having me stay here." He leaned over and kissed Warren on the cheek.

Warren was glad that he was under the covers, because his dick was hard, and he didn't want Thom to know it. "You're welcome. Anything for a friend, right?"

"You bet." Thom turned off the light by the bed and turned on his side, facing away from Warren. Warren felt acutely conscious of Thom's body beside him, his even breathing, then his tiny rippling snores as he drifted into sleep. It took Warren a lot longer than usual to fall asleep.

CHICKEN SOUP

Wednesday morning Warren awoke to find himself curled against Thom, his arm over Thom's shoulders. Embarrassed, he pulled away as Thom woke up. He turned to Warren and smiled sleepily. "Morning." He sat up and stretched. "Wow, I slept like a log. You have a really comfortable bed."

Thom got up to go to the bathroom, and Warren noticed that his friend had morning wood but didn't say anything. He was worried that he'd pop a boner too. He got up while Thom was out and put on a big terrycloth robe with the Jacksonville jaguar on the back.

He realized that he hadn't heard from Victor, and he checked his phone. There was a hang-up shortly after midnight from a number he didn't recognize. Was that Victor calling from someone else's phone? Or just a random wrong number?

"You want to go for a quick run?" Thom asked when he came back into the bedroom.

"Sure, we've got time." Warren forced himself to look away as Thom pulled on bright yellow running shorts and a purple and yellow FU T-shirt. He scrambled into his own clothes, and they set out down the street, establishing an easy pace. They made a big loop around Warren's suburban neighborhood, dodging moms in minivans and yapping dogs on too-long leashes. A big landscape company truck was parked at one end of the street, with a logo that read *Grass Kissers*. The workmen with leaf blowers looked like beekeepers, with big floppy hats, long sleeves, and scarves wrapped around their mouths.

"Dibs on the shower," Warren said when they returned to the house.

"Hey, it's your place," Thom said.

Warren half hoped that Thom would join him in the shower, but he knew that would be wrong for both of them. He finished up and then went out to the kitchen, where he made power smoothies for breakfast.

"I could get used to this kind of service," Thom said. "At the frat it's a free-for-all and mostly what you find in the kitchen is dirty dishes and empty takeout containers."

"Welcome to the grown-up world," Warren said. "When I got my place in Jacksonville, I realized I had to take control of my life, which meant watching my diet, having healthy food in the house, all that. I've been slacking off since I got back here, though."

"Maybe I'll be a good influence on you then," Thom said.

Warren drove them to work, and though they hardly spoke during the day Warren was growing to like having Thom there. He continued writing and polishing the copy for the new products. At one point he went outside with a printout and read the blurbs out loud, because he was determined that everything be perfect.

Then he forwarded the copy to Pritap for inclusion on the product pages, and went back to his research. He got a text from Victor late in the day. *Caught some kind of bug,* he wrote. *Gonna lay low until Saturday so I can be up for practice.*

Warren was disappointed that there was no apology attached, nothing about missing him or wanting to see him. But he sucked it up and texted back. *Feel better. Call me if u need anything.*

He and Thom went to the gym together that evening. It was good to have a workout buddy, Warren thought. He had been missing that since leaving Jacksonville. Thom made them both big salads with grilled chicken and lots of veggies for dinner, and then settled down to work at his laptop. Warren used his own laptop to follow up on some leads he had discovered at work, and he liked the camaraderie of having Thom around.

This was what he wanted with Victor, he thought. A guy to come home to, to hang out with. And with Victor, there'd be the added bonus of sex. Thom didn't seem awkward at all that night as they got ready for bed, and Warren felt foolish for thinking that they wouldn't be able to be just friends.

He and Thom slept together again that night, each on his own side of the bed. Warren was up first, and as he pulled on his workout clothes he nudged Thom to get up so they could run again.

During the day, Warren thought about Victor, but figured he was sleeping off the effects of his cold meds. Around noon, Buzz asked him to do some testing on the site. "I loaded in a bunch of those new products. I'll e-mail you our test account information. Can you log in and try to buy a couple of items?"

"Sure." Warren looked at the list of blurbs he had written and then started checking each item's page. The soccer mannequin page was all screwed up, with text on top of images. When he clicked the Buy button for the softball with the shuttlecock attached, he got a 404 error—page not found. And then when he tried to check out, the GetBalled window completely disappeared.

Warren was worried that it was something he'd done, so he went back over each step, and got the same result. He painstakingly typed up a list of exactly what he had done, and what had happened, and then attached it to an e-mail to Buzz.

"Holy shit," he heard Buzz say. "Man, Warren, you should be a website tester. This is awesome."

"Really? I was worried I did something wrong."

"No, dude, you did exactly what you should have. And your documentation is excellent. I know just what needs to be fixed."

Warren was pleased. He'd never worked in an office before, and his typing skills sucked, but he was managing, even doing a good job. By the end of the day he was still glowing with accomplishment. On the ride home, Thom said, "I don't have any work to do this evening. You want to catch a movie?"

"Sure. I haven't been to the movies in ages. What do you want to see?"

Thom used his cell phone to pull up the list of current movies and read them off. "What do you think?" he asked Warren.

"You're going to think this is really gay," Warren said. "But I'd like to see that romantic comedy." He named a movie about two strangers falling in love on a tropical island that had gotten good reviews.

"So it's a chick flick," Thom said. "Nobody says dudes can't go too."

They ate at a salad bar in the same shopping

center as the movie theater, and then settled into their seats with a tub of popcorn to share.

The movie was sweet, though Warren had to admit that he'd rather have seen a movie about two guys rather than a straight couple. But there weren't that many of those movies around, and the ones that played were usually at some offbeat small theater in a gay neighborhood. He wasn't comfortable enough to go to one of those places. Though maybe with Thom, he might.

Victor, he thought. He'd be going to the movies with Victor.

His hand met Thom's in the popcorn box, and Thom looked over at him and smiled. Then he looked away quickly. Warren figured that the reason why he got a boner was because he hadn't had sex in a while, and after all, it was Thom. In other circumstances they might have followed up the movie with a little performance of their own.

But instead they went back to Warren's house and sat up in bed together reading for a while before turning out the lights. "Goodnight," Thom said. "Thanks for having me as your house guest." He leaned over and pecked Warren on the cheek.

"*Mi cama es su cama,*" Warren said. "My bed is your bed."

Thom laughed and turned on his side. Warren was careful to do the same thing.

The next morning neither of them had to suggest a run—they both got up and pulled on their shorts and T-shirts. Warren practiced a couple of sprints, and was surprised that Thom kept pace with him. He wondered if Victor ran every morning, or if his erratic work interfered with a regular schedule.

They scrambled through showers and smoothies and hopped into Warren's car for the ride up to Broward. Thom asked, "Any way you can slip away a little early today? My car's ready, but the garage is only open until six."

"No problem. If I have any work left, I can finish it at home."

Warren was disappointed that Thom was going back to the frat. He had really enjoyed having him stay. Maybe he'd suggest to Thom that they get a place together up in Broward, if Thom's job continued with GetBalled. That would be fun, having a friend and workout buddy around all the time.

Have to be a two-bedroom place, though. Wouldn't be cool for either of them if they were sharing a bedroom, or a bed, if they were trying to date other people.

He was glad he hadn't been talking to Victor, because he wasn't sure what to say about having Thom as his roommate. They'd both been good, though he'd spotted Thom with a hard-on a couple of times, and he knew that he'd gotten boners himself. He wasn't going to screw up Thom's chances with this new guy, Dusty, and after all, he had Victor.

He worked through the morning, and just before lunch Leo called him over. "I have new project for you, Warren. You are good with social media?"

Warren shrugged. "I go on Facebook sometimes, but that's it."

"We have GetBalled accounts many places. I am making you in charge. You go online, post new products, updates, comments from customers.

Answer questions and such."

"I'm not sure I can do that," Warren said. "I don't know much about that stuff. And what if I screw up?"

"I'll help you," Thom called from his desk. "I've been using those sites a lot lately looking for jobs."

"Excellent," Leo said. "You work together."

Thom scooted his chair over to Warren's desk, and they spent an hour going through LinkedIn, MySpace, Facebook, and Twitter. "There are a bunch of other sites," Thom said. "But we can get to them later."

He showed Warren how to log in, and how to make posts. "You can't just jump into these groups and start posting stuff about products. Think of yourself as Dear Abby for jocks."

"You want me giving advice to people?"

"Say somebody posts a question about playing football," Thom said. "You make a suggestion. Here, let's see what people are asking about."

They scanned through a bunch of posts on a football forum. "There, that one," Thom said, pointing. "The guy wants to help his kid learn to tackle. What advice can you give?"

"The kid needs to keep his feet shoulder-width apart, and his head down when he takes off," Warren said. "And his knees flexed. Anybody knows that."

"Obviously this dad doesn't," Thom said. "So explain that."

Thom watched while Warren two-fingered the basic steps in football tackling. "All right, now for your signature," Thom said. "Type your name, then hit Enter, then underneath type former NFL defensive end."

"Really? I only played one year. I don't want to seem like a blowhard."

"Do it. Hit Enter again, then type your job title. What is it?"

"Product specialist," Warren said.

"Good. Type that, and then put the company website after it. That's it. Now you post."

"If you say so."

"See, what you're doing is participating in the community. You're not just trying to sell products. You keep posting, and people will see your name and your credentials, and the GetBalled name, and they'll start associating it with good advice and good products."

By four o'clock, Warren had jumped around to a bunch of Yahoo groups and social media sites, answering questions and occasionally recommending products. After making sure there were no looming crises, he and Thom left the office.

They were both quiet on the drive south. Warren was bummed that Thom was leaving, and he finally decided to broach the question that had been on his mind. "What would you think about getting a place together up in Broward?" he asked. "If you keep working at GetBalled, that is?"

"I like the job a lot, but I'm not sure how much longer they'll need me," Thom said. "I've been building the encryption routines with Pritap, and it's going well. But I don't see it having long-term potential."

"Oh," Warren said.

"Not to say I wouldn't want to move in with you somewhere," Thom said. "We get along, right? I just have to see how my job situation evolves."

"Are you still looking?"

Thom nodded. "Yeah. This GetBalled gig has been great because I'm getting actual experience at encryption, so more possibilities are opening up. The problem is I need to know my shit before I can get something worthwhile. Pritap is great—I'm learning a ton from him. He has the programming stuff down, but he's not so strong on the math, so we're a good match."

"I'm sure you'll get an awesome job somewhere," Warren said. "But you're smart to stay at the frat until you know what's going to happen."

After Warren dropped Thom at the garage, he went over their conversation in his head. Thom had seemed willing to share a place with him—it was just the job stuff that was keeping it from happening. There was nothing he could do about that besides wait.

When he got home, neither of his housemates were there and he felt lonesome, the way he'd felt in Jacksonville. He had used his free time there to exercise, and he did the same that night—went to the gym, did a circuit of the weight machines, then ran several laps around the track.

By the time he finished it was late, and he texted Victor and asked how he was feeling, if he needed anything. He got a quick response that evening, that Victor was recovering after lots of chicken soup and vitamin C.

But still nothing personal, nothing romantic.

Oh well, Warren thought. If he was stuffed up and sniffling and sleeping a lot, romance would be far down on his list too.

Saturday morning Warren did a quick run around his neighborhood then drove up to the practice field in Fort Lauderdale. He hadn't heard anything more from Victor so he assumed the practice was still on. When he got into the locker room, he found Victor and Brendan there, along with Pete and Jerry.

"How are you feeling?" Warren asked Victor.

"Great. Ready to kick some ass on the pitch."

"Your cold's all better?"

He noticed Brendan looking at Victor curiously. Huh. Guess Victor never bothered to tell his friend that he was sick, though he'd told Warren. That gave him a warm feeling inside.

He was careful not to say anything to Brendan that might set him off. The rest of the guys arrived, and Victor laid out a practice session for them. It was a tough workout, and Warren was tired by the time it was finished. But thinking about having dinner with Victor gave him a second wind.

After practice, though, Victor pulled him aside. "I'm going to have to take a rain check on our dinner. I thought I was better, but after that practice I realized I'm still not a hundred percent, and I ought to just go home to bed."

"Are you sure?" Warren asked. "Because I can come up and take care of you. Heat up your soup and all. See, if I moved in with you, I could do that."

"You're not moving in with me, Warren," Victor said, and there was an ugly edge in his voice.

"You need to take a chill pill. We've had a couple of dates, and things have been okay, but I don't have time for all this romance shit right now."

"Romance shit?" Warren echoed. "Excuse me for thinking you cared."

"Warren," Victor said. "I didn't mean it like that."

"How did you mean it, exactly? Are we boyfriends? I mean, I know that's a silly high school kind of term, but what else do you call it? Fuck buddies? Friends with benefits? You already have that with Brendan, don't you?"

"From the start, I made it clear to you that I wasn't going to settle down into some pseudo-heterosexual shit. I make my own rules."

"Yeah, well you can play your own game, then," Warren said. "Fuck you, and your pencil-dick fuck buddy too."

He stalked away, not bothering to take a shower and change back into his street clothes. He was so angry at Victor that he wanted to get a big bucket of chicken soup and drown him in it. He clenched the steering wheel as he drove out of the parking lot and stopped at the traffic light.

A plus-size Alice in Wonderland, complete with blonde hair and a light-blue apron, crossed the street in front of him, walking hand-in-hand with a zombie in bloody rags. Warren had seen some funky outfits in Miami, but that topped them all.

Then he watched them catch up with a furry blue monster, a Cher wannabe, and a muscular Tarzan in a loincloth. That's when he realized that it was Halloween. He saw a steady stream of people in costume heading into the center of Wilton Manors, and he was tempted to follow along. He could use a good party to cheer him up.

But he had no costume, he was sweaty, and he was in too foul a mood to have fun. So he got on the highway, thinking about what Victor had said, going over it again and again. Had Victor said that he was still having sex with Brendan? Or had Warren's temper gotten the best of him?

He was driving on auto-pilot, and he was about to take the exit for the FU campus when he remembered that Thom had a date that night.

Fuck. He wanted to see Thom, to rant and rave and tell him all about what an asshole Victor was. But he didn't want to screw up Thom's chances with the guy from the garage. Yeah, he was older and had a dumb name. But if Thom liked him, Warren wasn't going to get in the way, even if his heart was breaking.

He thought about going to that X-rated bookstore on Bird Road. He hadn't been back there in years. Maybe he could find some guy there, go into the back room, and get his rocks off. Or he could drive out to that truck stop, find some horny trucker who wanted to suck a monster cock.

He started to sniffle and realized that he was crying. He didn't want to have anonymous sex with anybody. He didn't want to have sex at all. He just wanted to go out on a date with a guy he liked. Was that too much to ask?

DATING

Sunday morning Thom called. "You want to work out today?"

"I don't know," Warren said. "I feel like crap."

"You're not getting sick, are you? There's a flu bug going around at FU."

"Nah, it's not that." He sighed. "I think Victor and I might have broken up. He told me he doesn't have time for any quote romance shit unquote right now. And I got mad and told him off."

"Ouch," Thom said. "You definitely need to work out. Take out all your anger and frustration on the machines at the gym."

"You just want to use my guest membership," Warren grumbled.

"Well, that too. You spoiled me for the crappy FU gym. But I know you, big guy. You need physical activity to snap you out of this mood. I'll pick you up in an hour."

Warren sighed. "All right."

When Thom arrived, he was way too bubbly and happy for Warren's lousy mood. "How was your date last night?" Warren asked.

"We had a good time," Thom said. "He took me out to this great restaurant on Brickell, right near where he works. The food was awesome—like you only see on the Food Network or something. It looked so pretty on the plate, all these blobs of sauce in bright colors, like a painting."

"But how did it taste?" Warren asked. "You can't eat art."

"A couple of the things were too spicy for me,"

Thom admitted. "But that was my fault, for letting Dusty order for me."

"Why'd you do that?"

"Everything on the menu was so expensive," Thom said. "I didn't know what to order without seeming like a pig. So I asked him to choose for me."

"Then you got what you deserved," Warren said.

"It didn't matter. We really clicked, Warren. He has an MBA, and he has this high-powered job with a bank on Brickell. He lives in this condo on Brickell Key with a view of the bay, and he drives a Jaguar."

"You went to his place?"

Thom shook his head. "We went out for a drive after dinner, and he showed me where he lived."

"Just don't rush into anything," Warren said. "See what happened to me with Victor."

"I'm not planning to have sex in the shower with him, if that's what you mean," Thom said. "At least not until the third or fourth date."

"Fuck you, Lodge," Warren said.

"You already have, Updegrove. Multiple times." He tapped Warren's shoulder. "I was just kidding. Don't get so sensitive."

"I'm allowed to be sensitive," Warren said. "Just because I'm big and strong and I used to play pro football doesn't mean that I don't have feelings."

"Whoa. Where did that all come from?"

"Sorry. I'm still bummed about Victor, I guess."

They went through their workout, talking only about equipment and reps. When they were finished, Thom asked, "Can I buy you a smoothie?"

Warren shook his head. "I just want to go home."

"All right. But you can't wallow in this, Warren. So the guy's a jerk. There are lots more guys out there you can connect with. Move on."

"I know. Just give me a day or two."

"Well, I have some assignments from Pritap I need to work on, and I want to be near the FU library in case I have to look stuff up, so I'm going to work from home tomorrow."

"Can't you look stuff up online?"

"These are obscure math questions," Thom said. "Some of the books are so old they're on reserve at the library."

"Jeez, you'd think somebody would have digitized them by now."

"You'd think," Thom said.

When he got home, Warren couldn't stop thinking about Victor. Should he send him an apology? A text, an e-mail? Call him?

Despite his workout, he still felt lousy. Was this what heartbreak was? This empty feeling in the pit of his stomach, this overwhelming feeling of sadness. He thought back to the last time he'd felt anything like this.

By the middle of his season with Jacksonville, he had figured out that he just wasn't playing well enough to get much time on the field. When the coach did send him in, it was often late in the game when the outcome wasn't in doubt. He replaced players who the coach wanted to protect for future games.

He'd figured he'd be cut post-season, but he'd still held onto the faint hope that a player would be injured, or that the team would focus on other positions in the NFL draft, and they'd still have a place for him.

He had to admit to himself that he hadn't played up to his full potential. He got into his head too much, worrying about what other players might say about him. Not just if they discovered he was gay, though that had been a big part of it. He hadn't wanted anybody to think he wasn't working his ass off, which in turn kept him from doing so.

He'd reported for training camp in early August, determined to play his heart out. He'd thought he was improving, and when the coach called him in toward the end of the month, he'd hoped for good news.

"I had high hopes for you, Updegrove. But you and I both know this hasn't been your year. I need to reduce my active list, and I'm afraid that means you have to go." He stood up, and Warren did too. The coach reached out to shake his hand. "You played in the NFL. Always remember that. You reached the highest pinnacle of achievement in your sport."

Warren thought being MVP of the Super Bowl was the highest pinnacle, but he was too stunned to argue. He took a deep breath and said, "Thank you for the opportunity."

Then he went home and got drunk off his ass.

He'd felt like shit for the rest of the week, and he wasn't sure if that was the effects of his binge, of not exercising, or of losing his job. It took more time to rouse himself to get out of his apartment lease, rent a van, and drive himself back to Miami. An FU teammate had told him about the house where he rented a room, and that he was leaving, and Warren had moved in.

After a while, it had stopped hurting so much, and he was able to focus on finding a future for himself. Getting back in touch with Thom had been a big help.

He allowed himself one beer with dinner, a healthy salad, and then watched mindless TV until it was time for bed.

Warren decided to keep up the routine of a morning run, though it wasn't as much fun without Thom beside him. He drove to work by himself, and when he got there he discovered that there had been a deluge of orders over the weekend for some of the new products he'd discovered, and he spent most of the day helping to pick and pack and ship products. He had no time to obsess about Victor and their failed relationship, though it all came back to him as he was driving home that evening.

How could he have been so stupid? Victor was a good guy, and a good match for him. So he got moody sometimes. So did Warren. The poor guy was sick, after all, and here was Warren yelling at him.

He was in the middle of a major beat-up on himself when Thom called. "Hey, I wanted to let you know that I'm still working on that stuff for Pritap. So I won't be going in to GetBalled tomorrow."

"Yeah, whatever," Warren said. "Just think of me as your limo service. Call me when you need a ride again." He punched the End button on his phone savagely and tossed it to the seat beside him.

You couldn't count on anybody, he thought. Not friends, not boyfriends. You had to make your way on your own. Do your own thing. He stopped at the mini mart near his house and picked up a six-pack of beer, and when he got home he drank four of them in quick succession. Then he started to feel dizzy and had to go into the bathroom to worship the porcelain god.

Crap, he thought. He was such a loser he couldn't even get properly drunk. After he rinsed his mouth with mouthwash he went to bed. He had a hard time sleeping, rolling around and messing up the covers, and it was the middle of the night by the time he dropped off.

Tuesday morning he forced himself to go for another long run, hoping to sweat the toxins out of his system. It worked to some degree, though every time he thought of Victor Ragazzo he felt nauseated.

He was looking forward to another busy day at work, but for whatever reason the site had settled down to regular order volume and all he had on his plate was more product research, which was slow and tedious and gave him way too much time to think. He made some social media posts, but without Thom there to advise him he wasn't sure he was doing everything correctly.

He kept watching the clock, waiting for quitting time. Maybe this wasn't going to work out, he thought. He hated being tethered to his desk, the background music in the office, the way Leo spoke too loud on phone calls. He realized he was being overly dramatic, but he couldn't help himself—and he hated that.

When the clock was finally about to tick over to five-thirty, Warren was getting ready to leave.

Michelle buzzed to say there was someone there to see him.

She didn't say who, and Warren didn't ask. He was surprised to see Victor there.

"I wanted to apologize in person," Victor said. "I checked with Leo to make sure you were still here."

"It's okay," Warren said. "I'm over it."

"But not over me, I hope. Can you give me another chance, Warren? Let me take you out to that nice dinner I promised you."

"Tonight?"

"If you don't have other plans."

His heart gave a couple of extra-quick beats. If Victor was going to throw Warren a lifeline, he owed it to himself to grab it. "No plans but to spend time with you."

He got into his car and followed Victor to a steakhouse in Fort Lauderdale near the Intracoastal. "Order whatever you want," Victor said, as they looked over the impressive, leather-padded menu.

Warren had been to a lot of fancy restaurants during his brief tenure in the NFL, but he still hadn't gotten over the sticker shock of some of the prices. He hesitated because the steak was so expensive, but Victor said, "I'm getting the twenty-four ounce porterhouse. You think you're man enough to handle one of those too?"

"Anything you can do I can do better, and bigger," Warren said, smiling.

Over dinner they talked the way they had on their first dates, sharing memories and experiences. "How did you ever get started with the luge, anyway?" Warren asked.

Victor grinned. "Would you think I was a real loser if I said it was because of a guy?"

"Not at all."

"Like I said, I was on the ski team, and I was crushing on this other guy on the team, a big bruiser, kind of like you. But he gave it up midway through the season to focus on the luge. I went to watch him at a couple of practices, and he invited me to try the two-man sled with him. Of course I said yes. I thought that was his way of telling me that he was gay, and interested in me. So he got on a two-man luge, and I snuggled up between his thighs. I leaned my head back against his stomach and held on tight. It was such an awesome thrill, sex and athletics all tied up together. I couldn't quit the ski team, because like I said I had a scholarship, but I went all out for luge too."

"And was he gay?"

Victor shook his head. "Nope. But it didn't matter. I was hooked."

It was great to listen to Victor, and to see how much the two of them were alike in so many ways. They were both groaning by the time they were finished, after buttermilk biscuits, shrimp cocktail, and monster loaded baked potatoes along with the big steak.

"I feel like they ought to roll me out of here," Victor said, after he'd paid the bill. "Jesus, I can barely stand up."

Warren leaned in close to him. "Don't tell me you're too tired for sex."

Victor grinned. "Never too tired for that. And my place is only a few blocks away."

They were both slow and lazy when they got into the apartment, kissing, taking their clothes off one item at a time. Warren had a raging hard-on, but he felt lethargic after that big dinner. He and Victor cuddled together on the sofa, both of them shirtless with their pants open, and they kissed and fondled each other.

Warren had one hand on Victor's dick, and his mouth on Victor's nipple, when he felt Victor stop moving beneath him. He backed off and realized that Victor had gone to sleep. His head was against the back of the sofa and his mouth open.

Warren was disappointed, but on the other hand he thought it was sweet that Victor trusted him enough to pass out in front of him. He tugged Victor's pants and shoes off, then laid him out flat on the sofa, his head on a square pillow. He found a comforter and laid it out over Victor.

He went into the kitchen to get himself a glass of water before he left, and he was surprised to see that Victor didn't have any orange juice or other vitamin C heavy beverages. Not good, Victor, he thought. You've got to take better care of yourself.

He realized that he had to piss before he got in the car for the long ride home, so he went into Victor's bathroom. While he was there, he noticed there were no cold medicines at all—not even empty boxes in the overflowing trash can. Victor sure had a curious way of taking care of himself when he was sick.

That night, his phone rang twice, and each time the caller had hung up before Warren could answer. It was the same number, with a 754 area code, the supplemental one for Broward County. Was it just some weird auto-dialer? Maybe a sales call that got disconnected?

But what kind of calls would be coming through so late at night? It was very curious.

CALLER ID

Wednesday morning Warren picked up Thom at the frat for the ride up to GetBalled. He was eager to tell him all about the date the night before with Victor. "He fell asleep in the middle of sex?" Thom asked, when Warren was finished.

"Yeah. But he had this really bad cold, so I bet he was just exhausted. And he hasn't been taking care of himself. No orange juice, no cold meds."

"You're sure he was sick?"

"He told me he was." Warren realized there was no evidence at Victor's house that he'd been sick, and he'd certainly played aggressively on Saturday. Then he remembered the odd look that Brendan had given Victor when Warren asked about his cold.

"You think maybe he lied to me?" Warren asked. "But why?"

"You can't go assuming that he lied. Maybe he really was sick. Give him a chance. You guys have a lot in common."

"How about you and Dusty?" Warren asked. "You having a lot in common with him?"

Thom shifted in his seat, and Warren read him. "You had sex with him, didn't you?"

"He invited me up to his house for a drink before we were going to go out. We made out on his couch for a while, and then, well, you know. Things went on from there."

"How was he?"

"It was okay. He's kind of controlling."

Warren thought back to his spanking episode with Victor. "Not like whips and chains controlling?"

"No, not like that. More like, no, I don't like that. Don't do that. I'm not doing that to you. That kind of thing."

"Doesn't sound like much fun."

"It takes a while to get to know somebody," Thom said, in a tone that Warren read as defensive. "And he's older than we are, so he's already had a chance to figure out what he likes and what he doesn't."

Maybe it was easier just to have sex with your friends, Warren thought, as they drove on in silence. He and Thom had never had any problems. They both liked the same kind of things in bed, they both liked each other, and everything was good.

Except for the love thing, of course. The way Warren had felt at first with Victor, like he was falling head over heels into passion, that he wanted to spend every night in Victor's arms. Look how that had worked out, though.

When he got in, he started checking Facebook to see if he'd gotten any response to his posts. One customer had bought a product and said that it sucked, and then went off on a rant about it.

Crap, Warren thought. He had to do something. But what? He stared at the screen. It was clear to him that the guy hadn't read the instructions, because if he had he wouldn't have had the problem. Warren started to respond, and then stopped himself.

His high school coach had a mantra: don't criticize, analyze. Don't just tell somebody he was doing something wrong, figure out what he was doing wrong and find a way to help him improve. Warren had to be the coach in this case.

He went back to the product instructions and figured out how to explain what the guy had done wrong in simple, positive terms. Then he posted his response. He spent the rest of the morning skipping around to various sites, sharing product recommendations, and making comments. People had started responding to his comments, asking other questions. One of them mentioned having seen Warren play.

That was very cool, he thought. Maybe he did have some credentials, after all. He had certainly listened to enough coaches over the years, in so many different sports. When he didn't know the answer to a question someone had posed, he searched online for an answer, then typed something in using his own words.

How lazy could people be? Some of the questions that were asked could have been answered with a simple Google search. He found that he was often copying URLs to put into his responses—for more information, click here.

By the end of the day, he was feeling pretty good about his work. He drove Thom back to the frat to pick up his gear, and they went to the FU gym together for a workout. As Thom lifted, Warren spotted him. "I keep thinking about Victor and wondering if he was really sick," Warren said.

"Don't," Thom said, panting, "obsess." He put the bar back in the rack with a clang.

"You can do another set," Warren said.

Thom wiped his forehead with the hem of his T-shirt. "Nope. I'm wiped."

"Come on. I'm right here; I'll help you if you

can't manage."

Thom looked up at him, and Warren felt something weird in his stomach. Thom smiled. "I trust you."

He lay back on the bench and lifted the bar, and did five more reps.

"That's awesome," Warren said. "I knew you could do it."

"We have more faith in each other than we have in ourselves," Thom said.

"Hey, that's what friends are for, right?" Warren said, and fist-bumped him. But he felt that odd sense in his stomach again.

They raided the salad bar at Whole Foods and ate in Thom's room; then Warren drove back home. As he was getting undressed for bed, Victor called. "I had a big job up in Palm Beach today," he said. "I've been there all day. But I wanted to check in with you. How was your day?"

Warren got excited all over again about the social media work he'd been doing. "It's very cool to be communicating with all these people," he said. "Like being a coach or a personal trainer, but more cerebral, you know?"

"If you get any questions about the luge, you can refer them to me," Victor said, laughing.

"Or rugby," Warren said.

"Oh, I'm no expert at that. I just love to play. You're coming to the practice this Saturday, aren't you?"

"Sure, why wouldn't I?"

"I was worried after you left on Saturday. That you were over playing with us."

"No, it's fun," Warren said.

"I'm glad you feel that way, because we really need you on the pitch."

Warren waited for something else—a comment about Victor needing or wanting Warren too. But it didn't come.

Thinking about Victor and worrying about what was going on between them, the way Victor seemed to run hot and cold, Warren had trouble getting to sleep. When his phone rang at two in the morning, he grabbed for it. "Hello?" he said. "Victor? Is that you?"

He heard the sound of TV in the background; then the caller hung up. When he checked the number, it was the same one that had been calling him and hanging up. So it wasn't some call center gone crazy. It was a real person.

He meant to tell Thom about it when they drove to work the next morning, but Thom was buzzing about some coding he'd done the night before for Pritap—a complicated computer routine he'd figured out, and though Warren didn't understand any of it, he was happy to listen to Thom be so excited.

They arrived as Michelle was opening the office up, and Thom went right to his computer to play around with his new routine. "Holy crap," he said, a few minutes later.

"What's up?"

"Didn't you tell me you were answering questions yesterday about that backyard soccer trainer?" Thom asked. "Come take a look at this."

He turned his computer monitor toward

Warren, who swiveled his chair over to look at it. "What am I seeing?"

"Sales for that trainer went through the roof last night," Thom said, pointing at a number on the screen. "And see that? That's the average dollar amount of each shopping cart over the last twenty-four hours." He hit a couple of keys and a line graph popped up on the screen. "People aren't just buying that item, either. They're buying all kinds of stuff."

Leo burst into the office a few minutes later. "What is happen with site?" he asked. "Where are programmers? Something crazy going on."

"Big sales, boss," Thom said. Leo leaned over Thom's shoulder as Thom explained.

Then Leo turned to Warren. "Is all you? What you do?"

"Just what you told me to," Warren said. "I've been going around to all those social media sites, Facebook and all, and answering questions about sports and about our products."

Leo shook his head. "Amazing. Wish you had been here for months. Keep going, Warren. You are superstar!"

Once the rest of the staff had arrived, Moises asked Thom and Warren to work together to figure out which sites had been delivering the most customers. Warren went through his regular routine, checking Facebook, Twitter, SportsFanLive, Bantr, Baseball.net, Chat Sports and others, with Thom checking each shopping cart for the referring site.

It was awesome to watch the stats as they developed—it seemed like whenever he posted a response to a question that included a product that might help, sales at GetBalled for that item went up. Sometimes the shopping cart didn't even contain the product that had been discussed, but something else entirely.

Thom's cell phone rang late in the afternoon, but by the time he answered the caller had already hung up.

"That's been happening to me a lot," Warren said. "All from the same number. At first I thought it was some kind of robocaller but last night I heard a TV in the background before whoever it was hung up."

"There's this service you can use," Thom said. "I'll find you the website. You put in the number, and it calls the phone and goes direct to voice mail. You can hear the person's message and figure out who it is."

He did some hunting on his computer and then e-mailed the number for the service to Warren. Then he swiveled his chair over. "Put your phone on speaker so we can both hear," Thom said.

Warren did. He dialed the number, and after a couple of seconds wait he heard, *"This is Brendan Auerbach, and I'm in the tax cave right now, working hard on client returns. But leave me a message, and I'll get back to you as soon as I finish wrangling with the IRS."*

Thom looked at Warren. "This is that crazy guy from the rugby team?"

Warren nodded. "Victor's ex. This is fucked up. Why does he keep calling me and hanging up? If he has something to say, why not just say it?"

"Maybe he's still pissed about the way you teased him."

"Come on," Warren said. "Really?"

Thom leaned close to him. "Look how angry you get when guys talk about yours. And they're being envious."

Warren felt himself blushing. "I guess. But I'm still going to talk to him about it the next time I see him. This has gotta stop."

"Be careful, big guy. You don't want to cause a problem. With him or with Victor."

That irritated Warren even more. Why was Brendan trying to screw up this thing he had going with Victor? Was he jealous? Didn't he have his chance, and screw it up?

But what if by confronting Brendan, Warren made Victor mad again?

Where was that fucking dating rule book when you needed it?

NOT RUNNING

Warren worked out with Thom again that evening, and as he stretched and lifted and ran, he felt his anxieties slipping away. "You sure you're all right?" Thom asked, when they left the shower at the FU gym.

"Yeah, I'm good," Warren said. "I'm not calling Victor, though. And if he calls me, I don't think I'll answer. I don't want to confront him over the phone about these calls of Brendan's."

"Good idea," Thom said. He started to sing, that song from the movie *Frozen* about letting go, and Warren couldn't help laughing.

Victor texted Warren late that night, just a check-in and a *See you Saturday.* Warren couldn't decide if Victor knew what was going on with Brendan and didn't want to confront it, or if he was just busy. But he was getting tired of giving Victor the benefit of the doubt.

By Friday morning, Moises had negotiated agreements to sell more of the products Warren had found at the trade show, and he was busy all day writing copy, testing the order process, and keeping up with his social media posts.

That afternoon all of them had to pitch in with shipping again. The big bay doors were open and a couple of tall standing fans were blowing, but the warehouse was hot and everybody was irritable. Buzz kept dropping things, and Jackie snapped at the slightest provocation, her Jamaican accent growing more pronounced and the beads in her hair clacking like castanets.

"Are you going to hire somebody else to help with this shit?" Pritap complained to Leo. "We all have our own work to do."

"Blame it on Warren," Moises said. "Most of these sales are from new products he found or what he's doing online."

"Hey, don't blame me," Warren said. "If we need extra help, I'm not the one who would hire them."

"No crying like little girl," Leo said, as he taped up a shipping box. "If this keeps up, yes, I hire someone else, all right?"

Thom cut his finger on a sharp edge of a tape gun, and Warren said, "I know where the bandages are. Put pressure on it and come with me."

They walked back into the office area, which was blessedly cool. "Things getting hot out there," Thom said as Warren opened the door to the small bathroom. "Must be tough for Leo to manage all this."

"Don't feel bad for Leo," Warren said, as Thom rinsed his hand. "He must be making money." That reminded him that he was supposed to get a commission on any products he found. "So am I. I can probably afford to move pretty soon. I could even cover you for a while until you find a job."

"That's great, big guy," Thom said, as Warren applied the bandage to Thom's index finger, over a drop of bright red blood.

Then he squeezed the finger in his hand. "You need to keep pressure on it for a couple of minutes," Warren said. He looked down and realized how funny it was, the way he had Thom's index finger inside his fist.

Thom must have realized the same thing, because they both started laughing. Warren let go of Thom's finger.

It really was good having Thom there, Warren thought, as they walked back to the warehouse. Everything was so easy between them. And it would be cool if they lived together too. A buddy to work out with, run with, hang out with. Screw Victor Ragazzo and his fucked-up relationship with Brendan. This thing with Thom, that's what friendship was about.

Victor called Warren late that night, once more as Victor was driving home from somewhere. "I've been thinking about strategy for Saturday," Victor said. "Let me run something by you."

Warren listened patiently as Victor laid out some practice drills and some ideas he had about helping particular players with their workouts. "Hey, when I was at that trade show I saw this cool set of speed hurdles we could use for practice, and a product sample came in yesterday. I'm going to bring it up with me."

"Sounds great. Some of the guys could really use some more speed."

Warren really wanted to talk about what the hell was going on with Brendan, but as soon as he tried to shift the conversation to the personal, Victor said that he was about to pull into a drive-through and needed to hang up.

The more Warren thought about Brendan making all those calls to his phone, the angrier he got, and the more he wanted to bust the guy's head. But he had started to like playing rugby—it was great exercise and a good outlet for all his frustrations. Since he couldn't play football any more, at least not at the level he wanted, rugby was a decent substitute.

So he turned on a meditation CD and forced himself to relax.

* * * *

Saturday morning Warren checked his phone to be sure that the hang-ups still showed. Then he drove up to the practice field. By the time he got there, though, Brendan and Victor were already out on the pitch, tossing and kicking the ball back and forth. He left his phone in the car and figured he'd handle things after the practice.

A couple of the guys were either busy or sick, so there weren't enough of them for a proper scrimmage, and they worked on drills instead. It was boring, and Warren was eager to get the practice over with. He couldn't get the physical release he longed for, and his anger continued to build inside him.

Even though it was the first week of November, it was still hot and Warren worked up a sweat. He finally walked off the field and out to his car, where he retrieved his cell phone. Then he sat on the sidelines until Brendan and Victor were ready to head for the locker room. "Hey, Brendan, can I show you something?" Warren asked.

Brendan shrugged.

Warren held out his phone. "See all these calls? That's your number, right? Why are you harassing me? Because I've been going out with Victor?"

"Come on, Warren, don't make a big deal." Victor turned to his friend. "Brendan, you can't keep doing this shit. Every time I meet somebody new, you screw things up."

"You're the one who's screwed up," Brendan said. "If you really wanted to date the incredible hulk, you wouldn't keep coming over to my place to suck dick."

"Shut the fuck up, Brendan," Victor said.

"Is that true, Victor?" Warren demanded. "Have you been fucking Brendan at the same time as me?"

"Sometimes a big dick isn't everything." Brendan snickered.

Without thinking, Warren punched him in the gut. Then he swung around and punched Victor too.

Both of them doubled over. The other guys from the team stood there dumbstruck. Warren didn't say anything more, just strode back to his car. Not running, he thought as he went. Not running away from anything. Just getting the hell out of here.

CALL ME SWEETHEART

Warren refused to think on the drive home from the field. He slid the Dalai Lama's CD into the deck and listened. *"Happiness is not something ready-made. It comes from your own actions."*

Yeah, he thought. He'd believed he'd be happy when he made it to the NFL, but instead he'd spent the year he was on the Jaguars worrying about his performance and struggling to keep his place.

"In order to carry a positive action we must keep a positive vision," the Dalai Lama said.

What was Warren's positive vision? What was making him happy?

The first thing that popped into his head was Thom's face, laughing the way he had the day before as Warren put the bandage on his finger. Yeah. Thom made him happy.

He was so into the CD that he didn't notice that he was on autopilot again until he was in front of the Three Lambs frat house. He put the car in park, looked up, and wondered what the fuck he was doing there. What did he want, anyway? Did he want to cry on Thom's shoulder about how awful Brendan was, how badly Victor had treated him?

No. He was over that. But he'd come there for a reason. Because he wanted to be with Thom. But he didn't even know if Thom was in his room. Maybe he was out somewhere with that new guy, Dusty.

That thought stopped him. He wanted Thom to be happy. What if Dusty was somebody he could really fall for? He had a fancy condo, an expensive car, the ability to treat Thom like a king. Warren didn't have that kind of money.

But money wasn't everything in life, was it?

He got out of the car and walked up to the frat's front door. He hesitated, but just for a moment. Imagine, two years ago he'd have been too scared to be seen in front of the gay frat. At least he was making progress on something.

He walked inside. The living room was empty, though there was music playing from somewhere in the house. Warren climbed the stairs to Thom's third-floor room and stood in front of his door. He listened for a moment, trying to make sure he wasn't interrupting something, but all was quiet. He knocked.

"In," Thom called.

Warren walked in and closed the door behind him. Thom was sitting on his bed in his boxers, reading something on his laptop. "Hey, big guy. Wasn't expecting to see you today. Don't you have rugby?"

"Fuck rugby," Warren said. "And fuck Victor Ragazzo and his butt boy Brendan."

Thom sat up and patted the side of the bed. "Come on over here and tell me."

Warren shook his head and stayed standing by the door. "That's not why I came here. I'm done crying over other guys."

He took a deep breath. "Ever since I met you, you've been the one guy I can count on. You've been my best friend. We can talk about anything; we have great sex. I just like being with you."

"I like being with you too."

"But I want more than that. I want to be your

boyfriend." Warren's heart was pounding as he waited to see what Thom would say.

"You're just feeling bad about Victor."

Warren shook his head. "I've been a big dope. All this time, riding up to work with you, working out with you, eating with you and sharing a bed with you. I was too dumb to realize it was you I wanted all along."

He waited. Thom didn't say anything, and Warren's heart dropped.

"I did learn something from Victor," Warren said when the silence had gotten too oppressive. "That in life, like in sports, you have to go all in. You figure out what goal you want, and you go for it. I'm sorry if I embarrassed you or put you in a bad spot, Thom. I understand if you—"

"You don't understand anything at all." Thom jumped up and walked over to where Warren stood. "When I first was assigned to tutor you, and I met you at the library, my dick was so hard I thought it was going to explode. I kicked myself up and down for falling for a straight guy."

"I didn't turn out to be straight, did I?" Warren asked. He stood with his back to the door, facing Thom.

"No, you did not. And it blew my mind when I realized that we could…you know."

"It blew *my* mind when we did." Warren smiled.

"And then I started to get to know you, and I discovered the sweet guy behind that big bull-headed facade. When you got the bid from Jacksonville, I was happy because I knew it was what you wanted, but it was killing me inside because I figured you were going on to some big football career, and I'd never see you again."

"I should have called you when I was away." Warren crossed his arms in front of his big chest. "I meant to, a couple of times, but I was so caught up in trying to make it to the first team, then scrambling with my fingernails to hold on to my place."

He looked down and realized that Thom's dick was hard and tenting his boxers. But this wasn't about sex, he reminded himself. He kept his arms across his chest, holding back from touching Thom until they had everything on the table.

"I wasn't that happy when you came back, you know." Thom leaned back against his desk, seemingly oblivious to the way his dick was sticking out. "I thought, oh, no, I don't want to get caught up in this same thing again, wanting a guy who doesn't want me. But I couldn't help myself. Then when you met Victor, I was almost relieved. At least I can get out from under Warren's spell, I thought. He'll be with somebody new, and I can do the same thing."

"My spell?"

"You don't realize it, but you have a powerful personality," Thom said. "And you're such a good man inside. Victor was a complete asshole for not recognizing that."

"But then you started dating Dusty."

Thom shook his head. "The whole time I was with him I kept comparing him to you. And of course he came up short."

Warren felt himself relaxing. "A couple of times when I was with Victor I thought of you too.

But I thought you just wanted to be friends, so I kept pushing that away."

"I do want to be your friend, Warren. I want to be your boyfriend."

Warren reached around Thom and lifted him up, twirling him around. "I was hoping you would say that!" he said, laughing.

"Come on, Warren, put me down!" Thom said, but he was laughing too.

"You don't have to call me by my name, you know," Warren said, as he put Thom down. "I like it when you call me big guy."

"I want to call you a lot more than that," Thom said. "Sweetheart. Honey. My baby. Love bug. I've got a million things I've been wanting to say that I've kept bottled up."

They kissed, and Warren felt the passion he had for Thom running through his veins. He wanted to gobble Thom up, kiss him and nibble on him until they were two parts of one being.

"Like that," Thom said, panting, when they finally pulled apart. "I've been keeping that kiss inside me, waiting for the right time."

"I hope there's more where that kiss came from," Warren said. "Because I'll be wanting that every day."

"I aim to please," Thom said. "I am so happy right now, big guy."

"So am I, sweetheart," Warren said. "So am I."

THREE LAMBS

Warren Updegrove first stepped into my imagination as a character in a series of short erotic stories about college students who belonged to a gay fraternity. I'd been wanting to write a collection of stories about overlapping characters, and came up with Lambda Lambda Lambda, or Three Lambs.

A wealthy alumnus of Florida University in Miami - also known as FU - funded the building of a frat house for gay male students.

Thom Lodge is the narrator of the story "Bull-Headed." But as I thought about Thom, who goes on to graduate study in math at FU, I realized that the story I really wanted to tell was about the guy he crushed on, football player Warren Updegrove.

They have an erotically charged encounter in *Three Lambs*. Turn the page for an excerpt from "Bull-Headed."

"Bull-Headed"

An excerpt from *Three Lambs: Erotic Tales of a Gay Frat*

Warren Updegrove looked like a bull. Broad-shoulders, thighs like tree trunks, a square head with an angry set to it. And he was so angry that I could almost imagine cartoon smoke swirling out of his ears and nose.

"I'm Thom," I said, reaching out to shake his hand.

"Fucking waste of my time," he said, ignoring my hand and settling into the chair across from me in one of the private study rooms in the campus library. He was so big and the chair so flimsy that I was afraid he'd smash it and then blame it on me.

"You've got to pass calculus if you want to major in business," I said. "You've already failed, what, twice? Third time and you're done. Bye-bye football team. Bye-bye FU."

"You're a pansy, aren't you?" he asked. "From the faggot frat?"

"Yup. Lambda Lambda Lambda. And I need to put in community service hours tutoring for my honors society. I waited too long to sign up so I got assigned to you. You've gone through, what, two tutors already? If you don't want to work with me you're SOL. So you need me and I need you."

"Just don't try anything funny," he said, pulling his calculus textbook out of his backpack. "Stay on your side of the table."

"You straight guys think every gay guy wants

to get in your pants. But you don't have to worry about me. I like a guy with a brain in his head, which lets you off the hook. Now, I see from the form you filled out with the tutoring center that you failed your first exam."

"It just doesn't matter," he grumbled. "None of it makes sense in the real world."

"Let's start with football. Suppose the quarterback throws a pass, and you catch it, and you run ten yards."

"First down."

"Yeah. Then the next time, another guy catches it, and he's not as fast as you, so he only goes 90% as far as you do. How far does he go?"

"Nine yards."

"Good. So there's another play, and this third guy catches it, and he's even slower, or runs into more defense, so he only goes 90% as far as the second guy. How far is that?"

I could see the wheels turning in his head. He wasn't bad looking when he wasn't angry, but there was no way he was my type. He looked like a movie action hero—square jawed, brown hair in a crewcut, those biceps bulging out of his T-shirt sleeves.

"I don't know."

We walked through converting nine yards to twenty-seven feet, then multiplying that times point nine. We kept on going, and finally I said, "Is your team ever going to score a touchdown this way?"

He looked at me like I was stupid. "Of course."

"Nope. Let's add up the numbers and you'll see." We did that, and I showed him that as long as a player was only going ninety percent of the distance to be covered, the team would never make it all the way to the goal.

He pulled out the test he'd failed. "So that's why I got this answer wrong," he said, pointing it out to me.

I looked at the problem, figured it out myself, and said, "That's right."

He smiled. "I actually understand. Cool."

We worked out a couple more problems, and then our hour was up. I stood up and stretched. "You work out?" Warren asked.

I didn't have anywhere near the muscles he did, but I wasn't any ninety-eight pound weakling, either. A bunch of the guys from Three Lambs ran together every morning, and it wasn't hard to find a workout buddy if you wanted to go to the gym, either. I had a fine coating of hair on my arms and legs which covered up the fact that I had some pretty decent muscles there.

"Yeah," I said.

"But you're - you know—gay. I thought you guys just liked theater and Barbra Streisand and shit."

"There are a couple of guys in the frat who can really flame," I said. "But most of us are just regular guys."

Warren looked like he didn't believe me, but I didn't care. He was just a project. Put in my hours, get my credit, move on.

We met a week later in the same study room. This time he came in with some homework problems he'd been having trouble with. I pulled open his textbook and paged through to the right section. "See this line?" I asked, pointing to a graph on the page.

"This represents the relationship between these two numbers."

"How can numbers have a relationship?"

I groaned inside but tried not to let Warren see how I felt. I started explaining, but it was hard to do when the book was facing him and I was reading everything upside down.

"Why don't you just come around to this side?" he asked, after the third time I turned the book around so I could see. He scooted over so there was more room for me to move my chair.

I couldn't help the feeling I got from being so close to Warren. We weren't touching or anything, but he was just so big, and he radiated a kind of masculine energy. My poor dick pressed against my pants as it stiffened but I was afraid to adjust myself in case Warren went ballistic on me. I suffered through the next half hour feeling my dick head pulsing against the keys in my pocket. It was a delicious agony, and a couple of times I found myself drifting off, daydreaming about going back to my room at the frat to jerk myself off. I imagined Warren's beefy arms around me, pressing my face against his prominent pecs. Would he have a dick that matched his musculature? Or would it be a cocktail frank? Maybe he was compensating for a pin dick by building up the rest of his body?

"Yo, dude. Earth to Thom."

I snapped out of it. "Sorry, Warren, I just spaced."

"Yeah, math does that to me, too."

He leaned over close to me and pointed at the page. "I don't get this question. All those symbols look like Greek to me."

"They are Greek, Warren. That's a sigma. Don't you guys have to memorize the Greek alphabet in your frat? We do."

"You kidding?" Warren said. "That's why I joined Alpha Beta Kappa. The letters look just like the English ones."

I wasn't sure if he was kidding or not. I looked at him and took a deep breath. "Fine. This letter here, that's a Sigma, the backwards E. In math it means to sum whatever follows. So ∑ 1-6 means to sum the numbers one through five."

He looked at me. "Add 'em up," I said.

Fortunately he didn't have to take off his shoes to do it. "Twenty-one?"

"That's right. Now this symbol here, that's the square root. What's the square root of nine?"

"Three."

"Good. Once you figure out the parts of the equation, you carry out the operation—in this case, division. Twenty-one divided by three."

"Seven."

Damn, he smelled good up close. A mix of soap, shampoo, and male funk. His hair was still damp, like he'd just come from a shower. "I think that's enough for today," I said, closing the book.

"Thanks, Thom. I think I'm starting to get this stuff."

"Cool." We walked out together, back toward Frat Row. It was a cool night in early November and I shivered a little as we walked.

"You cold?" Warren asked.

"Still getting accustomed to this Miami

weather," I said. "I grew up in Pensacola and I had this idea that it was always hot down here. I never think of carrying a jacket."

"Pensacola, huh? How come you came all the way down here?"

"Got a scholarship to FU. And I wanted to get as far away from my family as I could."

"They don't like your being – you know – gay?"

"Nope. They're Southern Baptist. Very religious."

"No shit? Mine, too. Jesus, I was glad to get away from that crap." We came to the ABK house and he held out his fist for a bump. "See you next week."

"Yeah, see you."

I scrambled the rest of the way to the Lambda Lambda Lambda house and went right up to my room. Fortunately my roommate was out, because I was so horny I thought my dick was going to burst if I didn't jack off right there.

Another of the characters from *Three Lambs* who wanted his own story was Gavin Kaczmarek, who began as a pretty boy invited to do his first modeling job. He insisted, though, that he was more than just a pretty face. Here's an excerpt from Gavin's short erotic story, "Head Shots."

"Head Shots"

An excerpt from *Three Lambs: Erotic Tales of a Gay Frat*

I was walking along Ocean Drive in Miami Beach with a couple of my frat brothers when this dude came up to us. He was some kind of old hippie with a ponytail, an earring and a Springsteen tour T-shirt. "You guys ever think about modeling?" he asked.

He handed us each a card that read BEACH BOYZ MODEL AGENCY. Chuck and Larry were like ready to book, but I kind of fancied seeing myself on the cover of some magazine. "What's the deal?" I asked.

"Give me a call," he said. "We'll take some head shots and see how you look on film. Then I'll see if I can book you any jobs."

"Cool," I said.

"You're not actually going to call that loser, are you, Gavin?" Chuck said, as we walked away.

"Why not? You think I'm not good-looking enough to be a model?"

"It's some kind of scam," Larry said.

We were all students at Florida University, living together in the Lambda Lambda Lambda frat house just off campus. It was the only all gay frat in the country, and we were lucky to have a chapter at FU. At other colleges, gay students still got bullied and teased, but at Three Lambs, as we called the house, we were safe from outside pressure, free to concentrate on studying.

And sex, of course. Most of the guys in the house had hooked up with each other at one time or another. Chuck and his boyfriend Fitz were among the first members of the frat, and they had an open relationship. Most of the other guys were single, hooking up whenever the need or the mood arose.

Every guy in the house was good-looking, in one way or another. Chuck had this Asian inscrutability going on, like he was a direct descendant of some Manchu emperor. His hair and his eyes were coal-black. Larry was a tall stringy bean pole with awesome abs and a mop of shaggy blond hair.

I flattered myself that I had a kind of all-American wholesomeness. I'd often been told I looked like I belonged in an Abercrombie & Fitch ad. Square jaw, close-cropped blond hair, and a body conditioned by years of high school sports and college workouts.

And the truth was that I could use the money. I wasn't the smartest guy at FU, and my parents were paying the full tuition because I didn't qualify for any scholarships. They kept me on a short leash cash-wise, and I couldn't take on a regular part-time job because then my grades would slide and my parents would pull the plug.

But I wanted to be able to afford the kind of clothes the rich boys wore, the fancy sneakers and the bits of bling. So Monday afternoon I called the number on the business card. I made an appointment for late that day, borrowed Chuck's old beater, and drove back across town to the beach.

The office wasn't much, just a second-floor walk up over a bodega on a side street a few blocks from the beach. But the waiting room was lined with head shots of good-looking men, and there was a receptionist and a buzzer and everything.

The hippie dude's name was Alfie, he said,

when he came out to meet me. "Come on back and we'll take some test shots."

He led me into a room with big windows overlooking the street, and lots of bright light streaming in. He positioned me in front of this big white sheet of paper and started fiddling with shades and cameras. "Big smile now," he said.

I smiled, and the camera flashed. He led me through a bunch of expressions—moody, sexy, relaxed, and so on. Then he asked me to take my shirt off.

I pulled it off, and he even took a couple of shots as I stretched, exposing my long, narrow chest. My shorts were hanging an inch below the top of my boxers, and he seemed to like that, talking sexy to me and snapping shots.

"You're a natural," he said. "I can tell. The camera loves you."

He put the camera down and looked at me. "I don't want to pressure you into anything you don't want to do-- but how would you feel about posing nude?"

"You mean like this?" I asked, dropping my shorts and my boxers with them.

He laughed. "Yeah, that's how I meant."

I felt myself popping a boner, and shifted.

"Yeah, that exactly how I meant," he said. "Stay just like that."

He brought over a couple of props—a chair, a beat-up calculus text, a baseball cap. Then he posed me in a bunch of different ways—sitting on the chair, straddling it, then reading the text, with the ball cap backwards on my head.

"Oh, yeah, this is great," he said. "Love your dick, baby. Touch it, will you? Yeah, just like that, your finger right below the head. Man, that's hot."

After a half hour of that, my dick was stiff as a rock and ready to explode. When Alfie finally stood up and put the camera down, I wanted nothing more than for him to come over and blow me. But instead, he said," I'm going to print these up, and see what kind of work I can get you. I'll be in touch."

That was all? No sex? Fuck, I was horny. Even though he was like a hundred years old (probably more like fifty, but it's all the same when you get that old) I was sort of hoping he'd make a move. I'd never had sex with an older dude and I was kind of wondering what it would be like.

But just my luck, Alfie was a hundred percent professional. Either that or straight, which was pretty much the same thing to me.

"Stop at the front desk with Tony and fill out an application form with your contact information."

I filled out the forms and drove back to the Three Lambs house. I didn't tell anyone what I'd done, because I didn't want anybody to razz me about it.

To read more, check out *Three Lambs: Erotic Tales of a Gay Frat* on Amazon.

I was interested in what happened to the children and grandchildren of performers. Did they inherit the family talent? What if Gavin's grandmother had been part of a well-known singing group when she was young? That led me to the plot of *Love on Stage*, where Gavin struggles to discover his talent with the help of sexy music producer Miles Goodwin. Here's the first chapter of Gavin's book.

CONTRADICTIONS

Gavin Kaczmarek expertly dumped a bag of organic Ethiopian coffee beans into the grinder, set the dial to Turkish fine, and flipped the switch. The alarm on the dark-roast pot was ringing behind him, and he turned it off and removed the glass pot from the burner. He pulled two shots from the tray of the espresso machine and poured them into a china mug, then reached for the pitcher of hot milk.

At six-one, Gavin was slim but muscular, with a tribal tattoo around his right bicep. He had been told often that he looked like a young Robert Redford, with a Nordic profile, a dimple in his chin, and a smile around his eyes. He kept his golden blond hair glossy and shoulder-length.

Humming along with the song on the stereo system, he placed a big spoon over the mouth of the pitcher and filled the mug. He pivoted to the grinder just as it finished and flipped the switch off with his elbow. Then he dropped the spoon in the sink and swirled the remaining foam in the pitcher into the shape of a leaf, finishing with a tiny doodle of his own invention. He handed the mug to the customer—an elderly woman in black tights and an electric-blue tank top, with a pink-tinged bouffant that had been lacquered in place.

She smiled a gap-toothed grin and took the mug, and Gavin bagged up the finely ground coffee beans for the customer behind her. He flirted with everybody—men, women, young, old. It didn't matter. A raised eyebrow or a sexy smile added to the pileup of coins and bills in the tip jar. And sometimes Gavin was slipped a business card or had a phone number written on the back of a receipt. The women never got a call back, but if the guy was cute or sexy or just different, Gavin often made the call, though he denied it to his boss—a Kenyan immigrant named Careful Handa.

Java Joe's, where Gavin worked the opening shift, was a funky fair-trade coffee shop a block off Lincoln Road. The place buzzed with office workers until nine, when there was a brief respite before the beauty school students, consultants meeting clients, medical staff in scrubs, and elderly java junkies showed up.

Gavin had unspoken nicknames for most of the regular customers, from Saggy Boob Lady to Hot Hasidic Guy to South American Soccer Mom. Because all of Java Joe's products were certified kosher, they did a good business with students and staff at the nearby rabbinical colleges, and Gavin was always amazed at how someone could live in twenty-first-century Miami and yet still dress like they had in seventeenth-century Poland.

Around ten, Music Dude came in for his

regular Jumbo Joe with extra foam. He was skinny and serious-looking, with hipster glasses, a goatee, and thinning hair, and had to be at least thirty. But there was something about him that Gavin liked, and if things were slow, he'd fantasize a bit about seeing the guy naked, and his dick would jump.

Music Dude always had high-tech earbuds, and when he'd pull them out to order, Gavin could hear all kinds of tunes, from Brazilian sambas to blue-eyed soul to rap. A couple of times Gavin had seen him working on a laptop with what looked like musical notations on the screen.

Gavin made the Jumbo Joe, a sixteen-ounce latte with two extra shots, and instead of his regular leaf, he drew a musical note with the foam and served up the coffee with a bit of song. "I love java, sweet and hot, whoops Mr. Moto I'm a coffeepot."

"Your voice has a nice tone," Music Dude said. "But you're losing your breath on the lower register."

"You know about stuff like that?" Gavin asked as he handed Music Dude his coffee.

"It's what I do. Digital music production."

"Very cool." Gavin struggled for something else to say, but there was a line of customers out the door, and he felt tongue-tied.

"Have a good day," Music Dude said. He took his coffee and left.

Gavin was bummed. He had hoped to impress the guy, though he didn't know why. It wasn't like he was super handsome or anything.

He went back to work, making coffees for Slope-Shouldered Tall Guy, Russian Realtor Lady, and a raft of others who weren't regular enough to have nicknames. At noon he signed out and walked to the corner of Lincoln and Alton, where a big orange school bus was idling in the crosswalk.

He signed in with the pimply-faced photographer's assistant and took a seat halfway back, across from Tate, another model he'd worked with in the past.

As the bus took off, he looked around at the half dozen other models and the mixed bag of crew members. He leaned over to Tate and asked, "You know where we're going?"

"I hear the underwear company rented out the locker room at the Miami Dolphins training center," Tate said.

"Maybe there will be a stray Dolphin hanging around," Gavin said. "I'd do a pro football player in a heartbeat."

"Too early for pre-season practice," Tate said.

Gavin had met Tate on his first modeling gig. He was a nice guy, despite having the kind of good looks that immediately put Gavin on the defensive—oval face, high cheekbones, tanned skin, and shoulder-length dark-brown hair. Gavin preferred to hang around with guys less good-looking than he was, but he made an exception for Tate.

When they walked into the locker room, the team's presence was everywhere, from the trophies along the wall, to the big sign that read THE ROAD TO THE SUPER BOWL STARTS HERE.

The stylist pulled Gavin's shoulder-length hair into a ponytail and slicked it down with gel. He was handed a red-and-black jockstrap studded with silver metal bolts, which he slipped on. The stylist fiddled with the position of the waistband, then sprayed his shoulders and chest with water so that he'd look like he'd just come from a sweaty workout.

He was directed to a bench in front of an open locker, and the stylist pooled a pair of slacks around his bare feet to look as if he'd just stepped out of them. There was an erotic kick to being in a place suffused with so much testosterone, and so far the photographer, a slim Asian guy wearing one of those vests that hunters wore during deer season, had chastised two of the models for getting boners.

Suddenly the photographer was right beside him, his lens up in Gavin's face. The camera's rapid shutter clicks reminded Gavin of the sound the crickets made back home in Wisconsin. He was looking forward to spending the Independence Day weekend with his family at their summer home at Starlit Lake.

"Don't think about anything!" the photographer demanded. "You are a blank canvas. An empty shell. A mannequin to display the clothes."

Gavin imagined that the photographer was his father, yelling at him for some screw-up, and switched to the distant-focused look he had perfected as a teenager. He emptied his mind and stared straight ahead.

"Excellent!" the photographer said. He snapped a few shots, then reached down and lifted Gavin's left leg, placing it on top of the wooden bench beside him. He moved Gavin's arm so that his right hand rested on the top of the half-open locker door. Gavin didn't understand why the guy couldn't have just told him what to do, but that was the business.

The photographer took some more shots, then sent Gavin back to wardrobe.

The wardrobe mistress was a plump Latina with dyed red hair, who had "fag hag" stamped all over her. She looked at her clipboard. "You're Havin, right?" she asked, giving the G at the start of his name a breathy accent.

"Yup."

"You're wearing the body shapers next." She handed him a T-shirt and a pair of briefs with some kind of reinforcing on his abs and waist.

"What are these?" he asked.

"They slim you." She rubbed her belly. "You know, down here."

"I don't need these!" Gavin protested.

"Of course not. If you did, you wouldn't be able to model them."

The contradiction confounded Gavin until he'd slipped into them. If they were tight on him, when he had single-digit body fat, he could only imagine how awful they'd be on a guy who needed them. He looked at himself in the full-length mirror in the dressing area.

The white fabric clung to him like a second skin. Not an ounce of fat pushed through. He felt like he was standing up straighter, perhaps because of the lumbar support. It was the least sexy underwear he'd ever modeled, but what the hell, he was making money and building his portfolio.

Want to read more? *Love on Stage* is available in ebook form from Loose Id, and available wherever e-books are sold. You can also order it in paperback through Amazon.com.

Another character from Three Lambs is Larry Leavis, hero of *Love on the Web*. Here's an excerpt from the story that features him.

"Three Little Lambs"

An excerpt from *Three Lambs: Erotic Tales of a Gay Frat*

Larry Leavis walked past the Lambda Lambda Lambda table at rush week three times before he got the nerve up to stop and pick up a brochure. There were two guys behind the table, a gorgeous blond preppy in an Izod shirt and plaid Bermuda shorts and a Chinese guy with straight black hair and skin so smooth Larry wanted to reach out and touch it. They were busy talking to a buff Jamaican guy with dreadlocks, so Larry stood there awkwardly, looking at the pictures of the guys studying, playing touch football, or hanging around the living room of the frat house.

They were all too handsome, he thought. Nobody at the Three Lambs would ever even look at him. He'd always been a scrawny beanpole, taller than everyone else in his class, and though he'd begun to fill out in college, he still thought of himself as skinny and awkward.

He stuffed the brochure in his pocket and turned away. "Hey, wait," the preppy guy said, breaking away from his conversation. "I'm Fitz. You interested in Three Lambs?"

Larry looked down at the table and mumbled,

"Yeah."

Fitz stuck his hand out. "What's your name?"

Fitz's hand was cool and his grip was strong. Larry felt a flutter at the pit of his stomach. "Larry," he said. "Larry Leavis."

"Cool. We're a new frat-- this is our first rush. The house opened last year with just a half-dozen guys, though we've got room in the house for twelve." He opened another copy of the flyer and pointed at the modern-style house. "An anonymous gay benefactor bought the land and paid for the construction, to create a support network for GLBT students at FU."

Florida University was a branch of the state university system in southwest Miami. Larry had felt swallowed up by the huge student body. He hadn't made many friends, just focused on studying and getting good grades. When he had free time he ran along the track at the football stadium or worked out in the gym.

He smiled. "It looks nice."

"You've got a great smile," Fitz said. "You should smile more."

Larry felt himself blushing. "Is everybody in the frat -- you know -- gay?"

Fitz nodded. "That's the idea. It's a safe zone, where you can be who you want to be without worrying about bullying or name-calling. It's like, really important, you know?"

Larry couldn't imagine anyone bullying Fitz or calling him any name other than some romantic endearment. His polo shirt clung to his chest like a second skin, and he was as handsome as a male model. "We're having a get-together tonight," Fitz said. "At the house, at eight. Why don't you come over?"

"OK," Larry said shyly. He looked at his watch. "Shit, I've got to get to class."

Fitz took his hand again, and Larry's heart fluttered. "I hope we'll see you tonight."

Larry's heart raced as he took back his hand. "Sure, yeah." He turned and rushed down the sidewalk toward the math building, only then realizing then that his dick was tenting his shorts like a flagpole. Oh god, had Fitz seen that? How embarrassing. He couldn't remember popping a boner like that in public since the time he snuck into an X-rated bookstore in downtown Miami when he was a high school junior. He swung his backpack in front of him and tried to concentrate on math problems.

Want to know more? Pick up *Three Lambs: Erotic Stories of a Gay Frat* wherever e-books are sold. And here's the first chapter of Larry's book, *Love on the Web.*

THE BIG PICTURE

Kermit the Frog sang that it's not easy being green. Well, it's no picnic being tall either. I had a growth spurt in seventh grade and shot up, still skinny as a beanpole. I was already starting to show signs that I was going to be gay, so a couple of bullies started calling me the Jolly Gay Giant. I'd be walking down the hall in junior high and hear, "Ho, ho, ho, gay giant!"

Julian was the first guy who made me feel like my height was no big deal, which was funny, because he was only six feet tall himself. From the moment we started to talk at Java Joe's, I felt, I don't know, normal.

It was close to nine thirty when I stopped at Java Joe's, on Lincoln Road. The owners had recently begun experimenting with serving alcohol at night, creating a new party scene. Sometimes I felt like a vampire; I slept late in the morning, worked until well after dinnertime, then hung out at bars with my roommates until the Beach began to go to sleep.

The bar was jammed with guys in their twenties and thirties, wearing the best clubbing looks from the new H&M store on Lincoln Road, formfitting shirts that highlighted their guns, ass-hugging tight slacks. I felt out of place in my ordinary jeans and polo shirt.

I looked around and saw my roommate Gavin holding court at a big round table in one corner, surrounded by his usual coterie of young male models and the wealthy middle-aged men who liked them.

If you looked up the definition of "male beauty" in the dictionary, you'd see Gavin's picture there. Six feet tall, with golden-blond hair that flowed smoothly around his shoulders. He was slim but muscular enough, with a tribal tattoo around his right bicep. He looked like a young Robert Redford, without all the wrinkles, of course. He had the same smile, a Nordic profile, and a dimple in his chin.

Does it sound like I had a crush on him? I did. But a tall, skinny geek like me had no chance with a gorgeous god like him. I've been told that I have a handsome face, but I think my scarecrow body negates it. My two older brothers are both good-looking, and I resemble them around the eyes and the nose, but they're more proportionate than I am—tallish, with a better ratio of body fat to height.

I got myself a chocolate martini and then wandered over to Gavin's table. There was an open chair next to a guy I didn't know, and I slid into it, trying not to kick anybody with my long legs. Gavin called over to me as I sat. "Larry Leavis, meet Julian Argento. He just moved here from Silicon Valley. Larry's a computer genius, so you guys should have a lot in common."

"Pleased to meet you," I said as I shook Julian's hand. "I wish I could move out there. Maybe someday."

"Are you a techie?" he asked.

"A programmer. I work for a company that makes custom mobile apps."

Julian was handsome in a Latin-lover kind of way. Wavy black hair, dark eyes, and prominent cheekbones. His five o'clock shadow had reached the perfect level of scruffy, and though his English was excellent, he had a very slight Spanish accent.

Way out of my league, of course. But so was almost every guy who made my dick jump. I had a history of falling for unavailable guys, from my high school science teacher to the captain of the football team to guys I'd meet online who would turn out to be older, uglier, or more married than they had originally indicated. It was almost a joke among my college frat brothers that if I liked a guy, he had to be either straight, committed to a relationship, or hiding some huge secret.

I heard my other roommate Manny's voice in my head. "You're a good-looking guy, Larry. You've got to get over your inferiority complex."

I knew objectively that my string-bean body had been filling out; I worked out at the gym every other morning. And I wasn't a troll in the looks department—I have an open, honest kind of face, like Opie from The Andy Griffith Show.

My biggest problem was an inability to make conversation with other guys. I got along fine with girls; all through my teen years girls had been my closest friends. But I had this morbid fear that every straight guy I talked to would think I was coming on to him and lash out at me for being gay.

Gay guys were even worse. I worried that my sexual need and inexperience made me seem like a loser who lusted after anybody with a dick—which wasn't that far from the truth. So I was confused when Julian said, "You and I should talk. I've got a start-up I'm trying to get off the ground."

"I thought that's what we were doing.

Talking."

Julian cocked his head, and maybe it was then that I fell a little bit in love. "I meant talk about how we could help each other," he said. "I had a programmer lined up, but he bailed on me at the last minute. I can do some coding myself, but mostly I'm the idea guy, the money man."

The rest of the table ignored us as we talked. "Seems like the wrong move to come here from Silicon Valley if you want to develop something," I said. "You've got a lot more resources out there."

"But a lot more competition too," Julian said. "For staff and for money. I want to build up a multicultural workforce and tap into some Latin American investment capital."

"And?"

"And I'm having trouble finding a programmer with the right qualifications. SQL, PHP, AJAX for the back end, platform independent on the front end..."

"Now you're talking my language," I said.

"I thought so," Julian said. "Gavin told me you were really sharp."

Gavin wasn't the kind of guy who looked out for his friends. He was all Gavin, all the time. So if he'd spoken about me to Julian, there had to be something in it for him.

Suddenly Gavin stood up. "Let's all dance," he said. "Come on." He took his boyfriend, Miles, by the hand and tugged him up from his seat. Miles was older than we were, nearly thirty, a skinny, serious-looking dude with hipster glasses and thinning hair. He was some kind of music guy, and he was helping

Gavin kick off a singing career.

"You want to dance?" Julian asked me. Java Joe's was a coffee shop in the morning, but when the sun went down, it shifted into a bar, and the back patio became a dance floor with a very gay vibe. There was a lot of that morphing and mixing on Miami Beach—you could buy parking decals at the hair salon, the woman behind the counter at the dry cleaner doubled as an Avon Lady, and the bodega on the corner of Collins Avenue advertised unlocked GSM phones and prepaid calling cards for Latin America.

"I don't dance that well," I said. I shook my arms. "Too gawky."

"I'll bet you'd be fine." He stood up. "Come on; we'll talk more later." Julian wasn't as model-handsome as Gavin; few guys are. But I got a real personality from him—something that was often lacking in Gavin.

I followed the group outside, where it was hot and humid and the music was fast and tropical. Julian took my hand, and we began to dance. He had an amazing sense of his body, and the way he led me made me feel like I was really dancing, not just hopping around and jerking my arms as I usually do. It was easy to follow his steps, moving when he did, swiveling my hips—or trying to—when he did.

The best part was when the music slowed and Julian held me tight, pressing his body against mine in a whole lot of very enjoyable places. It was almost a dry hump. After about an hour, I was sweating like mad, and my throat was parched.

I mimed getting something to drink, and Julian

followed me to the outdoor bar. It was jammed at least two deep with guys waiting to be served or waiting to see who came along. "Beer okay?" I asked Julian.

"Whatever you can get hold of."

One advantage of being six-six is that I could see over the heads of all the short guys in front of me, and I motioned to the bartender for two beers. I handed over the cash and got the bottles in return.

We took the beers and went back inside, where the air-conditioning was running and the vibe was much quieter. It was a big space with high ceilings, lots of comfy couches for conversation and wooden tables for laptop work. The walls had been paneled with fake brick, and the exposed ductwork hung from the ceiling.

Julian and I sat in big comfy chairs by the plate-glass windows looking out on Lincoln Road. A constant parade of drag queens, elderly women, and cute guys walking tiny dogs cruised past. "Tell me more about this business you're trying to start," I said, though business was the last thing I wanted to do with Julian. But I knew I was on firmer ground with geek talk.

He surprised me when he answered, "I love to read. In English or in Spanish, doesn't matter to me. You know much about e-books?"

I shrugged. "I don't have a reader, but I read technical manuals on my laptop with the Kindle app sometimes."

"There's been a huge explosion in e-book publishing over the last few years," Julian said. He took a sip of his beer and sighed with pleasure. "The

New York City gatekeepers have lost control of the business, and authors are publishing their books themselves."

"Yeah, I've seen a few of them," I said. "I'm not saying I've got the best grammar, but some of those are full of errors."

"Yeah, there's a lot of crap out there. But there are also amazing books. Only in English, though. Nobody is moving into that space yet, translating self-published e-books into other languages."

"That's what you want to do? Be a translator?"

He shook his head. "I want to create a marketplace for translations, like Amazon has done for audiobooks. A website where authors can register their books and hook up with translators, editors, and foreign-language publicity. I'm going to call it E-Books Everywhere."

"Hasn't anyone done that before? Like Amazon?"

"Not the way I'm planning. There are sites that will do translations using a combination of human and API, charging by the word. But that's not practical for independent authors. My site is going to be specifically focused on e-books, with specialized translators, and an author can hire a translator on a royalty share deal, rather than an up-front payment. I want to blast open the market for foreign-language novels and creative nonfiction."

"Sounds like a big undertaking," I said. "The database end isn't that tough, from what you've said. But recruiting all those people? And how do you make money?"

"I've got some contacts among translators

already," he said. "I know a woman who runs a translation certificate program at UCLA, and she could feed her students in. The people who sign up agree to let me be the distributor for their books—I'll sell them on e-book stores all over the world and take a tiny percentage on each sale."

"Sounds like you've got it all thought out," I said.

"Just the big picture so far. I have a long way to go." He leaned forward. "You interested in helping me out?"

Looking into those deep dark eyes of his, I would have agreed to almost anything. A little freelance programming in my spare time? That was nothing.

"Julian," I said. "I would be delighted."

The first character from *Three Lambs* who wanted his own story was one who's close to my heart. In the erotic anthology, construction management major Manny Garcia has a fling with an older man working on a project at FU. It was fun to write, particularly because of my background in construction management. And it set Manny's pattern of interest in older men.

Here's the beginning of Manny's story.

"Love with an Older Man"

(An excerpt from *Three Lambs: Erotic Tales of a Gay Frat*)

The chain link fence was already in place by

the time Manny Garcia began his sophomore year at FU. It surrounded a big hole in the ground, and the area crawled with bulldozers, piles of steel beams, and hunky men in hard hats, some of them shirtless in the Miami heat.

Manny's skin was the color of light coffee, his wavy hair black and lustrous. He had almost no body hair, something that always embarrassed him when he was around other guys. He thought he might be handsome, but he was never sure. His grandmothers and aunts had always cooed over him, saying how pretty he was, with his long eyelashes and delicate mouth.

But that wasn't the way a man should look, he thought. And he was a man; he was nineteen years old, and responsible for himself.

Which reminded him that he had no time to stop and stare. He was pre-med and he was carrying a full course load, including organic chemistry. He had received a full scholarship to FU after his parents kicked him out, and if he didn't maintain his GPA he'd be forced to drop out.

But he did stop, sometimes. Most of the guys were nothing special to look at—fat or ugly, skinny or worn out looking. But there was one guy, a foreman or superintendent or something, who Manny couldn't take his eyes off.

The guy had to be his dad's age, but where his dad was wiry and mean-looking, this guy, an Anglo with short brown hair, had a broad smile and even broader shoulders, which tapered down to a narrow waist. His muscular arms were dusted with a coating of light brown hair, and his smile was wide and frequent. He looked so friendly, even when he was criticizing someone.

One day in late September he saw the man talking to a workman who was laying cement blocks. The guy was doing something wrong—Manny couldn't tell what—but the foreman pitched right in to show him the right way to do it. No yelling or screaming, just kindness. It made Manny hard just watching. He wanted to be that workman, right next to the foreman.

Jesus, he was going to come in his shorts if he stayed there. He shook his head and went on to class. He had always been a wimpy kid, preferring to play dolls with the girl next door to football or soccer with the other boys. His voice didn't change until he was halfway through his teens, and it took forever for his pubic hair to start to grow. As a little boy his dad had begun telling him not to act like a *maricón*, the Spanish word for faggot.

He found his refuge in books. He studied all the time, hoping that getting straight As would make his father proud of him. But no luck on that front. Even after graduating at the top of his high school class and getting his full scholarship to FU, his father still acted like Manny was something on the bottom of his shoe.

A week after watching the foreman help with laying the blocks, Manny was there again when the foreman was helping unload some kind of equipment from the back of a truck. Halfway through he pulled off his T-shirt and used it to wipe the sweat from his forehead.

Manny thought he might swoon. The guy's

body was so perfect: huge pecs, with a trail of dark hair between them. His stomach was so flat and taut Manny thought he could bounce a quarter off it.

He kept watching until the truck was completely unloaded. He was just thinking that he had to pry himself away when the foreman turned and walked right over to where Manny stood at the fence.

Busted. The guy would probably call him a few names and chase him away.

"Hey, kid. You interested in construction?"

Manny wasn't about to say that the only thing he was interested in was staring at the foreman's naked chest. "Uh, yeah. It's cool."

"Want me to show you around?"

Manny's mouth dropped open. "That would be awesome."

"I'm Doug. What's your name?"

"Manny. I mean, it's Manuel, but everybody calls me Manny."

"Then I will, too. Come on around to the gate."

Doug tossed his sweaty t-shirt over his shoulder and started walking toward the gate in the fence. Manny trailed behind, awestruck by the way sweat had pooled at the top of Doug's slacks, trickling down to his ass crack. There was a thin dark line between his cheeks.

It was 3:30 and the lot was clearing out. Manny had to wait at the gate for a whole crew who were leaving. "Come on in to the trailer," Doug said.

Manny followed him across the lot. The sun was high in the sky and it was hot. He could see why Doug had worked up such a sweat.

Doug walked up a couple of wooden steps and opened the door to one of the construction trailers. It was just one big room, with a plan table in the middle and a desk and file cabinet at one end. "Gotta get out of these sweaty clothes," Doug said, crossing to the file cabinet. He tossed his T-shirt onto the chair and stepped out of his deck shoes.

As Manny watched, open-mouthed, Doug unbuttoned his slacks and dropped them to the ground, leaving him only in a pair of red satin boxer shorts. "Jeez, even the shorts are soaked through," Doug said, dropping them to the floor and stepping out of them.

If anything, his body was more perfect than Manny had imagined. He had a thick tube steak of a cock, half-hard against a bush of black pubic hair. His legs were dusted with light-brown hair.

"How old are you, Manny?" Doug asked.

"Nineteen."

"That's good." He looked at Manny. "You want to stay over there, or you want to come over here?"

I was intrigued by the trope of a character in love with his boss—something I wrote about in my first M/M romance, GayLife.com (available from MLR Press as an e-book.) In coming up with Manny's story, Love on Site, I was able to use a lot of details from my own experience, including sexy construction workers and homophobic managers.

Turn the page for the first chapter of *Love on Site.*

LEARNING THE CODE

"Now that's a hunk of man," my roommate Gavin said as we idled at the traffic light at the corner of Alton Road and Seventeenth Street on Miami Beach.

I looked where he was pointing. A shirtless Latin guy with tattoos decorating his biceps and his pecs sat on top of the cab of a pickup that was towing a pair of Jet Skis on a trailer. He was about our age, early twenties, with a mane of flowing dark hair and a grin that said he was on top of his world. He looked a lot like Gavin, though my roommate's hair was a golden blond and his muscles weren't quite as big. But both had that sense that they knew they were handsome.

"He's okay," I said. "Not my type, though."

"Manny, Manny," Gavin said. "We've got to get you over this thing you have for daddy types."

"Just 'cause there's snow on the roof doesn't mean there isn't fire in the fireplace." The light changed, and I gunned across Alton Road. It was true; I had a thing for older men, with more maturity and more going on than guys my own age.

An old lady in black tights and an electric blue tank top strolled out into the crosswalk, despite the fact that I had the green light. She had a pink-tinged bouffant that had been lacquered in place, and carried a purple yoga mat. I slowed to let her cross, even though Gavin yelled, "Hey, Yogi, try this position!" and gave her the finger out his window.

"Gavin," I said. "Don't you know it's seven

years' bad luck if you run over a yogi?"

The old lady stepped onto the curb and pressed two fingers of her right hand to her mouth as we passed. Then she turned and showed us her hefty butt, pressing the fingers there.

I guffawed. "She told you, bro. Probably show up and order a latte as soon as you start your shift."

I accelerated onward. My beat-up sedan wasn't much, but it had kept me going through four years of college, and I loved having wheels of my own.

Gavin knew a rich snowbird who had bought a three-bedroom condo on South Beach as an investment. As he and I were preparing to graduate from Florida University in Miami, he'd wrangled a deal for us to rent the place for a year, along with Larry, another of our frat brothers.

We had all met when we pledged Lambda Lambda Lambda, or Three Lambs—the gay frat at FU. Larry and I were ready to get started on our careers—he had a gig as a computer geek with a South Beach startup, and I had been able to parlay my bachelor's in construction management into a job with a real-estate developer.

Gavin had done some modeling while we were in college, and he was trying to build a career based on his fabulous looks—and while he did so, he prepared lattes and mochas at Java Joe's, a coffee shop on Lincoln Road. I turned off Seventeenth Street, alongside the parking garage, and dropped Gavin at the shop's back door.

"Good luck," he said as he hopped out. "I'm sure you'll kill it."

"Your mouth to God's ear," I said, echoing

something my *abuela* said in Spanish.

I was extremely psyched to be heading out for my first day of my first real job. Loredo Construction had recruited at FU, and when I'd walked into the tiny interview room and shaken hands with Walter Loredo, I knew his was the company I wanted to work for. Not just because he was killer handsome, with a smile as wide as Biscayne Bay, but because he was only thirty-two and already very successful.

We'd talked during the interview, and he'd seemed impressed with my résumé. Then his secretary called and invited me out to the site of his new project—a warehouse complex west of Miami International Airport—for further interviews.

* * * *

I cooled my heels in the construction trailer for a half hour as a succession of men in T-shirts and faded jeans walked in and out, carrying hard hats and rolls of blueprints.

I got quick glimpses of Walter that reminded me of how he floated every oar in my boat. So many Latin men I knew were short, topping out around five-nine or so, but Walter was six feet tall, an inch taller than I was. If I ever had the chance to kiss him, I wouldn't have to lean down. He had silky black hair with a gentle curl to it, and when he passed by in an open-necked shirt, I glimpsed the way his chest hair frothed up around his neck. I loved hairy men.

He had an air of confidence, from his firm handshake to his quick brain. He was the best-looking guy in the room and the smartest too, and he knew it, but not in a cocky way. He said a brief hello to me, and my skin tingled when his hand touched mine.

"I'm glad you could come out to see us, Manny," he said. "If you have any questions, let us know."

His voice was deep, with just the hint of a Spanish accent trailing through the words, and when he spoke to me I felt my heart leap. Though maybe that was just nerves. And after all, I was there for a job interview, not a date.

I spent most of that afternoon with Walter's two superintendents. Camilo was in charge of site work—a wiry Cuban in his late forties, about five-seven, who spoke to me exclusively in Spanish. My command of the language is pretty good, having grown up speaking it at home and with friends at school, but I stumbled over some of the technical terms he used, because all my education had been in English.

He took me out to the big, empty lot, hot and dusty, with planes taking off from MIA roaring above us. The first of four warehouses planned for the site was already under construction, though all I could see were the trenches for electrical conduits and plumbing pipes. Back at the construction trailer, Adrian, the interior super, walked me through the plans: four cavernous warehouses, built in succession.

Adrian was Colombian, but he spoke English with only a slight accent. He was about thirty, solidly built but not fat, with a skimpy mustache and a pair of aviator sunglasses perched on his buzz-cut head. "Not the most exciting stuff to build, but at least it's a job, and Mr. Loredo's a good boss," he said.

I ended the afternoon in Walter's office. I was

glad I had been given a promotional folder about the project so I could lay it over my lap to cover the hard-on that just looking at Walter Loredo gave me.

"What do you think about what we've got going on here?" he asked.

I noticed him appraising me and felt self-conscious. "It's very impressive," I said. I had studied the area in preparation for the interview. "The property is large, with excellent access to the highway, and I understand that rental rates in this area are on the rise again."

"You've looked into that?" he asked, and a smile played on his face.

"I may be an engineering student, but I've taken some business courses too," I said. "I wanted to pick the area with the best growth potential, and I think this kind of light industrial land use will grow in this neighborhood."

I had the oddest sense that Walter Loredo and I were flirting with each other, but maybe it was just my imagination. We talked for a few more minutes, until his secretary buzzed to remind him of his next appointment.

"I wish I could spend more time with you, Manny," he said when he stood and shook my hand. "I hope the future gives us that opportunity."

That was supposed to be my line, I thought. "I appreciate the chance to meet with you and your staff," I said. I was proud that I managed to get out of the office without stumbling or showing off my hard-on. When I got out to my car, I sat in the parking lot for a minute with the air-conditioning on full blast. It cooled everything except the tingle in my hand where

Walter Loredo had touched me.

I must have made a good impression, because Walter called the next day with a job offer, and followed it up with an impressive package FedExed to the frat house, full of forms and information on benefits.

Read *Love on Site* in print or electronic form from Loose Id.

Printed in Great Britain
by Amazon